ME_.

To Cath – for your love and support

MELT

Jeff Murray

MARY EGAN
PUBLISHING

Published by Mary Egan Publishing
maryegan.co.nz

jeffmurraybooks.com

This edition published 2019

© Jeff Murray 2019

The right of Jeff Murray to be identified
as the author of this work in terms of section 96 of the
Copyright Act 1994 is hereby asserted.

Designed, typeset and produced by Mary Egan Publishing
Cover art by Euan Macleod
Cover designed by Anna Egan-Reid

ISBN 978-0-473-47053-1

Part I

MELT

Jeff Murray

MARY EGAN
PUBLISHING

Published by Mary Egan Publishing
maryegan.co.nz

jeffmurraybooks.com

This edition published 2019

Designed, typeset and produced by Mary Egan Publishing
Cover art by Euan Macleod
Cover designed by Anna Egan-Reid

ISBN 978-0-473-47053-1

Part I

1

October 2048

Vai Shuster clung on. She clung on all night and well beyond that, and in the end she had nothing left.

The storm that broke her family and threw Vai south lasted eight days and overwhelmed the island of Independence. This was the world she knew. The ocean rarely rested, storm followed storm. Black skies dragged angry winds across the wild ocean. The island's reef broke up, bleached out. Surf surged through, sweeping away buildings. All the hoists and fish storage were gone from the little wharf that China had funded. The news that came to the island's people gnawed at their stocks of resolve. Myriad threats were combining into a pandemic across the globe.

The eight-day storm had come deep in the night. The wind tore at the house, getting its fingers under the blue sheets of iron on the roof and prying one off — and then, with that advantage, it took hold of two more and threw them into the night sky.

At the height of the storm Vai's dad, Moses, raised a hand to the broken roof. 'Everyone out!' He pulled his family into a huddle and pointed to the corner of the room. The intersecting walls were moving as if they had come to life beneath the finely patterned wallpaper. One wall moved south and the other went east, the crimson-rose paper distorting to red eyes. He took Vai's arm roughly and ordered her to lead the way, get them on the platform outside, above the ocean's reach. Then his eyes went

7

back to the walls that were parting company and he struggled to keep his jaw set.

The ocean surged against the foundations of the house and the family felt the house shudder and they groaned and surveyed their meagre treasures. Standing strong, legs braced as if she might take the storm on her shoulder, Vai looked out into the night and reassured herself that there was no monster, only nature itself. She put her mouth to Moses's ear and yelled, 'No, we'll stay here, Dad. Everything's here.' She looked at the gaping holes in the roof and heard another sheet of iron pull away from its nails in a long-drawn shriek. Unbelievable: this was one of the island's big houses, a stronghold. In her twenty-eight years Vai had learnt that everything could break, but somehow she'd never imagined that would include her home.

They formed a chain through the waist-deep water. As she climbed the platform Vai took comfort in the strength of her younger brother, Erfan, and her dad. Man and boy anchoring the line. On the platform their fingers locked on the hand hold. Vai's grandparents clung beside her, Moses wrapping an arm around them. On her other side, Erfan held his mother, Sonya, and twin sister, Emma.

Seven of them, desperate, all eyes on their home as it held against the sheets of water driving off the south Pacific Ocean. Curtains thrust out through broken windows into the dark and wrestled their way back inside, re-emerging ripped and defeated. Then the walls of the main room split asunder and their home made a final sound of anguish. The family dropped their heads as all the little things of their lives disappeared into the night or writhed in the water. Vai flailed at a photo album that floated briefly, their younger selves peering upward as the water took them down.

Vai turned to the last of their good fishing boats, a twenty-foot aluminium craft straining against the post it was tied to. They'd winched it onto shore before the storm struck, but the sea had followed and now the vessel swept forward in the surge and then

8

pulled back off to the side, surging and retreating. The ocean swung the back end of the boat this way and yanked it back the other. Then the boat was skimming seaward in silver profile under brilliant lightning. Vai couldn't fathom its flight: the rope had broken without a sound. Moses rose to his feet and reached over to Sonya. Briefly they touched fingers. She didn't try to stop him, despite the silent terror in her eyes. He launched off the platform with his arms above his head, then started swimming. For a while the family could tell where he was because he kicked up a plume with his feet, but then he was lost in the black tempest and cresting swells.

'Come back!' Vai yelled. She looked over at her mum. 'It's too wild. There's nothing to slow the boat.'

2

In the morning the wind dropped and the sea fell back. The family came down from the platform and looked out to sea. Their feet sogged into the ground, muddy to their ankles. Water rose in the gathering heat, steamy clouds of it along the foreshore and wisps rising from their clothes.

Sonya settled her mother-in-law on a log that had appeared in the remnants of the garden. Erfan, a big seventeen years, stood awkwardly in the gathering light, cleft between man and child. His eyes were red and he wiped quickly at the tears. 'I'll get help,' he said. His voice shook and he raised his arms above his head as if he might lift a boat and cast it into the ocean after his father. 'I'll get some people. We'll find Dad.'

Sonya wrapped her arms around the boy and pulled him hard against her. Looking up into his face she said, 'Run to the Afoa house. If they still have a boat tell them Moses has to be found. If their boat is gone, then go on further. Then come back. I need you with me.'

'I'll go on the boat,' he said. His face darkened and his eyes moved quickly around the faces of the family. 'How can I ask the Afoas to go out and no one from us goes out?' He waved an arm at the ocean and pushed away from his mum. 'Look at it, the waves.'

'He's right. The boy has to go too,' said Moses's father, Malakai.

Sonya glared at Malakai and turned to the ocean. Her arm wrapped around the boy's neck and she pulled at him, but he resisted and spun away toward his grandfather. Big plumes of water boomed on the reef at the edge of the lagoon: water, dirty with debris, continued to surge against the land. Sonya turned her face to the ground and her jaw moved silently, chewing on her lips.

'Let me,' said Vai. 'I'm out with Dad more than anyone. Erfan only goes when he's not at school.'

Sonya marvelled at this girl, unbowed and the calm in her eyes. Powerful through her athletic shoulders and right through her legs, standing tall and firm on the broken land. In her heart Sonya believed this daughter could achieve anything. But to risk this? She turned back to the ocean and said, 'Your Dad will have got to the boat. So he will have kept it afloat and he'll know what to do.'

Emma started to cough, hunched over on the ground, blowing red bubbles onto the mud. 'Oh, hell. Quickly, Vai, take her into the bushes. Keep it secret.'

Vai took her sister by the shoulders and helped her to her feet, hurrying them both in among the broken vegetation. She looked back in time to see her grandfather nod to Erfan and jerk his thumb in the direction of the Afoa house. The boy ran down the coast. Sonya walked knee-deep into the water and stood with her hands on her hips, examining the grey clouds above her.

Vai held Emma as the girl sucked at the air and spat red onto the leaves of the bushes they crouched in. 'You should go back on the drugs. Go back to the nurse,' Vai said. Emma's beautiful long hands pressed into the mud and Vai brought a memory forward, the two of them laughing in the shade of orange trees, fragrant in the warm sun.

The branches they crouched under were split in all directions. Beyond them Vai saw the fields of food everyone needed and now couldn't have. She thought about her sister's bloody coughing and her brother, and her mum who couldn't reconcile with the angry world. She twisted her heels against the soil as if to ground herself deeply and the weight of it all settled on her.

'The drugs didn't work,' Emma said between gasps. 'If I go back there the nurse will have to put me on the other list.'

Vai felt a surge of helpless dread, then pushed it away and nodded as if the path they were on was a sure one. She tucked Emma's hair into the back of her shirt and looked around the strewn branches and debris. The island had to be finished now, she thought, so all twenty thousand inhabitants could take up the decades-old promise that they could move to New Zealand.

'New Zealand will send a helicopter,' Vai said. 'I might have to go there and arrange things. I'm sure we'll shift now.' She took Emma's hand. 'We'll keep this secret for a few more months, that's all. Once we're settled we can find a doctor who'll help. There are New Zealand doctors who work in secret.'

3

Two days later a Chinese supply ship settled in the swell, a safe distance from the reef. Small craft were lowered and slowly made their way to the wharf. Island men bent to the task of unloading the emergency supplies, breaking open crates and lifting the contents by hand.

A medical team climbed onto the wharf and set up on the shore. Vai and Emma stood to the side of the group seeking medication and treatment. They waited in the shade while the line of local men carted away supplies on their shoulders and the cluster of the sick and the damaged flowed around the medics. A doctor beckoned to Vai and Emma but they looked away and slid further from the group. He walked a circuitous path and stopped twenty metres from them, not visible to the cluster at the medics' table. He smiled and waited silently.

'This is Emma. Her lungs. Her coughing.' Vai hesitated.

'The medication's not working?' The doctor directed his question to Emma, who nodded. 'I'm Dr Zhu.' He didn't leave a gap for her to speak. 'There's a new strain of TB in these islands. Nothing's working on it. Nothing yet. If you have TB you need to make sure you don't cough on anyone. Keep to yourself as much as you can.'

Emma nodded.

'I'm sorry,' he said.

'We don't want her on a list,' Vai said. 'We're going to New Zealand.' Then, 'We're going south,' as if it was final, as if they'd always been destined for there and they'd just stopped off here for a rest.

'I'm not interested in lists.' Zhu looked inland, through the twisted and broken branches. He lifted a branch at the point where it was broken, still thinly joined with the tree. The stretch of bark skin and flesh-fibre allowed it to hold onto its leaves. He pushed the sharp bits of branch together, but when he released his makeshift joint it parted. Annoyed, he said, 'I'm heading south too. A short stay in New Zealand and then Antarctica.' He looked out to sea and Vai followed his gaze to the horizon. The place that wasn't where they stood. 'A long journey south for all of us,' he said.

Vai heard a new tone in his voice. Excited and distant, as if he had something in mind. He'd moved on from the island and the cluster of damaged people. He spoke to the distance and Vai lent forward to hear him. 'You know that your people probably started out in Taiwan, and before that Fujian?'

'Yes,' Vai said. 'That's the story.' She was curious, standing here in this mess, being given a portion of popular history. The doctor's gaze was away from the people he had, presumably, come to help. 'We sort of used to be Taiwanese, so I guess we're family. And our Māori cousins too.' She watched him closely to see what he would make of that.

'Ah, of course, the Māori voyagers. They went as far south as anyone could at that time.' He returned his attention to Vai. 'They should have waited for planes to be invented. It would have been easier.' The women laughed politely. 'It took months for the Chinese goldminers to get to New Zealand in the 1860s, and now the Chinese middle class get there in a few hours.'

'Here we are being bound back together,' Vai said, pointing to the Chinese ship. 'The forces of integration and destruction working in tandem.'

'An historic journey,' Dr Zhu replied. 'A thousands-of-years journey to New Zealand. And now we pick up the strands that bind us — the southward journey continues.'

14

Vai recognised what he was doing: he was locating himself. Linking their histories and journeys. The awkward, slightly-built man was greeting her. Now she believed he would keep Emma's secret: perhaps because he had reached out as family, or perhaps because he couldn't help and Emma's disease would run its course, either on this island or the island they were trying to get to. Everything was on the move now.

'There's no refuge in China,' he said. 'You can only head south.'

'We know,' Vai said. 'We've been told about your food shortages, your famines.'

The next day a helicopter settled onto the school sports field. It was red and emblazoned with 'Aroha-NZ'. New Zealand government representatives disembarked to explain what was next. Those watching prodded at the ground with their feet and discussed in whispers the secret, invisible work of sea water as it dried on crop land.

Homeless, the Shusters had all moved in with Sonya's parents and now they walked together across the school yard and into the hall, which stood resilient in its warm cream with red window trim and red roof. No other school buildings remained standing. Buildings that had nurtured Vai since she was five years old, blown to kindling. She had borrowed a brightly patterned dress and straw hat with a red cloth tied around it. Sonya and the twins were similarly defiant for Moses. Vai walked beside her mother's father, Pa. The big, humble man gestured to her to sit in the front row: he would have sidled into a back seat but Sonya took him and Malakai and guided them to the front to sit beside Vai.

Vai glanced at her mother and shuddered in memory of the fight they'd had that morning. The older woman had made a point of taking them all to the coast to survey the wreckage of their home, their shop and the coolhouse that stored their fish and the catches of their neighbours – all gone. And now the fire was back in Sonya's eyes. She took hold of Vai, a firm hand on the neck, and said, 'You'll have to go to New Zealand again. Everything I worked for here, it's gone, wrecked like the house.' She looked along the coast at the places where other houses had been taken. Her gaze lingered on the houses that still stood. 'You are the Advocate for Independence,' she'd said, as if that were Vai's only burden and there was no waiting for Moses.

They stood when a thin woman from New Zealand approached and shook hands. Her light-blue pant suit and translucent skin had a ghostly effect, as if she might not be present at all. 'Good to meet you again, Vai,' she said.

Vai introduced Herieth Woodley to her family. Herieth said, 'One of the bright notes for today is that I can confirm your next visit to New Zealand.' She brushed a lock of white hair back into place and quickly resettled the thick bun of it, ensuring there were no more strays. 'The Adjustment Office is aware of the plight facing Independence, and it is time to do further planning and preparation.'

Vai's face flooded with anger. *Further planning and preparation. What the hell for? Didn't anyone look down as the helicopter dropped Herieth and her experts from the sky?*

Woodley mistook Vai's anger for fear and widened her mouth in what might have been a smile. 'Don't worry,' she said. 'You won't be in New Zealand for long. We won't have you leave your country so easily.'

Vai confronted her, eye to eye. 'The island's broken. We've accepted that. We're ready to go now.'

Woodley placed her hand on Vai's shoulder. 'You don't need to think that. Anyway, you're not really refugees. No one's out to get you. Really, you're survival migrants, so we can keep you here for another decade. Maybe more.'

Another decade? Vai brushed Woodley's hand away. 'What do you expect people to live on? You know we can't do ten years.' She rolled her shoulders, loosened her neck. The murmur in the room took her attention and she faced the people who had put their trust in her. Some faces were strong and willed her forward;

16

others were fearful and seemed to say, 'This is a knock-out tournament, and we can't afford to put one foot wrong.'

Herieth Woodley stepped back to stand beside Pa. Even though he towered over her, he looked small with his head bowed and his hands clasped. 'I think your grandfather understands the situation better than you,' she said. 'There's an arrangement. This time the sponsorship is for completion of the transition plan. See what you can do with that opportunity.'

Vai saw herself shuffling from one room to another in a shabby office block in New Zealand. Each room would have screens on the walls and outcomes frameworks and officials pitting her against other Advocates in a petty contest. Her mouth was dry and she tried to imagine ten more years but she couldn't comprehend how it might be. 'We'll be pigs in a pen,' she said. 'Look at us!' She cast her arm wide around the room of anxious faces. 'We didn't destroy this place. We did none of it.'

Woodley smiled a threat. 'There's a very long queue, Ms Shuster, and you need to secure an option for Independence while there are still options to be had. That's all you need to do for now. You can move later. But remember, the scale of the problem doesn't give any priority to Independence.'

Part II

4

Vai was exhausted. She passed through the arrivals gate at Auckland International Airport and leant against the wall. Her shoulders and arms ached and her eyes brimmed with tears as she considered her task and imagined her father adrift. She scanned the faces that peered at the arrivals but none of them looked right. Too official, family members too sure of whom they were meeting, too old, too young, private drivers. She was looking for her cousin Leon. About six three, lean with black wavy hair and a scramble of brightly coloured flowers tattooed on each arm.

The crowd thinned. She moved toward the centre of the room and cast about, uncomfortable in the too-tight dress she'd borrowed. Over by a coffee cart in a corner she saw a man her own age, mid-twenties, leaning close to a younger woman, one arm raised above his head, resting it on the wall, flowers from wrist to shoulder. Tight black T-shirt. Black stubble on light-brown skin, eyes alight. He was enjoying himself, all his attention on the woman backed up against the cart. Vai stood in the centre of the room and watched her tuck her purse under her chin, other hand creeping toward the barista.

Vai strode over. 'Leon?'

He turned to face her and ran his eyes, top to bottom and on down. 'Yeah? Oh, yeah, Vai?' Once he'd scoped her his gaze returned to her shocking blue eyes. Never the burn scar snaking down her neck that held a stranger's gaze, always the eyes. The unexpected eyes set against brown skin and thick black hair.

21

The other woman said, 'I'll just leave you, then,' and turned on her heel. Leon cast a sorry glance after her then leant over and gave Vai a brief hug. 'You're earlier than I thought. Must'a got the wind behind you.'

'Must've. I'm a bit early. Thanks for coming to get me.'

'No trouble getting through Customs? Where're your bags?'

Vai held up a small media device given to her by Woodley. 'Just this. I've got an Adjustment Office visa. No trouble with Customs. I spent more time looking at the hologram.'

'Haven't seen it. Haven't travelled.' He motioned toward the exit and they began to walk.

'It's weird, there are people playing at the beach and under waterfalls and if you stop they look up as if you might want to join them,' Vai said.

'I hope it's a good day, not too sunny in the hologram.' He took her arm and pushed into a crowd of cab drivers. 'I've got a car. It's parked a way off, though.' They emerged into the sun outside the terminal and Leon pointed at the slow-moving line of silent vehicles. 'Watch these,' he said. 'They're a trap if you're not used to them. Bloody electric, run you over.'

'I've been here twice before.' Vai looked over the people hurrying to and fro and wondered how much had changed in the short time since her last visit. What damage was panic doing to her prospects? What of the imaginings she had carried since high school, clear as if they were memories, of her negotiating late into the night, finalising the resettlement of her community? The heat changed the rules, changed what people were willing to feel.

They hustled across the roads that led away from the airport, dodging the silent cars and trucks. 'I always ask what the city looks like from the air,' Leon said. 'I ask different travellers and they all tell it different. Everyone sees the city different.'

Vai noticed swelling around his eye. She'd missed it in the airport but here in the brilliant sun it looked puffed up, slightly red. And his knuckles, cut and freshly scabbed. She turned her own hands upward and looked at the blisters, a reminder of the

22

worst night of the storm, puffy with blood.

'What'd you see?' he asked, slowing his pace and smiling quickly.

'It's two cities, really, isn't it?'

He raised a finger and nodded. 'Got that right.'

'I mean, you fly in over the Manukau Harbour and it's muddy brown, stacked living and factories, except on the ocean edge. On one side of the harbour mouth there's all the forest running to the ocean and on the other side there's dairy cows and then you're back to the city and it runs south as far as you can see.'

'Runs down to Hamilton now, just one long strip of houses and businesses. Place is full of migrants.'

Vai said, 'On the other half of the city, the Waitemata Harbour and out to the Hauraki Gulf, they're the gem. Always glistening. Even if there's a squall blowing through, the water seems to glimmer. Big yachts, big houses.'

'Last week, when I picked a guy up, the weather was turning bad. I asked him about it, what could he see from the plane? He reckoned all these black clouds blow up along the coast from the south, Antarctica clouds he called them, and when you think they're going to blow on past the city, missing it, they come to the Waitakere Ranges and halt. They group up on the ocean side of the hills and when they're ready they rise in one big black mass and drive straight through the city. Big scrum of them, throw a blanket over the lot, they're that close. Rain pounding down, blowing hard. Then it's back to being too hot to go outside. I'd like to see it from up high.'

'It's not too bad today.'

Leon laughed. 'That's not what you'll hear around this place. I hate to think what *you* put up with.'

Vai nodded grimly. 'Yes. We do a lot of work at night now, especially in the gardens.'

They came to a tiny white car with speckles of rust and little wheels to match. Leon scratched behind his ear and fixed his eyes on the footpath. 'This is us,' he said.

23

They drove away from the airport, proceeding at walking pace for most of the time; at other times they were stationary. 'Have you ever been to Independence, Leon?' Vai asked. 'Do you know the island?'

'No. Mum was born there, but she's never been back since she came here. She was small. Never talked about going back.' Leon's face softened and the skin around his eyes crinkled. 'Did they give you a hard time? Make you plead for the visa?'

'No, that part of it was fine. I know how to deal with them.' Vai gave a long sigh, as if she was emptying right out. 'I'm allowed to stay here and do what they call "further planning and preparation". Just a short visit.'

'Then you go back?'

'Not if I can find something else. The island's ruined. The last cyclone ripped it to bits, but it's been dying for years. Mum told me to try to set things up for everyone and then keep travelling, see what's happening in other places. See what others are doing to survive, look for other chances.'

'My Mum always talked about it as if it was some sort of paradise. But she probably just made it up. She wouldn't remember.'

Vai looked out the window at the warehouses and lines of vehicles. 'It *was* a paradise. I missed that time. But I can remember when it was good.'

Leon touched her on the shoulder and then put his hand back on the steering wheel. 'When Mum was pregnant with me, Dad moved over here for work.'

Vai glanced at Leon to see if he might say something about her dad. Maybe he didn't know Moses was missing. Leon kept his eyes on the road. Vai turned her eyes down, scuffed her shoes. She didn't want to explain why she'd left the island when people were still looking for him. She wasn't sure she could say it, even thinking it was wrong, thinking she'd be the one to secure the deal to move the people. A history-maker. Her face burned in a heat of guilt. 'Mum's parents farmed in the middle of the island,

24

on the volcanic soil. Near where the remains of the volcano sticks its big arm up into the sky, fist balled at the top.'

'Can it still grow food?' Leon asked. He took his eyes off the road to watch her face. It would have seemed such an odd question only a few years ago. 'What're they eating now? Sacks of rice and tinned fish?'

'Honey.' Vai laughed at the taste of the word. 'My grandpa had bees. He had dozens of hives and I was his apprentice.' Leon's soft, dark eyes smiled. 'Husbanding the bees, Pa would call it. He said that was because the bees were mostly women except a few men who did nothing, and so Pa had to help.'

'Sounds good.' Leon shifted in his seat, knees almost up to his chin.

'When I was little I watched to see if he was right, looking into the boxes to see if the men really did nothing. I wanted to pull their wings off when I found out he was right. They just sat around, only trying when they thought they might mate the queen. They just saved up their energy, outliving the working women by tenfold.'

'Imagine that — the natural order. That's our trouble, we've messed with the natural order.' Leon beamed widely and bobbed his head against the car's ceiling, rubbing his hair up against the black-stained bit.

Vai smiled too, just as wide, and punched his shoulder. 'I love the bees. On Independence plants try to flower all year. Used to be there was always some bee food.'

'And then it changed?' Vai nodded. 'Hear about it all the time. Places that were food bowls are no good. What they call flash droughts coming in fast and killing off a whole season of food. Unexpected. Places that weren't much good for crops getting a bit better.'

'The great reshuffle.' For once Vai didn't mind the bitter taste in her mouth when she used that phrase. Sitting in the little car with Leon she felt she was with a kindred spirit. 'The specialists from New Zealand used to come over and walk around with us.

Look at the crops getting sodden and then rotting at the stem in the heat. The thrashing the plants took when they were in flower and the fruit didn't set. Some type of malevolence on the edges of life.'

'Yeah, everyone's scared. We're right in it now. Dragon's breathing fire.' He put his arm out the window, tapping the side as they inched along. 'Turns out the worse things get, the better I'm doing.' Then he rhymed happily, 'I'll getcha, I'll getcha what ya need.'

'We get these volunteers come over to the island. They think they're advising us, but they've got their eyes on something else.' Vai shifted in her seat and bit a knuckle. 'We get ones from a group called Young Nature. They're all sad faces and important messages, degrees in sustainable development, which is just code for "you're all stuffed". They want the island for rewilding and they're just waiting. They have devices that cast holograms and they talk about new technology and how it's going to set things right.' She laughed as Leon shook his head. 'Then they show films of people from countries that're uninhabitable and we talk about refugee camps, people behind barbed wire and living in tents. The films are a menace to us, a warning that we have to comply with something.' Vai's voice grew angry and she cradled her chin in her hand. 'Mostly the refugees are frightened or sad but sometimes they're rioting. Parents with young kids talk about this at home. It's their responsibility, with the younger children, not to let things get too frightening.'

'Emissaries of a rough god.' Leon held up one hand, like a preacher, then used a booming voice, emphasising each word, 'Who does not hide his works.'

After nearly an hour they were in Ōtāhuhu and the large warehouses gave way to apartment buildings, mostly six or seven storeys high. The shops bustled with activity and the streets were dappled with shade where people gathered around little

26

fountains. Leon drove through the shopping area and down some streets then pulled up outside an apartment building. He pointed at an apartment on the third floor and said, 'We're in there.' Then he pointed to a dyed-blonde woman in her fifties lifting heavy bags out of a van. 'That's Queenie. She runs the apartment day-to-day, and the ones either side, plus upstairs. There's twenty people in each apartment, two bedrooms each, and then there's the ones who just pay to use the kitchen and bathroom. Come on, we'll help her.'

Queenie kissed Vai on the cheek and said, 'Moses's girl, good to meet you. When your Dad was working here, he stayed with me and my ex.'

Vai jumped back a pace, crying out as if she had been wounded. Queenie looked to Leon, expecting him to clarify, but he just shrugged.

'What's the matter love?' Queenie asked.

'Dad's missing. He went after our boat, in the storm. I had to leave before they found him.'

Queenie took Vai's face in her hands and peered at the younger woman as if she was searching for something but wasn't sure what it might be. 'Oh, honey, come here,' she said, pointing to the back of the open van. Scowling at Leon, Queenie took a handful of his oiled hair and gave it one sharp yank as if it was his fault that neither of them knew, or that at least it was his fault that he didn't know, hadn't asked after Vai's family when he met her.

The colour had drained out of Vai's face and tears sat fat in her eyes. She ran her hands slowly through her hair and said, 'I thought you'd been told. We had a storm you couldn't imagine. Ripped right through the island.'

'We know about the storm, love. But we didn't know about your Dad. Did you have to come now?'

'The island's finished. But they want us to stay up there another ten years. We'll be left behind in ten years. There'll be nowhere for us to come to in New Zealand.'

'Tell me about Moses, love.' Queenie gave Vai's hand a squeeze.

'You don't need to be down here just now. Maybe you should think about going back.'

'I can't,' Vai said. She fingered the silver locket at her throat, given to her by her mother. 'You can't imagine the pressure. It's like the days before war breaks out, the days remaining to make one last dash for safety. Dad wouldn't want me sitting at home, crying with the children.' She looked Queenie squarely in the face. 'I don't need to guess what you're thinking, but until we know otherwise, Dad's somewhere on the boat.'

'Your Dad's on the boat?' Queenie said this in the type of cautious, guiding voice you might use when you were trying to bring a stray horse into a yard.

'Didn't see him catch it, but he's a good swimmer, fast.' Queenie and Leon hung their heads quietly, hands clasped in front of them. 'People were a bit upset with Mum and me and the twins because we aren't in black.' Vai's voice was rushing along, hollow, as if the words were entering a drain. 'But it wasn't right that we should be.'

Vai studied the two people in front of her. They were clearly shocked that she hadn't stayed home. She thought of telling them about the row she'd had with her mum the day before she flew to Auckland. Mum, with her jealousies and her constant fights with families who were better off. Vai felt her skin prickle as if tiny, hot pins were being applied everywhere at once, not the baking all-over heat of the sun; this was a million stings of anger. Her mum's family had a small plot of land and that was all: they lived on it, ate from it, buried their dead near the palm-frond house. It wasn't something they could advance from. And when Sonya and Moses fell for each other she was off to his coastal family, striding and growing more important with each metre covered.

Back then Moses's family had five boats and they hired crew and ran a coolstore for the fish they caught, and also the fish caught by other families on that stretch of coast. Her mum's eyes would glow with pride when she recounted stories of hosting the neighbours and, without a hint of resentment, she would

28

describe the hours she spent cutting the grass and maintaining the garden so that the rows of hibiscus never had a dying branch or dead flower.

Then, by the time Vai finished high school, they were down to one boat. Moses and Vai worked it themselves, struggling to find a catch in an ocean that now belonged to the industrial boats. Vai knew that time as a blessing, the days spent working alongside her dad. But with growing panic, her mum realised she was going to become the head of a home that had grown into poverty, and she drove her clever, determined oldest child harder to save their fortunes.

Vai took on the role with pride. She had her own ambitions. It was her generation that would lead the island on its epic migration to New Zealand. Whether it was a lifetime of her mother fostering ambition, or something she would have grown to herself, before she finished high school Vai settled on the idea that she would navigate the migration. But after Moses was swept out to sea they fought a battle when Sonya told her daughter not to come back from New Zealand, told her to find a way to keep going, to make herself somehow necessary in the world, so that she would be the beachhead the others would land on. 'You think I'm going to be nothing but the Shuster wife who lost the house? Washing back up with my parents and nothing but a handful of kids?' Sonya raged. She looked at her daughter and placed the burden of Moses on her: 'You get us across that damn ocean. Land us in that long country.'

29

5

The apartment was full. Vai guessed that relatives from Independence might be putting on a welcome for her. A killing game was being played loudly on a big screen and men were gathered around laughing and calling out; boys were sitting on the floor. Leon introduced Vai to a very big man in his fifties and his pinch-mouth wife, Boss and Bossie. They managed the lease on the apartment and Vai wasn't sure whether to hug them or shake hands, but Bossie asked where her bags were and then said, 'Well, don't expect to borrow other people's things.'

'Good to have another sponsored tenant,' said Boss. 'Proper rent. Leon, sign her up with the bank. For a short stay, rent's in advance. Don't go to the top floor, that's the TB people.' He pushed past Vai and stood on the balcony and growled instructions into his media device.

'We stay out of the apartment unless we're sleeping or eating there,' Leon said, gesturing to the door. 'We try to make room.' As they entered the stairwell to exit the building Vai looked up at the stairs covered in old carpet that might have been red in some distant heyday. She listened for any coughing from the TB level. *How might the TB people live*, she wondered.

They walked to the shopping centre. Vai was subdued. 'I need clothes,' she said. 'Everything was lost in the storm.'

'Let's arrange your rent first,' Leon said.

30

Vai made the arrangements on the device she'd been given when she left Independence. Leon told her how much to transfer in rent and Vai sucked her cheeks in and whistled, long and slow while she did the maths. 'Twenty people plus how many casuals staying there?' Vai said. 'Two bedrooms. Someone's making a lot.'

Leon just nodded.

Then Leon took her down an alley and over a couple more roads to a second-hand store. 'Get the minimum, and a backpack so you can keep your stuff with you. If you leave it at the apartment it'll go into the general pool.'

Next to the second-hand store was a shop that sold fruit and vegetables and she bought some soft apples and a bag of chips. A white van drove past and Leon raised a hand in recognition. Vai saw Bossie in the passenger seat. The van was very tall: Vai could have stood in it. 'That's what they sleep in,' said Leon. 'They have about ten apartments that they run and all of them are crowded like our one, so they sleep in that van. It's their office. They mostly eat takeaways, I think.'

They walked back to the main retail street and sat on a bench in the park. The roses were flowering and their scent lingered like colour on the air. Scattered randomly amongst the café tables beggars shook cups, jingling a disrupting syncopation.

'You're young to be an Advocate,' Leon said. 'They must trust you on the island.'

'Half of them do,' Vai said, leaning her head on his shoulder.

'Why only half?'

She touched her hair as if she was checking it was set just right, 'A fishing company from Australia wanted to lease our mullet fishery. Some of our councillors wanted to take the money, but it was a scam.'

'A scam? How'd you know?' Vai noted the glint of interest in his eyes. Up to now it'd been a getting-to-know-you kind of day, keeping each other company, but here she had something, a *scam*. Just on that one word she saw his mind was off on a run, thinking about how a fishing scam might get set up.

31

'We couldn't get the numbers from them, just the lease fee. Couldn't see how they'd calculated it.' She paused just long enough for him to think about her preparing her next move. 'So I made a video call to a woman from Dar es Salaam. You know, in Africa?'

'No, never heard of it. Who'd you talk to?'

'This woman who runs a business buying fish and advising on commercial stuff. She's a lawyer. I told her what we were being offered and she told me what to look for in terms of how the maths should be done, what we might get per tonne.'

Leon nodded enthusiastically, 'I'm a trader. Got to have on-the-ground knowledge, comparable prices, even for mullet.' But he was a bit disappointed it was just mullet, she could tell. His voice trailed away as he said it: *mullet*. As if it didn't count, as if it should have been make-you-a-million fish.

Vai looked him over anew. A trader in all things new and used, she thought, and the smell of boxes that had been stored out of sight tickled her nostrils. 'Anyway, my African lady dressed in these bright dresses, long, flowing to the ground, silk, always silk. And she kept her hair in cornrows. So I was using her maths and her experience, and I did my hair just like hers.' Vai laughed. 'Black cornrows, brown skin, the eyes. I dressed like that when we met the fishing company representatives. You should've seen people looking at me like, "Who the hell is she trying to be?"'

She stood up and mimed as if she were appearing in court, giving her argument. 'I ripped into them, took twenty minutes to show that their numbers didn't stack up. We'd be better off fishing for ourselves.' She sat back down. 'They weren't ready for that. In fact, they weren't really prepared at all. They just thought we'd be desperate and take whatever. Then my Pa said, "Look at her, she's the one. Did her homework, got the facts right."' Vai touched her hair as if she could feel the tight plait of it. 'He recommended I become the island's Advocate. I wasn't sure about it, but what I learnt from my woman in Africa was get the right people to take advice from. That's number one.' She raised one finger. 'Two, a lot of people can be knocked straight over. Don't assume anything from their suits and grey hair and the nasty set of their mouths.'

Leon said, 'So that's your schooling? And only half of them wanted you to be their Advocate?'

'Well, I ruined it for the other half of them. They were in on the scam. But I have a law degree.'

'From where?'

'I did it on the web. Through a proper university. And I've been here twice advocating. I know how it works.' She looked over at the beggars. 'It's fricken awful.' Then she shifted on the bench, shoulders back and chin forward. 'But I'll be the one who brings everyone over, gets us all to safety.'

Leon heard the pride in her voice, the emphasis at the front of the sentence: '*I'll* be the one.'

'Floods and droughts, roads washing away.' Leon didn't hide his anger. 'There were promises that we'd take in all the Islanders, but now everyone's saying, "Oh, we've fallen behind in health. Oh, what about catching up on fixing roads, flooding, all that." So the government's been breaking its promises, not letting people in or making them stay in towns that are broken. Places Kiwis won't live in. Giving first choice to migrants from rich places.' He picked up a stick, thick as two fingers, and banged it on the bench until it broke, his face turning red, making snorting noises.

When it was nearly midnight they walked back to the apartment. The street was busy with people enjoying the relative cool of the night air. They passed groups of young men with big dogs on chains and Vai wondered at the aura of uselessness that hung off them, dogs filling in a gap where a man's vigour could have been.

When they reached the apartment three men were standing beside the little car. One called out to Leon, 'Hey, come and do a shift. Sam's not coming and we need one more.'

'What's the job?' Leon asked.

'Cleaning in the city centre, office block.'

33

'All right.' He turned to Vai and said, 'I'll work all night and I'll see you at Aotea Square in the morning, in the city centre. Let me know when you arrive, then we can walk to the Adjustment Office.'

The car had only two doors and the men laughed as two of them wriggled into the back seat. As the car trundled away Vai heard the men mocking each other over the sound of a scratchy radio.

Food was cooking on the stove and the killing game continued filling the space with noise. Queenie was in charge of the cooking and a boy and a young woman were helping her, buttering bread one slice at a time until the loaf was buttered and stacked on a plate. There was no room in the kitchen for more people. Queenie waved to Vai and said, 'Queen of the kitchen.' She waved her hands merrily around the space. 'Stay here, love, I'm serving in a minute.'

'Workers first,' said a woman in a blue shirt bearing the logo of a cleaning company. A short line formed behind her of people in the same type of shirt.

'These ones are going on a shift,' Queenie explained. 'Let them have theirs and then you get a bowl. It's soup tonight.'

Vai joined the queue and took a slice of bread and bowl of soup. It was almost clear liquid with bits of potato, carrot and cabbage chopped into it. As Vai ate Queenie said, 'Good on you, you're famished. If you want more, buy your own but keep it out of the apartment or it'll cause fights.'

By the time Vai had helped Queenie clean the dishes it was after one in the morning. Fatigue soaked into the ache between her shoulder blades. Some girls were sitting in the tiny bathroom so Vai said she would wait but the girls said they were just talking — it was a quiet space. After using the bathroom Vai went into the bedroom that had been pointed out to her and was surprised to find there were no beds, just wall-to-wall mattresses

34

with women and children sleeping. In an unused corner she set her backpack down and lay against the wall. For a long time she twisted in the grip of her obligation, the burden of her island now trebled by her absence from the search for her father.

She was woken by the shift workers returning and burrowing in among the mattresses. She realised she had overslept and rose to leave with an apology to the woman taking a space next to her. A small boy had wet himself and some bedding. His mother was dealing with the blanket and another woman slapped her quite hard and the mother slapped the boy.

Vai said she'd help and lifted the crying boy but the mother wrenched him back off her. Vai was startled by the violence of the motion. She took her bag and passed through the lounge area with its incessant gaming noise and went outside. She didn't stop in the kitchen; it was tidy and she guessed she had missed Queenie. It was about nine in the morning and the motorway was snarled up with traffic, the vehicles moving like ants, driven by pheromones to march in silent, orderly lines. The electric vehicles almost touched in the line; the few that weren't electric were distinguished by pockmarks of rust and kept a bigger distance, as if their combustion engines were contagious.

The main street of Ōtāhuhu was beginning to bustle and there was a queue of people waiting for buses to take them to the central city, every type of face you could think of — the bus terminal was its own little émigré centre of determination. On Independence it was mainly Polynesians, mixed with some Germans plus a sprinkling of others — and, more recently, the boat people. *Boat people*, Vai reflected. *An odd denominator: all of us are boat people.* Her aunt had married an Iranian who'd spent the better part of a decade trying to get to Australia: Erfan carried his name. Vai thought about the Germans, all through her brown-skinned family. Her Pa had travelled to Taiwan as a younger man, adding his DNA to the database that tied them there, right back to the originals who had walked across the land bridge from Fujian.

The silent bus bullied its way out of the terminal and crept toward the central city. Vai hadn't seen this part of Auckland before. The view of Maungakiekie from Manukau Road was an eye-opener, a 500-acre farm preserved in the middle of a city, spread over the highest volcano in the region. She could see cattle and sheep and a crop that she guessed to be pumpkins. On all sides of the farm, apartment buildings stretched up grey and higher than the ones she had passed earlier. There were tarpaulins tied to trees and tents scattered across the paddocks. A sheep hung by a leg from a tree, its carcass fatty-white and meaty-red; one man pulled on the skin while a second worked a knife. There seemed to be a lot of people, and she guessed they lived there.

When the bus deposited Vai in the middle of Queen Street she used her mobile device to contact Leon, who told her to wait in Aotea Square and he would come to get her. The square was shoulder to shoulder with people: it looked like a market day. Trestle tables were set out in long rows, and at the head of each was a trailer with large pots of food and large bowls of salad. Full plates were being distributed to the people seated, many of whom were very scruffy. Vai realised this was food being given to the poor. She guessed there were more than two thousand people being fed.

Leon arrived and said, 'Come on, let's get some.' He laughed at her look of surprise. 'You're one of the poor in this town and you've got to learn the tricks.' They hurried across the road and found a seat and were given a plate of rice and pumpkin with a cabbage salad. Along their row the people were of all ethnicities and ages and dressed in an odd assortment of clothes, having to manage warm weather and then wet from the southerlies. And they laughed and jostled in their diversity.

Around the edge of the square were balconies that connected in a whole layer of activity, and at the doors leading up to these were positioned large men in brown shirts and black pants, creases sharp. The people up there were smiling and laughing and eating and drinking too. 'Every day at ten,' Leon said. 'It's worth it.'

On the walk uphill to the Adjustment Office Vai and Leon passed the hotel where she had stayed on previous advocacy trips. He laughed when he saw the concrete-slab building. 'Now you're having to bunk in with us. Too bad! Why aren't you staying in the hotel this time?'

'Unscheduled trip, so it had no proper budget. I'm on the cheap with family,' she said, giving a friendly punch on his arm. Then her voice changed and revealed her anxiety: it was one thing to imagine the honour of settling the negotiations, but the reality of it burdened even her sleep. 'I have to secure a place for the whole island, and then try to hold it till we're allowed to come. I need a good place, maybe Hamilton, but if we can't come for ten years others might get it. We'll miss out. We'll get pushed to the bad places.'

'No way you're getting near Hamilton,' Leon said. 'Everyone's aiming for Hamilton. It's got quite good weather and farming's doing fine. There're chances down there where you can get cheap food, especially if there's a storm that damages a crop and they move it quickly. But the migrants with money, they're moving there and there are jobs in construction and all the high-rise food cropping, so there's citizens who're poor down there too. But they have tricks for keeping refugees out.'

Vai's face was set. 'I've heard about those tricks.' She bit her lip.

Leon took her arm. 'Don't let them put you in Hawke's Bay or Northland. See if you can get to Rotorua. There's no work there but the climate's all right so in future it will be one of the better places.'

Vai had plenty of time to observe the waiting room of the Adjustment Office, which was a sorting pen for advocates of nations that were sinking or burning. The linoleum on the floor had been white but now it was ripped and scuffed black in places and in other places was stained by water that must have leaked over a long period. She didn't have an appointment so would have to hope for a gap. Those who did have appointments didn't wait long; Vai filled in the hours reading her media device and mentally preparing for the work ahead. Every so often she stood and paced the room, stopping to shake first one leg and then the other, then breathe deeply and return to her seat. She would run both hands softly down the length of her face, breathing out all her air and then smooth her hands across her thighs before going back to the media device.

Eventually she was the last one in the room and a buzzer sounded and a red light winked. A man in his early thirties looked through a glass pane into the waiting room and motioned to her to enter the meeting room. He held out his hand. 'Mike Powell.' Then he scratched his tummy and crumbs fell to the floor. 'You'll appreciate we haven't prepared for your visit. But Independence is now a Category Three consideration.' He paused to let that sink in. There was dead air for a moment until Vai realised he was waiting for her to thank him. 'That sounds important. Thank you.'

Powell nodded. 'That's right, it *is* important. I've booked two workshops so you can work through options for settlement with the Needs Assessment and Options Review team. The first one's to set out the options, then you report back by satellite to your people on Independence. Make sure they're fully informed. You need to be able to show that you consulted and demonstrate what was agreed.' He smiled so Vai smiled too.

'This will be the most significant decision Independence has made since the island was first settled,' Vai said. 'The location we settle in next needs to have jobs and access to opportunities so that we are not a burden. We are people who stand on our own feet.'

'The Adjustment Office does its best.' Powell touched his nose and ran a hand over the afternoon shadow on his cheek. 'We will ensure as many of you as possible are settled together so that your culture is respected and the towns that are becoming available are long-term options. The government will give you outright ownership of the houses in the towns.'

38

Vai let her voice harden a notch. 'It's more important to access opportunities than to own homes in an abandoned town.'

Powell sighed and checked the time. Then he slid three thin paper envelopes to her. 'The Needs Assessment and Options Review team have identified three towns that are likely to be free in the horizon available.'

Vai didn't move her hands. 'I'm here to negotiate the future of a great many people.'

'No, you are an Advocate. This is not a negotiation. The workshops will not go ahead unless you read all the documents and consult with the people you are an Advocate for.'

A large man appeared outside the room. He walked with Vai to the lobby of the Adjustment Office and as she departed he spoke to her in the language of Independence. They both shuffled their feet in their own type of embarrassment.

On the ride back to the apartment Vai didn't look at the three skinny envelopes which had the weight of concrete in her bag. She alighted from the bus and sat for a while in the park, but the cafés were busy and it would be a long wait until midnight and she was hungry so she moved away. In the community centre she sought a toilet but it was busy with local families and there was a line waiting to use the single shower. Inside the library next door groups of school children were doing homework with tutors hovering over them, and a group of smaller children with a bowl of sliced carrots.

At ten o'clock the facility closed. Vai tried to be last one to use the toilet but the man who was there to lock up said only parents were allowed now to take their little kids. Vai dispersed with the others who were calling out and laughing, except the ones who gathered in the light of the veranda and had blankets. The woman who had been slapped in the morning was there. She kissed her little boy and handed him to another woman. She then took off her tights, handed them to the other woman and in her short

39

skirt walked along the footpath to where the cafés were bustling with trade.

Back at the apartment Vai waited to be at the back of the queue for soup. Queenie twinkled her eyes at her and they leaned against the kitchen bench together, eating.

'How well did you know my Dad?' Vai asked.

'He was pretty shy, always polite. Never had long talks, but I felt like I knew him through his silence and his hard work.' Queenie dunked her bread into her soup and watched the buttery stuff swirl. 'He worked construction, mostly. That was the main work. He was one of the few who only ever wanted to get back home. Just working for the money to improve your house on Independence.'

Vai thought about her family, Emma's red coughed-up bubbles. She took a deep breath then pointed upstairs. 'Those people with TB.' She stopped and looked at Queenie anxiously, as though she didn't know how to say what she wanted.

Queenie smiled. 'They're okay. Just so long as they don't cough on you.'

'I know,' Vai said quickly and then covered her mouth. 'I was just wondering. Are they from New Zealand? Are some refugees?'

'No refugees, love. The government stopped letting in ones with contagious sickness.' Queenie looked carefully at Vai. 'Lots of Pasifika people have TB.'

They cleaned the dishes and then Vai stood scrunching her hands together. Queenie gave her a big hug and said, 'What are you worrying about?'

'Dad came here to help our future, and now I have to.'

Queenie nodded. 'Yes, you do. There's no pretending otherwise.' She watched some boys squaring off in front of the kick-boxing game until one of the men growled. 'If you get up in time for breakfast tomorrow I'll take you on the shopping run. After that we'll swing by the house I used to own with my ex, the one where Moses stayed in the garage.'

In the morning Vai joined the returning workers for breakfast. While they were eating the woman who had been slapped came in smelling of alcohol. She was ignored except when someone had to walk by her, and then there was no compunction about bumping her out of the way.

Later, in the van, Vai asked Queenie if everyone hated that woman because she was a hooker.

Queenie laughed. 'Hell, no. You think Joanne's the only one does that? She has a smell about her of things going wrong, things that haven't even arisen yet. You gotta stay away from that trouble.'

The shopping consisted of rushing to three charities that sorted out food which was still good to eat, and then buying what else was needed. Then Queenie drove to Māngere Village, along the coastal road that provided wide sweeping views to the head of the Manukau Harbour. Vai was impressed and tried to think of how to ask how Queenie had ended up in the apartment.

'This place wasn't like this when I lived here,' Queenie said. 'We got a cheap house here because it used to have a sewerage treatment plant that didn't work very well and about once a week the stench hung in the air like a plague. Then they fixed it, but my husband lost his job and we couldn't keep up with the mortgage.' Her voice drifted to a halt at the edge of the kerb. They were outside a very large house. She said with some bitterness, 'That's not the one we owned. Ours was much smaller. I guess it got bowled. But there's the garage.' Behind the house the garage peeked out in the long grass, as if the wrecking ball hadn't noticed.

Vai hopped out of the van and watched the house for a while and satisfied herself no one was home. She went to the garage and cupped her hands around her face at the window to see inside. Queenie felt above the side door and got the key. Inside, the concrete floor was cold and the room was full of packing crates. There was little room to move and Vai imagined her Dad in here, relaxing with friends. She examined a label on a crate and beside the address of the house was a stamp saying 'London'.

41

All the crates were from London. Some had no lids and Queenie lifted a beautiful teapot that was a soft blue with a pattern of leaves. Vai ran her hand over it, she cupped it in both hands and held it aloft so that she could feel its weightless grace, its fragility. *How beautiful*, she thought. In the crate a group of items were wrapped in the shape of plates and others in the shape of cups. 'Spread them out,' she said and Queenie lifted each one carefully and unwrapped it. The light from the door cast a rectangle on the concrete floor and they set them out as if on a table. Vai imagined sharing tea on a hot day with her family, imagined them walking in the door and gingerly using the delicate tableware.

The next crate had a note placed under the lid and beneath that were framed photos of people. A picture showed a man and woman, in their late thirties. Beneath that a second picture showed the same people standing in snow and beside them stood two elderly people. The note read, 'Dear Julia, a new world unfolds, a new future with hope. Be brave. And don't forget we want to speak to a grandchild before too long (Oliver that's a dig at you). Love always, Mummy and Daddy.' And then it said Jonathon and Alison, as if the parents' names might be forgotten or the writer thought Oliver might have felt left out.

Vai began to wrap the crockery and asked Queenie who used to share the garage with her Dad. 'There were about eight beds in here back then, just single guys. Well, when I looked in the door, it was just guys,' Queenie laughed. She stared around the shed as if the beds were laid out there in a mess of blankets and men's underwear. 'We ate together whenever we could. We built a shelter outside, with no sides, just a roof and we had a table and we all cooked together and then carried the pots out and ate. And if it was the evening meal we would stay on late into the night. The boys would use the shelter for their weights.' She looked out the door as if she could hear the men. 'He missed you, your Dad. I guess he didn't really know you, but he loved you. He would play with other children and say, "My girl would be about this size," or, "My girl is smaller than this one."'

'Mum said he named me Vailea, "the water speaks", so he could hear me when he was away.'

After they replaced the crockery in the crate Queenie locked the garage and put the key back in its time-honoured location. 'I planted those mandarin and lemon trees,' she said. Turning to the new house she sighed. 'Better get the food home.' They walked arm in arm to the road.

6

The next morning Vai took her bag and went outside and sat on a wooden pallet under a tree on the berm. The sun was already scorching the tarmac. A skinny brown dog snuck along the silent road as if it hoped it could avoid the heat by moving with its head down and its tail tucked under. Vai reached her hand into the bag and prodded the edges of the three Adjustment Office envelopes. The boy who had wet his pants was sitting on the gravel driveway playing with a digger in the stones. His mother stood smoking nearby and Vai smiled and raised a friendly hand. The woman carefully flicked the burning ember off her cigarette, put it in the cigarette box then she walked over to Vai. 'Joanne,' she said, putting out her hand. Vai reached up and took the hand and gave her name. Joanne pointed at her little boy and said, 'Vaughn.'

He lifted his bright red digger and walked closer to Vai. 'That's a beautiful digger,' she said. He *broom-broomed* it, like a truck. His lank hair was short-cropped on top, long to his chubby waist at the back. Vai looked at his black T-shirt and imagined a pack of cigarettes tucked into his teenage sleeve, a girl not unlike his mother slouching nearby. He gave a gap-toothed smile and went back to pushing his toy.

'Leon gave it to him. Leon's good to him.' Joanne swivelled a ring on her finger then smoothed Vaughn's hair gently. 'He got us some sheep meat last week, didn't he, boy?'

Anxious for help, Vai said, 'I've got options from the Adjustment Office.' Then reconsidered. 'Not really options, basically just choices.' She held up her bag. 'I don't want to look at them. They might be no good.'

'Yeah, well, it sure as hell matters,' Joanne said. Then she brightened up. 'Envelope one, please.' Reluctantly Vai joined in and flourished an envelope in anonymous brown, one hundred per cent recycled paper, with sharp edges. It bore the name of a town and the next line said 'Region: Hawke's Bay'. Joanne groaned loudly. 'No, no. I came from near there. Next envelope, please.'

The next one had the name of a different town and then 'Region: Hawke's Bay' again. Joanne buried her head in her arms. 'Third one, last one, someone's gotta love you.' The third one said 'Balclutha. Region: Otago'.

Neither woman had thought of Otago. 'What's that like?' asked Vai.

'I dunno,' said Joanne. 'Crap, I guess. Otherwise it wouldn't be available. All I know is it's near the bottom of the South Island.'

Vai opened the envelope, took out a sheet of paper that said 'Balclutha Repurposing and Resettlement' and scanned the code with her reader. Joanne put her chin on Vai's shoulder so they could both read the details. The document opened with a picture of a garden in flower and a house that looked solid. They studied the photo, looking for sign of a trick.

'It's green,' said Vai.

'Yeah, it probably rains and snows every day except Christmas. If you don't get a town that's burnt dead you get one that's drowning.' Her eyes scanned the picture. 'You've gotta be careful,' she whispered. 'There's no free towns that are just green. Show me a map.'

Vai found a map showing the town and some of the rural area around it with a river curving around three sides of the main area of town. 'There it is,' Joanne said in triumph. 'I'll bet it's the river. It'll flood every time it rains and wreck the town.'

Sure enough, a clipping showed that the river broke its banks in 2042 and had done the same three years earlier, and after rebuilding the stopbanks a third time the insurance companies wouldn't let the town be rebuilt. Vai scrolled down and Joanne stabbed her finger at a photo of houses with floodwater marks over their window sills. Other documents showed that it was quite a big town, built for ten thousand people, so all of Independence could fit in if they held their breath. Vai didn't speak while they kept scrolling through the documents. Joanne poked her finger and commented like a tour guide, even though she had never been anywhere near Balclutha. Then they found a map that showed the area available for settlement. Joanne said, 'Oh, there you go. They're just offering the low bit on the curve of the river. You'll have New Zealanders looking down on you from the hills either side.'

Vai put the device in her bag and asked what it was like in Hawke's Bay. Joanne's tour-guide demeanour and enthusiasm fell away and she sighed as she fished in her bag for a plastic rubbish-bin liner. The sky had become overcast and now it deepened into black. 'Come and sit up against the building. It's going to rain and we can get some shelter. I'm not going inside.'

Once they were settled and Vaughn had accepted the shelter of the bin liner with a hole ripped so he could see, Joanne said, 'Well, it just burnt the hell up. It was always hot but the summer eventually extended to the end of winter and spring just didn't show.' She shook her head. 'You're going to have to be tough, Vai. You're going have to fight like a cornered rat, 'cause that's what you are. Just look at my lot, we nearly got our heads up. Down where I'm from there was investment in forestry and farms, we had health and Dad pushed all us kids to education, but the whole thing was being eaten away. No one wanted to know about it, but the dial on the oven was turned on high and we just started to cook. Then it turned out that everything we had invested in needed water, and you'd be surprised at how quickly it all fell away. There was two hundred of us all tied together in the family businesses.'

Joanne stood heavily and stepped out into the rain that was

falling steadily now and pointed to the two unopened envelopes on Vai's lap. 'If you saw the photos in there you'd see land that was ashamed of itself. Barren soil, orchards that are a collection of sticks, and if there's any cattle they'd be a disgrace to proper farming. But the farms are mostly just rabbit runs now anyway.'

Vai stood beside Joanne and, reaching her arms out, tried to think of some comforting words, but Joanne shoved her off. Vaughn peered out from his bin liner then sploshed over to his mum and held her leg. 'You have Vaughn,' Vai said, as if she were making an offering of the child. 'And you have everyone here in the apartment.'

Joanne made a sound that was half-yelp, half-fury. She ran to the tree on the berm and bent against it as if she were vomiting.

Vai waited uncertainly while Vaughn sat down in the mud. The tree was poor shelter, its branches scraggled upward and were broken off in places where they might have been large. Black-purple and full, the clouds stood over the city and dictated. Then Joanne strode back to pick up her boy. 'They're Vaughn's father's people,' she said. 'Vaughn's Dad got killed by some prick who wouldn't pay me after a job and his family think I'm poison.'

'That wasn't your fault,' Vai said. 'Can you go to your own family?'

Joanne's face was red and water ran all over her so Vai wasn't sure if there were any tears. 'What for?' she asked. 'You can't imagine the way a change like that affects people. If you start out poor it might be okay, but we came up thinking we weren't going to be poor any longer. Then the way everything turned barren and came to no fruit, one by one bits of the family blew away like the dust. Each one tried a different place but it was just scratching around like chickens. There were no jobs for rural workers. We had a place in the forestry where the pine trees stood in their rows like soldiers, all along the sides of the valleys and across the river flats. They kept their green coats on but when you walked along the tracks you could smell the dry. The brittle clay was cracked open and if there was no wind you'd get the feeling that the whole

47

place had stopped dead still, like a deer that thinks it might have heard a hunting dog.'

Joanne leant against Vai in a close embrace. 'Then one day it caught fire. Took a week to control it, burnt right around the house. Then we got overrun by rabbits, the only crop that grows down there. Dad said we can't get anywhere till we've cleared out the rabbits. He spent every day walking the hills shooting them but they bred faster than he could walk. Then he took to shooting them from the house, which meant he stopped going out, and then he hadn't been outside for months, just shooting out the door, out the bedroom window, sneaking through the kitchen and blasting from where he crouched down in the laundry. Then he started making Mum go and get each one and cook each one with beans. He'd shoot twenty in one day, but we were all scared of him. Then my older sister left and I hung on because Mum was getting around the house like a small child. But then I started sneaking out and staying in town.'

Joanne lit a smoke and blew a big belch of it into the wet air. Then she said how she stopped going home and even though she liked school she started this work, but she didn't think she was very good at it, she never got much business, no repeats.

Probably right, Vai thought looking at the farrow lines on her face and a chest that promised no bounty. She remembered the deep rich soil of Independence and shuddered at the girl in front of her, depleted before she made her second decade.

'Anyway, one good thing about that,' Joanne said, 'is I know who Vaughn's father probably is. He used to look after me and some other girls from school.' She looked along the street, which was flooding around the blocked drains, water pooling over onto the grass. 'So I don't recommend you take your people there.'

Hearing that, Vai felt a familiar skip in her heart. Just then Leon scuttled through the rain and opened the car door. Vai called out anxiously, 'Can I fit in too?'

'I've got to meet a guy at the wharf. It's business and I don't know how long it will take.'

48

'That's okay,' She placed a hand on Joanne's shoulder and said, 'Thanks for the advice.'

Inside the car was fuzzy with damp and old shoes. Vai said, 'I'm soaked. Is there a towel?'

'Probably. Have a look.'

Vai rummaged through the detritus in the back seat, found a towel and rubbed her hair dry. 'Joanne's had a hell of a life.'

'Yeah, but everyone gets hit. It's attitude that matters. Did she talk to you about rabbits?'

'Yeah. Why?'

'Because that's how she sees herself, a prey animal, a rabbit.'

'She said you look after her and her boy. Get them food.'

'When? Nah. Oh, yeah. It was raining the other night and I went up the peninsula and got a sheep. Real sheep's like gold and I got one. I stuck it in the front seat here, where you're sitting. I put a wig on it so it looked like a girl.' He pushed Vai's shoulder back and she sniffed the seat. There it was, a faint scent of lanolin. 'A green-hair girl with her throat slit and her guts out. Everyone had that sheep.'

They pulled to a stop near the wharf and Leon pointed to a steel-hulled ship painted black and emblazoned with a sword at the head of a school of marine animals: whale followed by shark, followed by seal, followed by various smaller fish and birds flying above. The sword had a thick, wicked blade and underneath the words 'Ocean Warrior' were painted white. 'Come on, I'll introduce you to a few people, then I've got to take something to look after for them. They're going south to Antarctica.'

The ship was called *Taniwha* and was about the size of the ships that had connected Independence to the world, but possibly faster, Vai speculated. The foredeck had water cannon mounted and above them the bridge would provide the captain with a three-sixty view. The open deck running the length of the ship was wide and there were other cannon mounted at evenly spaced distances through to the rear deck. A long mechanical arm was being used to load supplies.

A thin man of mid-age and mid-height watched Leon and Vai approach. His head was shaved and his thick beard bristling over his chest emphasised how skinny he was. He had a hammerhead shark tattoo that ran tail to head from his elbow to his wrist and a ring on each finger of the same hand. His other arm and hand were bare of any adornment. 'This is Robert Negri, captain of the *Taniwha*,' Leon said, 'and this is Vai Shuster. Vai is family. She's advocating for Independence.'

The captain leant forward and hugged Vai. 'I heard about the terrible storm that hit not long ago. Were you there?' His bushy black eyebrows furrowed and then lifted like friendly pets.

'Yes,' Vai responded, 'it wrecked the place. We can rebuild but the soil is in terrible condition.'

'I heard there were deaths. Are your family safe?'

Vai shook her head and explained what had happened. Tears, her sadness a raven perched on her shoulder, guilt. 'Good God,' the captain said. 'And you're here advocating? It's relentless. Merciless.'

'It's desperate now. We're being kept up there like convicts.'

He rubbed her arm. 'Come in and have coffee. Leon will be twenty minutes. I guess you're familiar with ships?'

As they climbed the stairs to the deck Vai took in the familiar smells of diesel and salt, the rhythmic pulling of the *Taniwha* against her ties. Stores were set out on deck, neatly stacked boxes waiting to be taken below. Vai was impressed by the orderly set-out of equipment and supplies and the fresh paint.

Negri noticed Vai surveying the ship. 'Are you from a fishing family?'

'Dad's a fisherman, and I'm his first mate.' She motioned around the deck. 'I've worked on boats this size, boats trading between islands. I'm good crew. I've sailed through some big storms out on the open ocean. It's a tidy ship, this one here.'

'Of course. There's no room to be casual. We might not be carrying weapons, but this is a fighting ship. We're going into the Southern Ocean, to Antarctica. We're going to shine a light on what everyone's doing. The sea's warming and there's bugger-all law there. It's a wild frontier.'

Vai nodded and pointed to the water cannon. 'Are they weapons?'

'They'll kill you if you stand in front of them at less than twenty metres, but technically they're fire-fighting.' They stood still and studied the cannon as if they might transform into military weapons. 'Will you go back to Independence when you finish here?' Negri asked.

'No, I don't plan to. I don't need to know more about that island. It's finished. I need to know more about the world.' Vai looked at him hopefully. 'Do you need crew? This is the type of ship I know about, and if Antarctica is changing then it's worth seeing now. How long will you be away?'

'We'll be in the Southern Ocean for about five months, but it depends on the weather. I don't mean to say that I wouldn't want you on crew, but wouldn't you learn more from staying here?'

'I can't, unless I overstay. They're very careful about holding us off until the last minute. My role as an Advocate would be finished if I overstay. I have too much responsibility to do that.' Vai tugged a lock of her hair. 'I hope this doesn't sound wrong, but I don't have any money. I'm here on a sponsorship and back home we just live day to day. I need to work and I—'

'You don't need to explain,' Negri said. 'Some of what we do is dangerous and there's the risk of being arrested. In safer waters we're direct, violent. It's action, action, action but the Southern Ocean is too isolated and dangerous for a lot of that, and it's hard to escape after an attack on another ship.' He pointed skyward. 'Easy to follow us.' Then he leant back against the rail of the ship and opened his arms wide. 'Mostly, down in the Southern Ocean we're just exposing criminal activity. Or publicising exploitation, even if it's not strictly illegal, shaming nations and their navies into action.' Then he took a boxer's stance and threw a snappy combination of punches toward Vai. 'We hit them if we can. If we can get away with it. Sink the bastards.'

Vai was grinning, nodding along, feeling the punches land and the thickness of blood.

Negri's eyes lit up. 'I think you'll fit. You won't earn much, but it will be enough to help you keep moving.'

'I'll need to clear up what's needed from me here in New Zealand. Have I got time?'

'Few days.'

The kitchen was empty. As Negri looked around the room his face settled comfortably in a way that reminded Vai of peace and they helped themselves to coffee. He described some of the journey to Auckland, and lingered on the stopover at tiny, uninhabited Malden island. 'I don't know if Independence is like this,' he said, 'but Malden's teaming with bird life. I've never seen anything like it, abundant nature like we read about from the past. Boobies, terns, frigate birds in large numbers and others as well. The island's very low so no one lives there, but it has an immense, enclosed lagoon, then the surrounding land and then it plunges into deep, deep water. Unimaginably blue and clear. I guess you know what it's like, but for me these places are breathtaking. We dived and saw sailfish hunting, shaking out their magnificent sails and rounding up small fish. They could flash their sails from browns to reds and purples and even silver. They were like something from a child's imagination.'

7

By the time of the first resettlement workshop there was unanimous agreement from the team on Independence that they were going to fight the options. They knew they needed to get to jobs and, if they could stay together in one of the cities, Vai said they could do what others were doing, band together in apartments and support each other, work as a team, hunt as a pack.

Vai was met at the Adjustment Office waiting room by a kindly-looking man with grey hair and soft hands. He wore a mauve shirt with a deeper, purple tie. His name was Andrew and when he introduced his associate Vai only noted her hostility. Mauve Andrew and a woman in a summer dress with hostile eyes. Vai wanted to say how unhappy she was with the options but Andrew beckoned them all to remain standing in the meeting room and opened the workshop with a prayer. While they were still standing he welcomed Vai and extended his greeting to all of Independence and then they each had a scone with jam.

There were three options to consider and they only had an hour and half, so thirty minutes for each option. Andrew distributed an agenda. 'For each location we will look at the quality of assets, infrastructure such as schools, water and wastewater, parks and medical facilities. Once we understand the asset base we can discuss how each location can be configured to accommodate twenty thousand people. We'll need to think about budget for additional buildings over time.' He looked at Vai to check she was following. 'It's crucial to know about these things. We've tied settlement to the provision of health and education. You have to stay put to get those services. It's how the government makes sure existing assets are used fully and limits demand for new ones. Once we've discussed each place we'll rank them to see which best meet the needs of Independence.'

Vai said, 'Everyone on Independence agrees that none of these places will work for us. We really appreciate what the government is offering but we'd rather be in a city where there's employment. Wouldn't it be cost-effective to build homes near jobs?'

'I'm sorry,' Andrew said, 'this can't become a negotiation. We're not building new homes for refugees when there are quite good ones lying empty. The political door would shut.'

Vai started to state her case. She'd rehearsed it. 'Wouldn't it be cheaper—'

The woman cut her off. 'Look out the window. What you see now is just the beginning. Climate breakdown hasn't even kicked in yet. From here on things really turn to shit and decisions are going to be made about leaving millions upon millions of people to die. It's not like a world war where the political leaders can turn it off when they get sick of it. Two hundred years! There's two hundred years of calamity baked in place and there's no hero to just turn that off.'

Vai shoved her chair back and was about to walk around the table and knock the woman down, but Andrew stopped her: 'Vai, just get your people over here. Who knows how policies evolve?'

He said there would be a reception the next evening for all Advocates of Pacific Island nations and the advisory board of the Adjustment Office: a mix of senior business people and community leaders, supporting the Minister of Population. 'Please come. It's important.'

*

54

Vai exited the Adjustment Office at a quick trot and contacted Leon. She needed good clothes. 'Easy,' he said. 'We'll do that this evening.'

On the bus back to Ōtāhuhu, Vai put her bag on the seat next to her and spread herself out. There were noisy schoolkids and little kids with runny noses who were tired and hungry and everyone had on clothes that were worn at the collar and might as well have had second-hand stamped across them. A couple in the seat behind were arguing, not even taking turns, just belligerent.

Vai alighted outside the café strip and hurried toward the apartment, arriving breathless at the car where Leon waited. 'Squeeze your arse in here,' he said, and she was trundling deeper into the side streets. She explained what she was looking for: skirt, blouse, jacket and good heels. A handbag if possible.

They drove down a long access way and stopped in front of a building that was too large to be a shed but not much use as a warehouse. Vai screwed up her face and waved her hands in exasperation. 'I need *good* clothes.'

Leon laughed. 'That's what we're here for, unless madam wants to pay top dollar.'

Inside there were boxes of big screens and electric bikes and an area marked off with clothes and an area that seemed to have some of everything a person could want. The woman who greeted them knew Leon well enough to peck him on the cheek. She wore a purple plastic cowboy hat on bright red hair and her pink dress looked like the skin on a saggy sausage. Leon told her what they were after: she looked at Vai and smirked. She rustled in some boxes and came back with a skirt that covered about six inches of nothing, a pair of stilettos and a tight blouse that buttoned down the front. Vai looked at her dead flat and said, 'No, I'm a lawyer and I'm meeting business clients.'

The woman laughed. 'I'll get you another six inches, then.'

Leon pointed at some unopened boxes that had a high-class air. 'What about the stuff in there?' The woman sauntered over and said she'd only open the boxes if they purchased, otherwise they'd lose value. Leon said, 'Yeah, that stuff would be right,' and he selected a skirt that dropped below the knee, matching blouse and jacket, then pointed out a handbag and shoes.

Vai asked about a necklace and the woman pointed out a selection but Leon said, 'They're too expensive.' Vai said she'd better try the clothes on and the woman said, 'If you must. There's no changing room here.' Vai stripped to her knickers and bra and the other woman pretended not to admire Vai's shoulders and legs, her swimmer's build. Vai paused to flex the muscles on her legs and pulled her belly tight and was pleased to see the other woman's scowl. Leon helped himself to a look before she stepped into the ensemble.

The mirror sparkled at her in the dusty room and she took stock of the new woman reflected there. *Very good*, she thought, and asked how much. No way could she pay the amount. She looked at Leon. 'Can you lend me some of the cost?'

He turned to the woman and said, 'How about she rents it? She can pay you twenty per cent and return it unmarked.'

The woman tilted her head back and crossed her arms. 'Well, you could earn the cost of the whole thing if you didn't have such a high opinion of yourself.'

Vai said, 'I'll pay you fifty per cent and keep it for the week.'

The woman poked a fat finger at Vai. 'If it's marked you pay the whole lot and if you don't come back it'll come off Leon's docket, so it doesn't worry me.' Then Vai changed into her old clothes and while the woman packaged everything up Vai dropped a small box with a necklace into her backpack. She ignored Leon's angry look.

The reception was held on the waterfront at Mission Bay in the historic stone building that used to form the Melanesian Mission but had long since been a restaurant. Vai cut a striking figure, her hair braided and piled high on her head: the doorman was unable to avoid staring into her eyes, set against a dusting of purple make-up on soft brown skin. She paused at the door, settling her nerves and rehearsing the names of the people she hoped could help her. The doorman smiled encouragement and she stepped into the high-ceilinged foyer. She took a glass of peppermint water as she walked into the main room and sighted the Minister of Population, who had a small gaggle of Advocates around him. He was renowned for staying two steps behind the voters and Vai didn't break her stride as she headed for the business leaders.

Jim Wang, chair of the advisory board, ran the largest meat and milk products wholesale company in the country. Vai checked his photo on her media device and scanned the room. Wang stood near the waterside door, talking to a middle-aged man whose stocky build emphasised Wang's tidy, neat demeanour. She introduced herself and congratulated him on securing a new deal with China. He smiled, happy to give her his time. 'Yes,' he said, 'ten per cent more product from next year. Let me introduce Adam Walker from the Prime Minister's Office.'

'I'm here to talk with the board,' Adam said, 'and get their sense of the willingness New Zealanders have to take on a great many more migrants. It's not strong, I'm afraid. And what do you do when you're not advocating for Independence?'

'It's my full-time role,' Vai said. She turned to Wang. 'You must have a very good reputation to continue securing such important contracts. I guess your business is run very efficiently.'

'Thank you, that's very kind. I feel a deep responsibility.' He moved his hand as if to dismiss his role. 'Tell me. What is being grown on Independence?'

She assessed him quickly: was that a polite question or did he really want to know? 'We have a lot of volcanic soil. We could grow so many things. It was a living grocery.' She folded her arms. 'The sea's been washing over. Washing over nearly half of it, all around the edges. The salt's wrecking it.'

He put a hand on her arm. 'That would break your heart.' He let his arm drop. 'My family are farmers too. We go back two hundred years here.' Vai nodded. His words took her back home

57

to her Pa's land and then she thought of her Dad. Tears brimmed in her eyes. 'I'm sorry,' he said, 'I didn't mean to be so thoughtless.'

She replied that they had recently suffered a massive cyclone and they needed to move quickly, that the New Zealand government was telling them ten more years but they couldn't wait. 'We are being tethered by funding policy to places with no jobs.'

Adam ran through the reasons, but Wang shook his head. 'This is a big mistake, we will all reap a poor harvest from that policy.'

Vai turned to him hopefully. 'We need to move near jobs. Will you be expanding your workforce?'

'No, it's almost all robotic and automated. We need to be as efficient as we can to get food across the world at a reasonable price. New Zealand is still the world's farm.'

Vai smiled. 'Yes, that makes sense. Perhaps I can correspond with you? Just to get a better idea of the changes that might occur in future.' She took a business card from her bag.

Graciously Wang took it. 'I don't carry cards myself, but I will ensure someone from my office makes contact.' Adam produced a card and Vai quickly fished out another one of hers for him.

The maître d' beckoned them to their seats and Vai found herself in the middle of the table away from Wang, who sat at the top. Miriama Hunter, head of the country's largest property company, sat on Vai's right; on her left was the Vice-Chancellor of Waikato University. Vai introduced herself and repeated her story, this time mentioning her dad.

Miriama said, 'You're obviously respected by your people. They chose you despite your youth and suffering.'

Vai tried to stay calm. She knew Miriama was a powerhouse in the nation's property world. *God, she could settle Independence before the week was over.* Sixty-two and no attempt to hide it: Vai had checked Miriama's age before the dinner began. Black hair run through with grey, face weathered and creased, shoulders straight, dark eyes digging into a person's centre. 'Perhaps,' she said. 'I feel like I've been thrown by the storm. I can't make any mistakes.' She hesitated. 'I met with staff at the Adjustment

Office yesterday. You should have seen the anger of one of their people. Yelling at me about how appalling things are about to become. How we're locking into the death phase. I nearly got up and belted her.' Vai hesitated again, checking Miriama's reaction. 'Government policy. It's got us trapped. It's calculated, almost cunning.'

'Yes, the policy is a disgrace. It's a capitulation to failure.' Miriama took a sip of her wine. 'We've shifted to taking migrants from the countries we need as partners, the big and the powerful. We're telling the failing countries, "Sorry, no room."' She took in Vai's frightened face. 'Except the little Pacific Island countries, we're still promising to take you.'

'The policy is to put us in towns that are failing. Do you know Balclutha? That's one.'

'Yes, I live not too far away, in Dunedin. It was a very beautiful town, but now . . .' She shook her head, 'Well, everywhere is in flux.' She looked Vai in the eye. 'You could make a go of the place, but you'd have to make a real commitment. The bit that's up for grabs needs more protection, raise the flood banks, there's a lot of work to do. But don't underestimate Otago, and don't think you're too far from jobs.'

Vai felt warmth and the first inkling of a chance. 'What about agriculture and cropping? We're farmers.'

Miriama shook her head. 'That's only a path for people with capital or for people who inherit. There will be many more jobs near Dunedin eventually, and not only low-skilled ones.'

Vai nodded eagerly. 'Yes, that's the path. Jobs near a city.'

'When can you all get here?'

'They're saying ten years.'

'No, no. Ten years is too late, much too late. You'll lose that spot. Balclutha will be taken by another group of refugees.' Miriama patted her mouth with her napkin distractedly. 'Left behind,' she said, looking through the glass to the sea.

'We need to move now. We aren't asking to stay, we're asking to get out.'

'Here, take my card. We must meet before you return to Independence. Call that number.' Miriama turned to the person to her right and Vai basked in the glow of possibility.

After the meal the party moved into the adjoining room where there was to be a brief presentation on urban resilience, which struck Vai as insulting given this was a meeting of refugee Advocates and they were all being blocked from city jobs. The presenter was a youthful man, thin across his shoulders and lean, with an expensive cotton suit that he mentioned was organic cotton and coloured with vegetable dyes. 'Let's acknowledge the facts,' he said. 'We're in a tough spot, but those aren't the facts that matter, they're the facts that scare us. Let's review the path to victory.' On the wall screen a couple were pictured riding graciously through a city on electric bikes. A vista unfolded of tall buildings festooned with vegetation. Birds flew among the verdant growth. Elegant street rail mingled with healthy people and food that popped with colour. He reviewed the technological achievements that took tonnes upon tonnes of carbon from the air or removed the need for that carbon to ever burn at all. The achievements were impressive and Vai nodded along with the narrative of hope. The images lifted her soul and the anxiety that followed on her heels stepped back for the first time in weeks. Real change was being implemented; technology was only just getting started. The real challenge, the presenter pointed out, was to believe in the radical transformation that was taking place and drive it harder. The visual journey above his head continued to unfold: the couple were joined on their cycle journey by six bearded men in tight tops and shorts and the eight of them rode effortlessly upward along a winding road.

Standing beside Vai, Adam leant in and mock-whispered, 'It's called anaesthetic.' He shook his head in disgust. 'The gentle ride to Eden.'

'Well, I guess so,' she said, 'but can't you enjoy the soporific feeling, just for the evening?'

'To hear him talk you'd think the beautiful eight on their beautiful bikes have tipped the balance, propelled us into the promised land. These people will let you have your cake and eat it.'

Vai felt a hand on her arm. 'Excuse me,' a man's voice said. It was the doctor from Independence, the man who had acknowledged Emma's illness and kept his silence: Dr Zhu. Vai felt as if a friend had made an unexpected appearance. Such a pleasant man, in his fifties. Thin, but with an air of something, not weakness, not strength, perhaps stamina. Vai imagined he might be an ultra-distance runner. The sort who find something inside themselves, an ability to lock into motion and be stoic in pain.

Vai introduced the two men. 'The doctor was in the team from China that helped us after the big storm.'

Dr Zhu touched his chest, hand across his heart. 'I'm so pleased you've got to New Zealand and you're here for this meeting. People should help you.' He turned to Adam. 'I'm a stand-in — the head of our consulate couldn't get here and since I have a lot of experience supporting refugee settlements I was asked to attend.'

They all turned back to hear the speaker prosecute his case in favour of technology that was on the cusp of bringing an end to climate change. *Fair enough*, Vai thought, *so many achievements, but it doesn't account for the existence of me.*

As soon as the presentation finished Adam said, 'How is there so much achievement, knowledge and wealth while at the same time, and often in the same locations, so much of the population is in poverty, generation after generation? Every day I read about some fantastic new advance in a field I didn't even know about, yet someone is working away sorting something out so that we can all progress. And then I read my morning briefing and the torrent of miserable souls, seeking nothing more than food and a roof that keeps out the snow or the belting heat, well, that torrent continues to flow.'

Vai looked at the ground, a wave of shame flushing over her. Then anger at her shame. She thought of her task and steadied herself. 'It's turning into a complex story,' she said. 'When I was younger I thought things would get fixed by people in New Zealand or somewhere else. Then I thought, well, we'll just have to move to New Zealand. Even though I was angry, I thought that would be okay. Now it's turning into a maze.'

'People like that presenter tonight should be shot,' Adam said. 'It used to be quite simple. There were two ends on a single rod, the experts stating we were heading for a crisis, and those who denied the whole issue existed. The everyday people arrayed themselves at various points on the rod, and as people shuffled up and down the line it was easy to debate and set policy.' He took three canapés from a passing tray and juggled one into his mouth, wine glass steady in the other hand. A fleck of pastry hung on his top lip. 'Then we got the green-growth crew, and their walled gardens. Everyone was invited in but no one could see out. All we had to do, they said, was wait for technology, implement it as it arose and price for change. It was laughable. All our projections showed catastrophic failure but the snake-oil salesmen were in full cry.' The fleck of pastry wobbled as Adam spoke, but held on. 'Instead of a rod we got something that resembled a hammock, and everyone went to sleep. The green-growthers stuffed us right up. One day they'll face a court and I'll be there to see them. It won't be the deniers, not the honest deniers.' Now he was poking his finger in sharp jabs, leaning in close. 'It'll be the bullshitters who faked the maths.'

Adam's breath had that older-man smell, like yesterday's dinner. Vai took a step back and said, 'Well, the achievements he listed are real. Why shouldn't he talk about those things?'

'Sure, but only if he discusses the scale of change needed and the time available to make the change.' Adam nodded toward Dr Zhu. 'Only China did that. Think how rapidly we need to drive carbon out of the economy. Now think how much time is available to do that. People have been telling each other we can rely on pricing pollution and cap and trade since 1992 at least, but nothing effective was done. We were anaesthetised by people

62

like him and his half-informed mates. Everything just trundled on.' He rolled his eyes. 'All he did was distract us with happy talk when we should be screaming. Scale and time, Ms Shuster, that's the heart of it now, the enemies that have been avoided for too long. Too late, I fear.'

Dr Zhu nodded and said quietly, so that Vai had to lean in to hear, 'We're in a new phase now. Arranging ourselves for the crash. Making preparations for the changes and the opportunities.'

'What's your response to that, Adam?' Vai asked as he finished his wine and took another from a passing waiter. 'I mean, for a place like Auckland. Do you know the city well? Do you see how this story is developing, for ordinary people?'

'I'm starting to understand it. Auckland's never been my favourite city. Wellington's for me. Or Europe — if I could live in Prague I would be a very happy man. It's the geographic centre of Europe, has a reasonable climate, and now it's the political centre too.' His face came to life as he mentioned Prague: his eyes sparked but then grew distant.

'What keeps you busy when you're here?' Vai asked.

'Reading, I read a lot, and walking. Sometimes I finish my work and walk for hours, to midnight some evenings. I might pick up a book and walk along the harbour and then find myself crossing a few streets and looking at the gardens, if I'm in the right suburbs. Then I stop for a meal and read a few pages. Or I might people-watch. I see couples strolling together and I try to imagine their lives. Sometimes I look into their living rooms. It doesn't matter if I don't know where I'm walking, in fact that's part of the fun. Then when I'm tired I find my way back to where I'm staying. I often stay in a bed and breakfast — the company can be good.' He rubbed his chin and looked embarrassed. 'What about you?'

'I have my advocacy, but I think I'm staying in a different Auckland from the one you visit.'

'Yes, I guess you might be. What will you do after your right to stay here ends? Will you go back to Independence?'

'No, I want to see what's happening in the world. I have an offer to go to Antarctica. It might seem a strange place to see the changes the world is experiencing but I've been told it's a frontier.'

Adam gestured toward the doctor. 'With the Chinese?'

'No, with a research ship. I've got a crewing job.'

'Good choice,' Dr Zhu said. 'Antarctica will tell you a lot about the future. You will see what's happening as we race toward three degrees of change, if not more. The ban on mining there has to be renegotiated, since the Madrid Protocol only ran to 2048.'

'The big prize is on the table,' Adam interjected. 'The real climate impacts are only emerging. What we've seen so far is child's play. Wait until China, America and India reveal their hands. The big three.'

'We're past the point for fear,' Zhu said. 'And there's no reason we can't move at pace. Pace and scale, isn't that what you recommended? We can do that.' He waved at a man nearby and excused himself.

Adam checked the time. 'I guess this reception will start to wind down. Can I buy you a drink? There's a good wine bar just one block from here.'

Vai thought about the second workshop she had to attend and Balclutha and said, 'Yes, why not, but I'm not drinking alcohol. Not tonight.'

At the bar Adam took his time with the wine list. He selected a shiraz from Alice Springs in the heart of Australia. 'Who'd have thought,' he said, raising his glass, 'who'd have thought shiraz from the red heart of Australia? Very good.'

Vai's drink arrived in a long glass with a straw and a little coloured umbrella. Adam reached over and took the offending items out. 'It's not school break, is it,' he said. 'Anyway, where was I? Yes, Alice Springs. It's become one of the more interesting places to visit. Hot, of course, but they found an enormous lake of water deep under the surface and they've used it to create an enclosed world with thousands of acres of residential, food production and leisure activities. From the outside, when you fly in it looks like a giant warehouse, but it's very clever, very safe. You can only get there by flying and you can live free of all the stress that dogs us in our home lives. Inside living, it works perfectly well. Adaptation, that's what it is, from the shopping mall, to the apartment, to computer games. Nobody really misses the outside.'

'Is that where you imagine living?'

'In the desert? No, never. Prague, as I said, it's the centre of Europe now. It has its own inside living, but of course you can move between streets to the art galleries and museums and theatre. You'd love it. Perhaps one day I could show you?'

'I've got a big entourage, I'm afraid,' Vai said, forcing a laugh. 'There's twenty thousand people I need to house. Can we discuss that?'

Adam placed his elbows on the table and his chin in his hands. 'I can't get Independence a special dispensation, if that's what you're going to ask. You have to work within the system. I know you want to migrate soon, but that will only happen if things get very much worse on Independence, and I assume you don't want that.' He beckoned for Vai to lean in close to him. 'What I *can* tell you is that soon there will be demand for labour in New Zealand on a scale never imagined. You could try to get your working age people here on work visas and build from there. I can't give you any detail, but I saw you with Miriama Hunter. Stick with her if you can, she's the ticket.' He leaned back and raised his glass to his nose. Fixing his eyes on Vai he smiled. 'Perfect. Excellent.'

But she didn't want him to focus on her and she didn't want to let him go, so she leaned forward with big eyes and said, 'What needs to be done? How do we respond to this?'

Adam swished his wine in the glass. 'Look at this thing, look at what we're facing. We're on the verge of the apocalypse and it's, well, let's face it, it's ordinary. We're adapting and accommodating and avoiding. This should be the greatest thriller ever written, but it's not.' He held one hand up high and indicated the words with his fingers, annunciating loudly, 'Apocalypse. Quite. Soon. Not very energising, not very scary, is it? Imagine that, the Apocalypse as a box-office flop. So long in the making and it turns out to be manageable. We just shuffle around.'

Bile surged in Vai's throat but her smile remained pinned in place. 'I don't follow,' she said.

'It's like this. Things are going wrong piecemeal and the rich and their mid-level support system have discovered they can adapt. Each threat is countered, the pawns are going to have to go, but it looks like the rest can survive. It's amazing. We're fantastic in our macabre, organic response.' He swept his hands across the cloth in front of him, clearing the land, then arranged his wine glass, blood red, and placed her glass opposite. 'Think about this. Forget the gentle walk to Eden. We should have said, "This is a war." Not a shooting war, but think of Winston Churchill in the1930s. He was in World War One and in the 1930s he sat down with the British public and told them he believed they needed to fight a second war. They knew the reality of war, the carnage, and he was asking them to send their kids into another. Eventually he convinced them to do this for the sake of their grandchildren. That was the type of action we needed, courage and sacrifice. Instead we were sold nonsense, tactical failure. We were told to talk up the successes but that made people think we were succeeding. It left no room for politicians to drive the scale of change, and there was no risk management. We ate up the time, ran down the clock and had no scope to recalibrate. Fatal, fatal.'

He took hold of the two glasses, swung the blood-red wine glass against the insipid light green of her mixture. 'As if this was war,' he hissed. 'A short, decade-long hit, hammering at the problem, driving the curve down, as if it was the only problem on Earth. We could have done it, could have smashed it. In the manner of a war. We could have accepted the sort of infrastructure casualties that come with war. We should have agreed to strand

66

solid assets like coal power, even if they had decades of economic life. Take the hit for our grandchildren. The narrative was wrong and we failed.'

Vai could see he was excited by this theme but his device rang and reluctantly he looked at the caller ID. 'Just one minute,' he said, annoyed to be interrupted, and hurried to the door. He spoke rapidly and looked back at Vai and put up his hand in a stop sign in case she might walk over to him. Then he ended the call and indicated his watch and held up five fingers to Vai, so she waited. Soon he was joined by a short Asian man in a well-cut suit. Adam stood between Vai and the other man so she had a poor view of him, but he appeared to be giving instructions and Adam appeared to be non-committal, moving his hands sideways, palm down.

When Adam returned to the table there were beads of sweat on his brow and his attention had moved away from Vai. 'Damn job,' he said. 'I'm constantly being lobbied. Anyway, Miriama, she's the one.'

But he didn't seem angry: his mood had turned to anxiety. Then he said, 'I hope you don't think I'm rude but I'm going to walk.'

Vai watched him walk away, shoulders hunched forward, no longer the assayer of a battle plan. How quickly he'd fallen back, she thought.

8

It was nearly one in the morning when Leon waved at her from beside a van across the road. He hadn't been happy to come and get her. He was busy, he'd said, so she had waited in the bar by herself. Then, when she stepped onto the path beside him, he took her arm and said, 'The guys inside are a bit bashed up, but they're mates.'

Vai took a step back and looked at him, his glistening eyes, mouth fixed in a hungry grimace. 'What's happened?' she asked. 'Your knuckles are cut.'

He flexed them, opening and closing his fists, looking at them as though they were someone else's. 'There was trouble, but we're fine. It's like this some nights. Mostly the city simmers, but some nights it boils.' He was breathing hard and his eyes were bloodshot.

Inside the van she felt dread, felt surrounded by violence. Blood ran freely from a cut above one man's eye and across his snow-white skin, so translucent that she felt the red flow might seep back in to rejoin a vein. 'This is my cousin,' Leon said to the men and then, pointing front and back, 'These guys are Kiwis.'

Vai tucked in against him and surveyed the half dozen men who had the look of a pack of dogs that were part-way through a hunt. 'Just dealing with some lice,' one called out. The others raised their heads up and laughed, but they could just as easily have howled. *Lice*. Vai was familiar with the term and looked at Leon in horror, crouching in tighter against him.

One of them opened a small glass vial and sniffed its contents. 'Didn't you hear the news?' he said. 'We're under more pressure to take in lice from all over the globe. The government's thinking about it. We're doing some doing about it, making sure they know how we feel. I don't mind if you're Pasifika, that's as good as one of us. Leon and Sai are part-Pasifika, we'll look after them, but if anyone thinks we're an open door they can take a message from tonight.'

The man with the cut over his eye hit the roof of the van with his fist. 'Not just us. It was all on across the cities tonight, coordinated.'

Vai kept her fear hidden, stayed expressionless.

'Don't curl up and be shocked, girl,' he said. 'There's tens of millions of them, and soon there'll be hundreds of millions. All of them starving and fighting. If they think they'll be welcome down here they'll swamp us all.' But he wasn't talking to her any more; he was working the boys back up, 'Did you see anyone stop us? Did you see anyone say, "Oh no, take my job away"? Brodie, did it matter when you got laid off and now your job gets done at night on the sly by the lice? Now things are happening.'

'There's already millions of them here,' another man yelled out the window. He turned to Vai. 'The government won't say, won't publish the numbers. But you can see them all the way south to Hamilton and over to Tauranga. Migrants, refugees and migrants. That's not us, not community.'

'That's right,' said the bleeding man. 'India, China, America. They've got a plan and we have to do our part. Whatever it is, we have to do it.'

The interior of the van was burning red energy and the men were grabbing and shaking each other and from the music speakers a man was screaming above the sound of guitar thudding. Vai put her hand on Leon's neck and pulled him in front of her. He felt the threat and moved with it, hitting his own hands on the roof and Vai wasn't sure if he was protecting her or just caught in the heat.

They were coming up to the wharf and Vai's reader showed that captain Negri was nearby, probably on the boat. 'I'll jump out at the wharf,' she said. 'I know someone down there.'

'Good,' said the bleeding man as the van came to a halt. His face crumpled, lips twisted, piggy eyes. 'Who're ya meeting?'

'The captain from the Ocean Warrior ship.'

'Hoo, yeah. They're fighting the wrong enemy but at least they're fighting. You can learn to make an explosive device if you spend more than a weekend away with a hard green.'

The next morning Vai cornered Leon before he could get into his car. 'Aren't I lice?'

'No, you're Pasifika and you belong here. Anyway, I don't care about it. I just do it for money. The other guys are into it. They're trying to stop the country getting overrun. There's already a million and a half migrants and refugees here.'

Vai sucked in a loud breath and bent forward, hands on her thighs. 'Rubbish. There's nowhere near that many.' She peered up at him. 'You're doing this for money?' She stood and grabbed him by the collar. 'Do you take money to beat us?'

Leon curled his lip and snarled, 'The panther strikes.' Then he turned serious. 'The trouble here, in New Zealand, is the climate apocalypse is mild. We're getting it mild, so everyone's coming to hide here.'

9

Wednesday was scheduled for Vai's second workshop at the Adjustment Office. She knew what she would advocate for and she had clearance from the team on Independence. But first she needed to see Miriama again. Shaking and urgent, she dialled the number Miriama had given her. Miriama laughed at her gabbled request and said, 'Yes, of course. I'll book lunch for us both at the Cherry Garden.'

Vai invested in another top to go with the clothes she was renting. It was a soft blue and made of silk, which felt great in the humid weather. She hoped the little mark on the collar wasn't obvious.

The restaurant was at the bottom of Queen Street. It occupied a large, privileged space facing down the harbour to North Head. Cherry trees stood in large planters and tables were arranged beneath them; above, a glass roof held back the weather. A mosaic of birds cast into the glass threw shadows onto the floor. Vai realised she was early: she felt light-headed amid the wealth and held back a desire to skip among the bird-shadows.

She had called home before she left for the restaurant. Her mum and the twins crowded to the screen, Pa quiet in the background. They were all pale and thin. Moses's absence hung over everything they said and all that was not said. Erfan explained how the search had progressed and ended. On calm days he still took the Afoas' boat far beyond the reef. Vai asked, 'Are you searching a grid?' He said, no, he mostly just sat out there.

Vai nodded at Emma. 'What about you?'

Emma began to avoid the question but Sonya said, 'Tell her. She needs to know.' Sonya stared into Vai's eyes and said, 'She's worse. It's settling deep into her lungs and it's resistant.'

Vai sighed. 'I could tell.' She put on a small smile. 'I've met someone who can help. I'm having lunch with her. A property developer, the chair of the Otago Development Trust. One of the richest people in the country.' Sonya drew in her breath, leaning in. 'Something's happening in the south, near Dunedin,' Vai continued. 'It's to do with Antarctica. I don't know what it is but there's a town near there that we might get to settle in, and if I'm right we can get jobs. It could be a new home. It's called Balclutha. But I have to leave in a few days. I've got a job on a boat, an Ocean Warrior boat. We're going to Antarctica.'

'A fighting ship?' her Pa asked.

'I'm out of money and I can't stay,' Vai said.

He nodded, as matter-of-fact as his granddaughter. 'Do your share.'

Miriama entered the restaurant and waved cheerfully. They embraced warmly before being seated next to a window. Vai asked Miriama about her work on the Advisory Board and led this into a discussion on the future of Otago. 'If we settle in Balclutha, will there be work nearby?'

'Yes, watch what happens in Antarctica. The changes there will settle the future of Otago.'

Vai watched Miriama's face closely and said, 'Developing Antarctica will require development in Otago and Dunedin.' When Miriama nodded Vai sighed and said, 'I'm leaving New Zealand soon. My advocacy task will be complete after my workshop today and I can't stay on. I've been offered a berth on an Ocean Warrior ship. We're going to Antarctica.'

'Well, I don't know what you know about Antarctica, but take careful note of what's happening there. The answer to your question about Otago and Dunedin lies in the changes down at the bottom of the world. But it's too early for me to explain.'

Success, an idea of success, was creeping into Vai's head, snuggling against her anxiety. She slowed her breathing, letting Miriama carry the conversation. She looked around, imagining anxiety as a small creature hiding in the room somewhere. It was easier to think of it as a something, otherwise it had no form, no blood coursed in its veins and it couldn't be contained.

'If there's a sudden demand for labour,' Vai said, 'somewhere in New Zealand. I'm just wondering, would you be able to advocate for us, to get us over here quickly to take up the work?' She fidgeted with her hair. 'It's just, well, this afternoon at the Adjustment Office, I'm going to try to secure Balclutha. But if it turns out that Balclutha's close to jobs then others will go after it, and I don't know what might happen. I don't think we can hold that location if we can't move straight in.'

'I can't promise, Vai. You have every reason to worry and I'll do what I can.' Miriama's tone grew angry, 'New Zealand doesn't understand the role it's being asked to perform, the scale of it. The harshness of what's about to unfold. But we'll go through a period of integration, I'm sure of it. We'll be a new world, a better one in the end.' Miriama nodded, as if to put a full stop on that thought, and looked up at the birds on the roof, sprigs of green in their beaks. 'A better world, but we'll need help.' She watched Vai, as if expecting another request, but Vai was thinking of Dr Zhu. He'd mentioned he knew a lot about refugee settlement. She asked Miriama if she knew him.

'Yes, he's famous. He worked in Greece. That's where he made his name. Europe has this population of people who have been broke for generations. They circulate around inside the free-movement zone. Winter on the Mediterranean then inland as the weather gets too hot.'

'Like gypsies? Caravan people?'

'Not gypsies, but mobile people. They were lost after the cycle of financial crashes. They didn't get back on their feet and began moving from country to country so that no one country got sick of them. They had a basic life, being fed but not getting work, not much work. Then countries got the idea that they would stop feeding them so they wouldn't visit and eventually they got hemmed in, down in Greece. It was like a slow-moving trap.'

'And China's big in Greece.'

'Yes. China owns a lot there. It's their base in Europe. Zhu was put in charge of working with these people who had a culture of moving and here they were, hemmed in. He spent a lot of time talking with them and helping them talk with each other. The story is he didn't have a plan and didn't see anything wrong with them travelling. But they knew that countries wouldn't tolerate them, that they had to make some changes. Zhu knew that all over the world there was a need for people to work in detention camps and the tougher refugee camps. Usually the work was done by locals but they didn't always do it well. The locals were antagonistic to the refugees. He trained these people to fly in, fly out, do the work well without any antagonism. They had no stake in it. They stay based in Greece, mostly up near the Bulgarian border, and travel around the world.'

'Like a little army?'

'Well, no, like professional aid workers. It's inter-generational. They're becoming like a guild.'

Vai wasn't sure what to think. This guild, it could be sent to Independence.

Their meals arrived and Miriama said, 'Let me tell you a different story.' Once Vai had a slice of warm duck on her fork Miriama recounted a visit she had made to Bangladesh in advance of five thousand migrants moving to homes she had built in Dunedin with government funds. 'I flew to Bangladesh to meet with the migrants before they came here.' She took up her fork and thrust it into the air. 'That was a shock. A radicalisation, my son says, but I can't claim that. I've tried to infect others but mostly no effect.' She put the fork down and made a half-circle in the air with her hands. 'Imagine a coastal river valley. Just what you'd expect these days. Inundated by the sea after the river delta is eaten away. The hills adjoining the valley were already inhabited

74

and so the valley community moved onto the steeper areas that had previously been forested. Their efforts at agriculture came to nothing. They had subsisted on handouts and aid for over a decade. They lived in tents and the near-constant rain and wind meant landslides were an ever-present risk.'

'We see that on the media all the time,' Vai said.

Miriama shifted in her chair. 'The older hill community had erected a makeshift fence between them and the refugees from the valley, to keep thieves and thugs out they said, but there was a shared sense of community. They shared a faith. The poor hillside originals shared resources as well as they could with the valley refugees. The poor rallying to support the poorest. They were all exhausted from living under these conditions — the kids were underweight, tiny, the women had constant tasks around meagre food and illness, the men were listless.' Again, Miriama curved an arc with her hands, but this time it was a bomb exploding. 'I was curious, so I asked to meet some community representatives, from those who were being left behind in Bangladesh. They assembled in a large tent, community leaders, but also children and the more vulnerable adults, including some pregnant women and older people. Outside the tent a crowd gathered.' She laughed. 'Don't ever underestimate people. I was put in a solitary chair in the centre of the tent and a small girl was placed on my lap. A man introduced himself in English, a school teacher, he was going to do the translation. They were polite, but—' She banged her fork down hard on the table. 'Straight to the point. Here's some of the questions they asked. First one, straight off, "How is it that New Zealand is the same size as the United Kingdom but has fewer than six million people?" What do you say to that? The UK has eighty million people.'

Miriama took a small tube of hand cream from her purse and massaged her hands. 'Next question, "Why are you taking so few refugees? Your country could take all of those here on these hills." From there things began to really tip over. These people weren't petitioning or begging. Straightforward people with straightforward questions. The mild effects of climate breakdown for us, and we're hiding. All the while the little girl is stroking my face and playing with the buttons on my shirt.'

Vai's hands were cupped over her ears. 'We see refugee camps on the media. So many of them.' Her voice small, distant in a wilderness.

'So there I was, the wealthy benefactor, sitting in a tent and the rain started pounding down and the mould-speckled walls begin leaking. I thought I was going there to look into their little schoolhouse or something, watch the kids draw and sing.' Miriama waved her hands theatrically, 'What was I going to say?' and Vai twisted one of her own slender fingers as if she would break it. 'So I'm there for half an hour and I realise I'm sinking into the mud. I mean, really sinking. There are rivulets of water running under my chair and the child has got bored and gone. I'm completely exposed.'

Miriama leaned across the table and took Vai's hands. 'Eventually there was nothing left to say. The questions ended, the flooding continued, my chair was listing as if a hand had it from below. The people peering in from outside the tent were drenched. Then I trudged through the mud to the bottom of the hill, where my car was. Irrelevant, even complicit.'

Vai was surprised to see the older woman's eyes were red. She stood and walked around the table to hug Miriama. Feeling an unexpected intimacy, she took Miriama's hand and said, 'I have a poem to share, it's a poem for the middle of a scary century. It is called The Half-Finished Heaven by Tomas Tranströmer. It's the story of the world we live in.' Then she recited the poem from memory, standing with one hand resting lightly on the table, pitching her voice as if she were giving her summation.

When Vai finished Miriama said, 'Yes that's right, that's how we must be. Despondency breaks off its course, and there is something for everyone.'

Encouraged Vai said, 'This is what I believe, and your story confirms it. I see all the refugee camps and I see the future. I see the most courageous, diverse, determined people in the world, all birthed in a crucible. And they belong to no land, but they form a new society. They are an embryo of a global society, one that has its roots everywhere. Each camp and refugee is a chrysalis, and when we emerge we will be a new people. We haven't chosen this, but you watch what we make of it. We will be what the world needs. We're a new type of nation, one hundred million strong, and we're the future for a world that needs to be global.'

Part III

10

Taniwha rose and fell on the long, grey swell of the Southern Ocean. Breathing in, breathing out, swells rising above the ship, then passing under it in graceful motion. The air was still and the ocean slid away gently beneath her hull.

Vai stood on *Taniwha*'s open deck, both hands holding the ship's rail. She turned to the woman beside her and said, 'We're a ghost ship, a raiding ghost ship, Paris. We'll emerge out of the fog onto an unsuspecting pirate fishing fleet and wreak havoc upon their nets and lines. We'll free the workers and sink the rotten hulks. What do you think?'

Paris bumped her head against Vai's shoulder to acknowledge what the taller woman had said. The little birds, tattooed in a flock that ran from beneath her shirt, up along her neck and across her left cheek, took on a strange life, in flight in the wet air. Paris's blue-dyed hair peeked out from under the hood of her thick jacket, the strands shimmering despite the dull sky. 'I think we should sink them,' Paris said. 'Why wouldn't we do that?'

Vai considered her new friend's statement. *She's a little pirate herself*, Vai thought, *and so are the rest of them*. 'You'd be locked up and miss these wild places. That's why not.'

'True. I live to see the wild places, in case they disappear. I hate being away from them, but when I am in such a place I say, These are not wild places. Not like they would've been. But then I think, That's not right. Humans are congregating in cities and food-growing areas. The rest are abandoned, rewilding and

81

becoming beautiful again. Then I think, No, they're degraded. No humans, but not much else either. But then I travel to wild places and even if they are not abundant, they can be beautiful. And I argue with myself like this.'

Vai hadn't met a woman like Paris before. The Young Nature activists on Independence were people of faith who wore their knowing as a badge pinned to their chests. They had an orderly vision, with humans in certain places, wild nature in places that the world had allocated through accidents of geography, history and climate, and in between, bucolic landscapes with their own varieties of harmony. Dogged management of change was the vocation of the Young Nature activists, and extinction, or even just fear and starvation, was background. They embraced the great reshuffle, a rearrangement on a scale never before undertaken, but there was order and purpose in their vision.

Paris had rambled her entire life. Her stories were littered with references to people who appeared to be family and then appeared to be lovers or acquaintances. An indeterminate childhood merging into the near past that involved animals and mountains and deserts and movement. Campaigns in the Amazon, escapes from remote ports with ships going down in flames, danger, and wildlife set free and property wrecked. It wasn't clear to Vai that Paris had anything approaching a home or a place she returned to. Her stories never settled and a new one might just be the continuation of a story that seemed to have ended in the telling a few days earlier. Then there was her name, possibly the only burden she couldn't drop in a recycling booth. She was born on the fourth of November 2016, the day the Paris Agreement went into effect. She'd told Vai about her name as if it was an embarrassment, not a notation of her parents' hope. Vai had smiled and Paris had felt a need to explain: 'Yes, I was born on the day of the happy narrative. It seems like a marker of failure now. The day that the world agreed to strike out for a future that gave everyone something and the animals a fighting chance.'

People didn't speak about accords like that any more. They

were for earlier times, when the future was unwritten. A new structure was emerging: the big three had reached an accord of their own, had set out a framework to shape the planet. A basic, almost federal, hierarchy was established in which the big three set out the essential terms of interaction, with regional and lesser agreements beneath this. Only Antarctica sat outside a formal, regional accord. But that didn't mean that south from New Zealand, into the deep Southern Ocean, where it might have been imagined a frantic world had no urgent concern, the nations of the world weren't busy. When the sea was free of fog or storms, many ships could be sighted hurrying south in the long, extended period of summer.

The *Taniwha* had left New Zealand waters the previous evening, south of the Campbell Islands. Captain Negri and his navigator watched their radar for any ships that moved away from a regular line to Antarctica. Any boats that were changing course, tacking and back-tracking, were likely to be hunting for fish or whales. Captain Negri called his crew together to celebrate: it was game on. The captain motioned to his First Mate, Hika Black. 'If we attack I'll make all the decisions. But if I want an opinion, it'll be his. No one else. So don't bother me when we're fighting.'

Vai stood near Hika, close so their fingers touched. In the tense room she smiled at the memory of their first conversation. Late one night leaning on the bow rail, they'd discussed silence. He'd spoken for several minutes about the smell and sounds of silence as if they were tangible, secrets that could only be accessed on the ocean breeze. Later, in his cabin, she snuggled against his warm back and tried to listen to the ocean in the way he had described, to hear the immensity and depth and the possibility of resting at that point where the water density held a body motionless.

From that point the crew were anxious and excited, scanning for a boat to attack. All of them were experienced deep-ocean sailors. They talked about what's next. How they'd handle a confrontation with a whaler or illegal fishing boat. Training for it and showing Vai what her role would be when they attacked. Until then, Vai worked with Paris on the mundane jobs, as deckhands, helping in the kitchen, and delivering meals to those on other duties.

From the outset the crew debated the future at full volume, cliques forming around possibilities and reforming before lunch, side-issues threatening to pull them all apart over breakfast. Vai joined in as best she could. All of them had an intimate knowledge of nature and they imagined in detail how the coming calamity could unfold. Abundance was the straw man of the debate. The Warriors lifted it up high and gutted it with relish. Vai knew that off the ship abundance advocates set themselves a big goal. They intended to restore the world in all its diversity and beauty. They had strategies and plans, and in this respect they were something like the Young Nature people, except more chaotic. The Warriors flew around the idea like moths loving it and destroyed by it, unable to bear its pain. They imagined themselves realists, campaigners for what could be done, and they had no time for the utopian ideas of abundance. They could only believe in a fight that produced a victory here and there. But despite themselves, they couldn't help imagining that the future could be put right. Back and forth they'd go, arguing all on the same side, mocking the weakling advocates of abundance. Diving in and describing abundance with relish and joy and spitting it out. The debate raged like a fire that might sweep the ship.

Initially Vai was drawn to the campaigners, but the more they argued and fought the sadder she felt. The loneliness of them, like magnets facing the wrong way, repelling each other and bouncing across to another kindred soul, but never together. Listening to them going at it Vai yearned to be home, with the gentle hand of her father, standing with the rest of them, facing down the catastrophe, community, together. Vai looked at the crew and saw each one alone, laughing and eating and bedding together and not able to hold, and Independence, not able to hold either. The tasks and arguments on board allowed her anxiety to slip away, but she was beginning to sink into melancholy.

In her minor role Vai could spend time with Captain Negri. On one evening shift when he was alone at the wheel she talked to him about her growing melancholy and the loneliness that tied them up. He took his woollen hat from his shaved head and ran his hand across the shiny dome. 'I'm a campaigner,' he said. 'It would be nice to hold to the abundance line, but there's too much loss in the world. You must've realised what's going on down here in the Southern Ocean. Every day we see ships racing south, and it *is* a race. They're working for nations and companies that are staking claims as the ice on the continent moves back.'

'Yes,' Vai said. 'Everyone on this ship is talking about it. The rush to Antarctica. On my own island we had the Young Nature volunteers, and they ran various programmes but I couldn't help thinking they looked at us like we were ghosts, gone from the island in all but fact. Only half-present, with our fate already set out for us. Our efforts at gardening and fishing were the actions of an apparition that might move around a house with a lit candle. They had plans for the island.'

Negri snorted and looked carefully across the ocean as if he could penetrate the blackness beyond what the spotlights illumined. 'They disgust me. Adapting to anything, fighting for nothing, celebrating each compromise. I'll go down in anger, soak my hands in blood.'

Vai sat forward in her chair. Negri said, 'No doubt you've felt the tension on board. It's not an easy ship to lead. I've already turned down various opportunities to harass ships nearby. We can go for the ones that are genuine pirates and we can go for the ones from countries that probably won't take action against us. Can't or won't, places like Thailand that have rogue fleets. But we have to pass on the rest.' He sighed. 'I'm trying to run a dog-sled team, but the dogs only want to get off leash and run something down for slaughter.'

'I know. Over the last few days, when people call you Black Bob, it's not always just a name, like it was when we left port.'

'It turns into Black Bob, the prick who stops anything from happening. Well, bear in mind that plenty of countries won't hesitate to capture and sink us.' He reached across and punched Vai gently on the shoulder. 'You came to me to shake off your melancholy, and I just gave you a sample of my own. Hell, don't you take any advice from me. You could do a lot worse than take after your mate Paris. She'll have lived a life to admire before she's old.'

'You see me like that?' Vai asked. Laughing lightly, not wanting to break the mood, cut the bond they had established. 'You think I could settle my people in New Zealand then take up a bow of my own? Roam the world like a fighting monk?'

'You have to choose, young woman. Either you go community or you go solo. I'm as solo as I can manage, and Paris is on her own. Most people on this boat are drifting.'

Vai took some time to look into the night and think about how the black ocean lost its own form where it merged with the black sky. 'This abundance idea seems something to live for. I have a place I love, and I accept that the *place* has to be left behind, but that is not the end to the community. I will always have people, and we might have a place to go to.'

'Abundance is about a lot more than people,' Negri said. 'It's about finding a way to get all the species and all the people, and everything else that can be carried, through this narrow hole we have in front of us.'

'What hole is that?'

'The next two hundred years is a hole we have to squeeze through. Anything that doesn't fit goes extinct. Each thing that goes extinct is one more slash on abundance. Too many slashes and it dies. Two hundred years, that's the period of abomination foretold. That's how long it will take for the major changes to occur, so the abundance people have to have a plan to get through that hole.'

They sat for a while, watching the calm sea. Vai wished the clouds away so that the full magic of the ocean could be revealed beneath its blanket of diamonds. In the poor light of the cabin Black Bob chewed on dried fish, his beard dancing in silhouette against his chest. 'Tell me one story about you,' he said. 'Not a sad story. I know about your island sinking etcetera.'

'I have plenty of good stories,' Vai laughed in happy memory. 'This is a good ocean one. And not long.'

'Good, then I'll tell a short one next.'

'My Dad and I had a place we would go to gather crabs. It was near the main island, perhaps one kilometre out to sea. Our island and this island both used to be volcanoes and they eroded or blew up. Anyway, not much was left of this one, just parts of the rim stabbing out of the water and dropping straight to the depths. No one lived there, just birds and crabs and fish. It was early in the morning, before the heat of the day, and we anchored about two hundred yards into the sea. The anchor sat on a rock uplift.' She looked at him. 'You can imagine the morning light?'

'Yes, I think so. In the tropics the sea would be light blue and, depending on how early, the sky might be orange against the ocean.'

'Yes, like that. We swam to one of the rocks that rose out of the water and we began diving under and hooking crabs with a piece of wire each and putting them in a bag that Dad held. We were concentrating on hunting among the weeds and in the cracks of the rocks. The crabs were disguised the colours of the weed — reds and blacks and oranges. And then, deep below us, a killer whale grabbed hold of a stingray and bit it in half. Then there were others. A pod of them had come to hunt and they had the rays sort of trapped in the rock circle.'

'And you were there. Amazing. Go on.'

'Dad pushed me against the wall of the rock and we stayed motionless on the surface. We watched the whole thing. The visibility was great. There were more than ten killers and they were feasting. Then one of them grabbed a ray and swam slowly up the rock wall with the poor thing in its mouth, still alive. And the killer stopped beside us, horizontal in the water, head out, eye to eye with us, and Dad took out his knife. It looked like a toothpick. And then the killer sank back down and swam off. When they were gone we swam to the boat and when we were lying on the bottom of the boat Dad said, "Did you see the look on its face when I took out my knife and it remembered that it's just a big dolphin?"'

'That is a good story,' Negri said and Vai snuggled her back into the warm rug draped over the seat and could imagine him and her dad being good mates, and her dad saying to her, 'He's a good man, that Black Bob, a man who loves the ocean.' Her dad often said that the ocean was a thing of great passion, and it took a special person to love that wild place.

Negri said, 'Us ocean people, we always have good stories. That's one reason I became a captain, so I could choose to travel with people like you. My story's about my father. He told certain stories so that we would learn some lesson or other that he wanted to pass on. He was surfing in a remote place by himself. There were big waves at the end of a point and then they reformed, smaller, near the beach. Of course Dad was alone at the end of the point. Then, after a while, another man paddled out and began to ride the smaller waves, close in. But he was not very experienced and he lost his board and the current took it out to near my father. Dad caught the board and sat where he was, just waiting. The other man was not a strong swimmer and he was in trouble, but Dad didn't go to help him. By the time he reached Dad he was exhausted and furious. So Dad agreed to paddle beside him to the beach. As they started the journey the man complained because the current was pulling out around the point, so Dad said to him, "OK, we'll move wider into the bay where the current is weaker." Then as they paddled a wave came from an unexpected direction, a much bigger wave even than the ones Dad had been riding, dragging spent foam along its face and making it ugly.'

'A rogue wave,' Vai interrupted. 'Imagine the struggle now.'

'Yes, the man now had his exhaustion and this thrashing to deal with. Dad said they were separated and after the wave broke there was a lot of water moving in the bay and the man was swept back toward the rocks on the point. The water had to exit and it dragged around the point, so the man was dragged back to where Dad had first caught the stranger's surfboard. Only now he was more exhausted and Dad was still in the middle of the bay but not so far from the beach. Again Dad sat on his board and waited. He didn't go to help. After a long struggle the man made it back to him and he wasn't able to be angry because of his great exhaustion. Then they paddled together to the beach and the man was crying on the beach for a while, then he went home. That was his story. That was the end. I thought there must be a message, but I still can't think what it was.'

'I think he was making a point about being out of your depth in the ocean. To always be cautious.'

'A good guess, and I thought about that, but Dad never preached caution. He advocated risk.'

Vai wrinkled her nose. 'Do you love the ocean, do you love its passion? Or is it frightening?'

Negri laughed. 'Yes, I love the ocean, but passion can become your master.'

11

Thumping boots and excited voices woke Vai. People were running on the steel steps leading to the big cabin. She could feel the relief of the crew as clearly as she could hear their loud voices, but she stayed with the dream that had occupied her sleep. Deep under her blankets she had visited Balclutha and taken the time to explore its streets and opportunities. She had watched the flood protection works be put in place, seen the small children playing in the schoolyard, stood in the rain and realised that there were plants that would bloom regardless of the cold. The flowers of Wintersweet stood delicate on bare, thin branches, and, close to the ground, little crocuses blossomed brightly. She took some flowers and gave them to her mother and then they were in a vase on the table and she could almost smell their scent. Emma came into the room and sat by the winter flowers and their mother ran her hand through her younger daughter's hair, combed her fingers gently through the waist-length hair, and Emma turned to Vai and started to cough. She coughed with her shoulders shaking, a rag over her mouth, and then Vai could see her sister's lungs, red and splotched black. Vai wrestled against the dream and then Emma held up the rag with blood all over it and there were splatters of blood on her lips.

Then Vai was changed and she leapt up the stairs in her heavy wet-weather gear. Inside the big cabin it was crowded and the crew were eager with anticipation. Captain Negri stood on the bench chair that ran along one wall and said, 'There's a South

African fishing fleet nearby. We've heard it communicating and they're talking about getting their catch back to Zanzibar. They've got to be breaking the law or else they would go to Cape Town or Durban.' The crew called out in anger as he described the zigzagging of the five fishing boats as they moved back and forth, travelling in circles to lay out nets. The sea was not so calm but nor was it dangerous, and the crew knew that the swell enhanced their chances, and there was fog so the fleet might not know they were being attacked until it was too late.

'This is how we're going to do it,' Negri said. He set out how they would circle the *Taniwha* back around to the north of the fleet then run straight south as if toward the Antarctic. That way the fleet would have no reason for concern based only on what they saw on their radar, and the heavy fog would be *Taniwha*'s friend. They were aiming for the nets, so it was important to hit the target area exactly when a circle was being pulled. Moving quickly, *Taniwha* would drag fouling gear through the nets and wreck them. Then, if the fishing fleet abandoned the nets, they could be recovered with equipment designed for that purpose. Such nets were very expensive and a fleet would only carry a small number of them. One successful attack could be followed by harassment to ensure that any remaining nets would not be deployed. 'And if they bring in their navy I'll have to make a fast decision on what to do. And I'll expect your full support on whatever that decision is. We're down here running as a team.'

Vai was not part of the team that would run the fouling gear. That was a sophisticated task for experienced brigands. She would be up front on the water cannon, helping to hold off any counter-attack by small boats.

Paris grabbed Vai's jacket. 'I'll be with you! We'll run a cannon together. Get your safety harness! How else are ya going to stay on board when they start hitting back at us?'

Vai ran to get her harness and then she stepped out onto the deck and registered the pitch and sway of the ship as it swung north. The air was ice-cold and ocean spray needled her face each time the ship drove its bow into a wave. She clipped onto a safety line and walked carefully to the front, spray from the bow rising in plumes. Paris was there and together they ran the cannon in practice, left to right and back, bracing their feet to manage its weight.

The ship laboured to reach a position above the fleet, its black hull secret in the fog. Captain Negri was on the bridge, his beard jutting forward and back and side to side, his bald dome on top. He spun the wheel just as the ship topped a wave. As it slid down the back of the wave it pivoted and they were heading straight at the fishing fleet.

Two ships of the fleet were making a circle in opposite directions and laying a very long net. And then ships from the fleet began to sound their sea horns in long blasts that shattered the bleakness. Vai knew they had been sighted on radar. Holding on to Paris she heard a rumbling and clanging from *Taniwha*'s stern as the ship ran her fouling gear out behind her.

Vai and Paris crouched against their water cannon and hung on as best they could. The noise from the fleet was aggressive and loud: Vai thought she would see a cavalry charge when they crested one more wave. Then *Taniwha* slowed and the fog lifted back far enough for her to see that they had driven into the centre of a half-formed circle and were now turning into the nets that were beneath the surface. By moving slowly the fouling gear would have time to catch.

The fouling mechanism was a work of art. It consisted of a series of independent units, each with its own motor, gears and series of blades, and together they worked like a cat-o'-nine-tails. A unit would tangle in a portion of the net, the motor would kick to life and the mechanism would cut its way up the net until it sliced the big rope at the top, whereupon the net would be almost impossible to haul in. And if the fleet cut it loose, the mechanism could be used to secure and hold the mess.

Negri's head was out the window and he was yelling instructions to Hika Black, who had the wheel. They were nearly above where the captain estimated the net was. The fouling gear grabbed the net and *Taniwha*'s stern swung to port. A wave hit the starboard side and she leant over almost to a point where the rail slid under the water. Vai and Paris swung against each other on their harnesses. A loud bang signalled the wire ropes snapping tight against the ship. *Taniwha* was almost stationery but Negri had kept her facing onto the waves: she strained forward and was steady enough.

Now the two women were crouched against their cannon as the deck shuddered under their feet. The fouling units shook the stern as they climbed the net, ripping it with their vicious blades. Negri called through the speakers, 'Get ready — there's a boarding party coming!'

Vai saw a rubber boat bouncing across the ocean at speed. Paris fired up their cannon and they hosed it left and right to get their range. Negri yelled, 'They won't come close in case we tip them over. The ocean's too cold.' But when they were within range of the cannon the boarding party fired automatic weapons into the air. Negri said, 'They haven't got the guts to kill us. One of our navies would come after them. Just keep them away until the nets are cut.'

Paris stood up and hit the little boat hard enough that its crew were unsighted and turned to run parallel with *Taniwha*. Vai put her arms around Paris and together they kept a river of ice water on the boat as it passed. Black faces glared up at them from the rubber boat. Inside the wrappers of their red dry-suits the South African crew were impotent, mouthing threats that were lost in the noise. One took aim with his rifle and Vai's heart choked for an instant but then the river of water was on him.

The rubber boat tried to close on *Taniwha* at other points, but each one was guarded well enough to raise the risk of tipping the little craft, so while they threatened with their weapons they did not board. Then, without warning, the net was cut through. *Taniwha* lurched forward and began a wide circle to ward off the rubber boat as the fouling gear clanked its way on board.

The fleet ships that had been laying out the nets could be seen hauling the mess back on board and the rubber boat went back to its parent. *Taniwha* turned south and the fog engulfed the fleet.

Inside the ship, the crew were wild. Wet and cold, they grabbed each other in long hugs, the smell of damp clothes and fear and elation mingling into an ecstatic drug. Music began to pump loud, hard, metallic, and the crew yelled at each other as much to participate in the mayhem as anything.

The ship powered through the fog, lifting and thumping on the swell. Vai was hugging and yelling and caught flashes of Paris's blue hair in the heaving turmoil of bodies. And all the little animosities and the anxiety that nothing would be done, the fear that the marauders wouldn't find a fleet they could hit, were all washed away in the southern cold.

The mood of excitement and purpose didn't abate for days. Everyone was on alert for the next opportunity; sleep couldn't hold anyone for long. Vai took the first chance she could find to climb up beside the captain when he was at the wheel on a night shift. 'How about that?' she said.

'Thank God, it couldn't have gone better,' he replied. 'We made an impact, the crew are all focused and we got clean away.'

'Why didn't we stay and harass them?'

'They were up to no good, but the South African navy still would have come for them. We had a big enough win and we've got good coverage across the media.'

'What about the boarding party and their guns? Why didn't they shoot at us?'

'Those fleets don't want to precipitate a crisis. It might bring more governance and rules.' He sat forward in his chair and looked at the distant glow of lights from a ship. He pointed out other lights in other directions appearing and disappearing in the swell. 'You see the ships, you see the activity? Let me tell you a story about the games being played down here. I was at the annual gathering for Ocean Warrior, where we elect our board and stuff like that. This time it was in Goa. You know Goa?'

'On the coast of India?'

'Yeah, used to be a Portuguese trading town, about the only bit they got on the sub-continent. It's got fantastic bars, and when you step onto the street you can smell the sort of spices you would expect, a bouquet of many colours. And then there is the smell of poverty and the smell of everything that ever moved or was made. At least one of everything gets traded through Goa and can be bought at a reasonable price. Goa has basically left India, seceded as they say. It's anarchic. I don't mean in the sense that it is out of control. I mean in the sense that every free person lives as they see fit. You can see it in the way the streets and river edges are going wild with vines and undergrowth and the monkeys run the city from the rooflines to the trees. Although if you are not a free person, it is an indenture that is a foretaste of the future. But don't think it's all bad. People like me live there, if we live anywhere.'

'I've never thought about you living somewhere. I imagine that if you're not on the ship, you're in a bar, I see that. Was Goa your home?'

'No, but it suited us. All the Warriors could meet up, including the ones that are on the run. Which is not me. I'm not on the run. I don't know if you know about these sort of get-togethers. People talk about strategy and funding, which is important, but most of them are like me and aren't interested. So a lot of us move around the bars telling stories and talking about campaigns and exploits. Most of it's lies. But not all lies, you pick up good ideas. That fouling equipment we carry was first drawn on the back of a menu by an engineer who was so drunk he couldn't stand. This is where the practical work gets done.'

He rubbed his dome. 'At these events there's always spies from different countries and corporations, and even rival environmental groups. Each year some spies are uncovered, and they can be dealt with pretty severely. There's a competition among the crews to see

95

who gets the first spy, who gets the most, and so on. Only off-the-record competitions — it's not like we parade them on stage. And I'm with some old mates, Wayne and Barry from Perth, and we have this Indian guy who keeps joining up with us at various bars, but only once we're quite drunk. Of course we decide he's a spy, and we hatch a plan to nab him and find out whom he works for and if he's worth anything to sell back to his bosses.'

'Really? Kidnap?'

Negri folded his arms and glared at her. 'Yes, kidnap. These people are dangerous. It's a crazy world.' Vai shook her head but he ignored her and went back to his story. 'Barry's with his wife, who's great and she gets in on it. Barry and Keisha rent a ground-level room a short walk from one of the bars we go to. And the three of us guys start drinking at the bar one night, late, and the Indian turns up and we tell him we're going to another bar just up the road and he comes with us. Keisha's dressed like a bar girl but she's got the lights down low because she and Barry are nearly sixty. The room has a door to the street, an entrance area and then a door to the main room. This allows us to get him in off the street and drag him inside before he sees he's not in a bar, but he's fairly strong and we have a hard time containing him. I'm only a little wiry guy and Barry's knee's no good. Wayne's got a big gut so he hops on the Indian's back and eventually we get the guy on the ground and Keisha binds his feet with tape. Barry and me have got a hand each and we need to get them together behind his back so Keisha can tape them. He's been to the gym — you can see his muscles while he's wriggling around. I'm thinking this is no good, one of us is going to have a heart attack, then into the room comes this black guy with a gun and he's yelling in a language I don't know.'

Negri's voice is excited now. 'Do you think we're in trouble now?'

'I don't know,' says Vai, not sure whether the story can be true.

'Turns out he's the man Keisha rented the room from and they both speak French. He'd spent time in Algeria when he was trying to get to Europe. So thank God for that. We say the Indian's a spy and we want to know what he's up to. Well, the black guy's face splits open in a grin wider than *Taniwha*'s back end. He helps us get the guy properly secured and then he says hang on or something in French, and whips outside and comes back with a hand-operated contraption that delivers an electric shock.'

'Don't tell me you tortured a man! That's horrific!' Vai rose to her feet.

'Hang on, this story has a point to it. Sit back up. The guy can see what's going to happen and he's sweating big beads in the heat. Goa's hotter than hell, even with the coastal effect. Keisha asks the Indian what he's doing and what he's finding out and he tells us that he's just listening, it's general surveillance. Then Wayne hooks him up to the machine and we tape his mouth shut. Wayne gives it a crank and the Indian's eyes roll around and he struggles. Wayne keeps going. Keisha disappears into the kitchen. I thought she didn't want anything to do with it, but she comes back with bowls of salad that she put together earlier and we all sit down and eat with the black guy. Turns out he's from Sudan. His name is Hamid.'

'I'm not liking this. You're not the man I thought you were.'

'Don't get like that,' Negri said angrily and pointed a finger at Vai. 'You think you're on a fantasy pirate trip. Don't sulk when you learn that fighting for the environment involves shit like this. For all of us, not just me. Stay and listen. There's a worthwhile ending.'

Vai could hear the noisy mirth of the crew nearby and the thumping of the ship against the deep ocean. She scrambled back into her chair and Negri resumed.

'Anyway, like I said, it's hot and we all have a glass of water, and one for the Indian. Keisha's makeup's running into the wrinkles on her face, turning it into a black and red and blue horror mask. After we've eaten we agree we need to try harder to see if the Indian has anything we need to worry about. Also, if there's anything that indicates he's higher up so we can get more for him. I get on the crank handle and give it a good hard go. The Indian's struggling and his breathing through his nose sounds like a bike pump going flat out. It's hard work and I stop after a while. Keisha takes the tape off his mouth and he gives us a bit more about wanting to know the Warriors, who's important, what we plan to do and when. But what he tells us he could have got from a website, so now Barry has a go on the machine. Then we ask him again and he tells us a bit more that doesn't help him. Hamid gets up, a strong man, good biceps. Away goes Hamid on the crank handle, like a seasoned pro, which I'm sure he was. The Indian's thrashing away and blood starts to run from his nose. Hamid stops and this time the Indian says he can tell us that the Indian government wants to find out what we plan to do in the Southern Ocean. He says they've got plans together with America and China.'

Negri scratched his beard and leant back in his chair, enjoying the memory. 'He said the three have a plan for Antarctica that involves them blocking all the nations from the northern hemisphere getting a role down there, except themselves of course, and leading the southern hemisphere nations in a federal arrangement, just for Antarctica. The northerners get to deal with the Arctic and all the land being freed up in Canada and Kazakhstan and across to Ukraine and Belarus and north of that area — the places that have very little population but are getting warmer. The three see a big future in Antarctica as the melt gets properly underway. That's nothing you couldn't guess from looking out the window here.

'The thing is, the Chinese and Americans are looking for an excuse to get the plan underway quickly. They want a reason to block the northerners and initiate the federal arrangement, but India's trying to slow them down. India's a long way behind the other two in terms of ability to run things in Antarctica and they fear being put in third spot instead of first equal. They were worried that we might precipitate a crisis and give the other two an excuse to get underway. That's why he was getting alongside us.'

Negri got up and stretched. 'But they can't set up much of anything on Antarctica for the next thirty to fifty years at least. The weather's still going to be too harsh. So they're likely to set up in New Zealand, Tasmania and Argentina, the next-best close options. The thing for you to think about is, if you move to New Zealand you might be part of a new colony. The big countries might just take you over. And that might not bode so well for New Zealand being a peaceful place to live.'

Vai considered this in silence for a while. 'It would have helped if you just told me the ending. I didn't need to know how you got the information.'

'You're not a baby, Vai. I see you on the ship, saw the way you fought the other day.'

'I'm trying to find something that works,' she said but this time her voice was a snarl.

Negri laughed: she had confirmed his view that she was no weakling.

'Anyway,' she said, 'what about giving the Americans and Chinese an excuse to take over down here?'

'I don't care if the Indians aren't ready,' Negri replied. 'I don't care if America wants a crisis tomorrow and China wants one next month. As Antarctica melts, a bid for control will be made. The timing is irrelevant.'

'You tortured the man for information that you could have figured out from reading the news.'

'I know, but it helped us fix a price to sell him for. His people bought him back.' He rattled off a laugh that would have pleased a hyena. 'The prick's paid for most of this campaign.'

99

12

The crew were hungry. It was two weeks since the attack on the South African fleet and Captain Negri was on edge again. Vai watched the heat rise around the dining table. Standing in the steel corridor, in front of the red door to the dining room, she could imagine a furnace, insinuations escaping and bouncing down the corridor in their haste to breathe.

They pushed further south and there were many more ships than Vai had imagined. Icebergs became a constant threat: every day *Taniwha* passed close to these strange, blue-white giants. They saw whales and followed them at a distance. Then the whales would be lost in a long dive or ice would divert the ship one way and the whales, more or less free to choose a path, might take another.

The crew stood on the decks, holding the ice-cold rails and watching the ocean pass beneath them while the busy activity of other ships grated on their minds. What were they doing, those other ships? Moving quickly and with purpose. Somewhere on each one would be a document that set out the purpose of their journey, the days, the budget, the fuel requirement, what to do when they reached their destination, even how to do it. There would be detail.

Taniwha had a mandate to hunt set out in plain language so the crew knew, for example, that they should attack quickly and fight fiercely. But *Taniwha* was mocked by the purposeful drive to the continent of the other ships. The Warriors watched and observed. Everything was wrong, yet there was nothing to be attacked: nothing was outside the bounds.

The sea sat grey under the burden of clouds and the ocean worked through its moods. Storms put the ship in lock-down, then there were rolling swells, hard on the legs, bracing and releasing, bracing and releasing until muscles demanded sleep. Paris spent her free time with a group planning a later campaign and Vai imagined the movement of the people of Independence to New Zealand. She could see in her mind's eye the long, slow journey from settlement to wealth, the stories future generations would tell about the historic journey, the swelling status of the pioneers who found the way forward.

One evening *Taniwha* found herself alone amid ice, out of sight of any lights from other vessels. The captain posted crew on the four corners of the ship for extra safety. The ship moved cautiously through the brief night with its floodlights blazing, the light casting magic on the ice. By morning Negri was ragged and his black beard worked in a constant rhythm with his anxious jaw. He hove-to with an iceberg moving toward the ship on the port side in a steady wind and a jumble of ice in front of him. His warm beanie and big beard poked out the window and between them were two angry black eyes. 'Back it up, back it up,' he called to Hika and the ship's propellers churned the water. He looked, Vai thought, like a hungover bogan from the Auckland suburbs.

'You all right, captain? You know where you're going?' one of the crew yelled at him.

Negri flicked a stiff finger at the man and bellowed to Hika, 'Hard to port.'

As *Taniwha* emerged into more open waters Vai put soup into a cup from the ship's kitchen and took it to the captain. At the cabin door she smiled as she caught him looking left and right in a hangdog way and guessed he was hoping other ships' captains didn't know he had taken his ship into a funnel with a blocked end. He'd be happy for the fog now.

Negri slumped in his chair. 'I spent the whole night with my head out the window staring into the wind to look for icebergs blowing into us. Thank heaven the night's so brief. It's a bastard's nightmare.'

'I slept through,' said Vai. 'I didn't realise it was so dangerous until you backed out.'

Hika said, 'There's a boat about a mile in front of us. It's moving fast and weaving. Can we take a look?'

Negri lurched to his feet, eyes dilated and lips pulled back to reveal his teeth. 'What do you think it is? Let's see.' He looked at the radar screen for a few minutes, grunting each time the blinking dot on the screen changed direction. Then he got on the intercom and told the crew there might be another ship to intercept. 'Maybe a whale chase boat, the way it's moving.'

Taniwha rounded an iceberg that stood as a tall sentinel, a race marker rising thirty metres above the water into the grey sky. The ship rolled in the swell and Hika pushed her to top speed. They closed quickly on the other ship, whose erratic chase was limiting the distance it moved forward.

'Yep, a whale chaser. It's Japanese!' Negri shouted. 'Get there before they catch anything! Prepare to block the hunt and drive the devil from the sea!'

The cabins and corridors snarled with crew preparing: Vai could smell the pheromone of the pack. On the deck, clipped to the safety line, she joined Paris at the water cannon. Paris put back her head and howled into the wind and Vai bayed with them all as the sound spread down the boat. 'This is going to feel like it busts every joint you've got,' Paris said. 'We have to keep each other psyched, adrenalin all the way to the end.'

Now the smell was of a burning house on cold air. Negri had his head out the window barking orders, then ran to the other side of the ship and did the same there, grinning wide.

The whale chaser was close now. The whale pod was blowing

and diving and the chaser would slow to pick any change of direction and anticipate where to put herself. *Taniwha* had the advantage of maintaining speed and when she pulled alongside the Japanese boat she was so close that Vai thought she could have jumped the gap.

As *Taniwha* went by her crew fired a narrow-gauge net across the chaser's deck and tied her deck crew in a clutter; the water cannon took them off their feet. Then Negri put her in front of the chaser and slowed down. Vai braced for a collision but the chaser pulled to port and turned back to where the whales had blown, five hundred metres away.

Taniwha made a big arc to limit the loss of speed and came in behind the Japanese ship but now they were too far back to catch up before it reached the whales. The net *Taniwha* had fired was thrown from the whale chaser; *Taniwha* moved around it and fell further back in the race. On the angle Vai was able to see the whales breach again and a harpoon slam into the largest one, which had dropped to the back of the pod.

Never in her life could she have imagined how much venom she would feel in that second. She took the impact of the harpoon in her own heart and watched the whale's blood through a red mist across her eyes. The Japanese ship slowed quickly and *Taniwha* came up on it at full speed. It seemed as if the vessels would pass each other within a whisker and then Negri drifted the back half of his boat against the smaller whale ship, rending the air with a screech of metal that sent both vessels bounding apart.

Paris screamed at Vai to get hold of the cannon. Blood ran on her cheek where the cannon had swung against it, and the flight of tattooed birds looked as though they'd taken a shotgun shell.

Now *Taniwha* was parallel with the thrashing whale and the long metal spike that stuck from its side and charged electricity through the creature. This time Paris and Vai both forgot their tasks and cried out a bitter, savage sound and the cannon swung free.

As Negri slowed alongside the whale the crew swung the crane arm over the sea and lowered its mechanical scissors, whose magnets dragged the blades onto the cable above the spike and gripped it tight. With a bang the cable was cut and snapped away and the whale dropped below the surface.

'Will it live?' Vai asked.

'No, but damned if the Japs are having it,' Paris yelled.

Then the air exploded as the whale chaser fired canisters of noise on *Taniwha*. This time Vai and Paris held their positions and swept the deck of the Japanese ship with a wall of water. The ships moved apart and sped toward the pod of remaining whales. Negri was thumping the window of the bridge, his spittle raining against the glass. Along the rail of the ship the crew were braced for the next assault.

The whales had dived and the chaser had slowed to see where they emerged. As *Taniwha* closed the gap the whales blew, showing themselves on the outside of *Taniwha* with the chaser further from the whales. The Japanese ship accelerated and swung toward *Taniwha*, aiming to cross her bow. Negri slowed down and let out a roar. The veins on his neck were popping; foam ran from his mouth. Then he drove *Taniwha* forward into the side of the chaser's bow and slammed it sideways.

The metal on the chaser's hull rent with a sound like hell opening up. Vai and Paris and all of the crew on deck swung in their harnesses and slammed back against the superstructure, all of them bashed to the point they could hardly move. The captain's mad, hyena laugh cut across the mayhem and Vai realised she was hanging upside down over the railing.

The whale chaser had turned sideways and *Taniwha* had bounced to run parallel to it. Vai was feet away from the other ship and could almost touch it. Paris stuck her head and one arm through the railing, blood running from her forehead and dripping off her nose. Vai righted herself, grabbed Paris's hand and together they hauled her back on deck as the ships drew apart.

The chaser slowed to a crawl: the gash on it was below the waterline. *Taniwha* circled her; Negri put his head out the window, his eyes fixed on the defeated whaling ship, his mouth set in the snarl of a hunting tiger. Fog settled close around the vessels.

In the main cabin the able-bodied helped the damaged out of their heavy gear. Vai helped with bandaging and everyone who could stand stared out the windows at the Japanese chaser listing in the cold ocean. The realisation dawned that it was sinking and eyes turned to the First Mate. 'Get ready,' Hika said. 'We'll need to take them on board. There'll be some who need medical attention.'

'We'll need the guns, Hika,' someone said. 'There's as many of them as there are of us, and I'm not having the pricks just climb on board.'

Vai looked across the room at the crew and could see that the anger that rippled in her was the same for all of them. She had been ready to fall to the ground, exhausted, but the thought of taking the Japanese crew brought with it a cold fury.

The first life-raft began to descend from the Japanese ship with its burden of sailors, but it did not touch the water and hung, suspended over the sea. Then it was raised back onto the ship and without warning the air split with a deep blast of sound. A ship's horn, shockingly loud came from the opposite direction to that of the whale chaser and continued with enough depth to shake *Taniwha*. And then her windows were blanked by the shark-grey steel of a naval ship running by at great speed and she was tossed like a toy.

'Corvette! It's a Japanese navy corvette! Damn them!' Negri yelled.

The corvette spun hard and slowed to move between *Taniwha* and the chaser. Immediately small boats began to descend from the corvette and Negri ordered his ship south toward the ice. The corvette's small boats had not yet set off before *Taniwha* was engulfed in fog and moving at her top speed. From the rear the sound of chasing engines came for five minutes but then they gave up. Doubtless the corvette was confident it would soon catch the slower ship once it had rescued the whaling crew.

A half hour later the captain climbed onto the bench seat of the cabin and surveyed his exhausted and damaged crew. 'I apologise,' he said. 'I lost control when you needed me to keep you safe. There's no excuse.'

One of the older crew members stepped forward. 'No, damn that for a coward's way. We sank the murdering bastard and that's what we live for.' A woman with a broken arm stood up off the floor and said, 'Hell yes, that's us. That's what we signed up for.'

Negri allowed himself a grin. 'Thanks. But we're still in danger.' There was silence in the room. 'We are off the coast of Marie Byrd Land, which is claimed by no country. We could run for Scott Base, where New Zealand might give us some protection, but there is no law down here. We're going to have to get back to New Zealand waters where we can seek fair treatment for your broken bones. I'm going to go into port in Dunedin and we'll reassess from there.'

Some of the crew nodded their agreement; nobody said anything. Their campaign was probably over.

Vai kept her heavy gear on, if only so she didn't have to look at the bruising over her aching bones. She wanted to see how the captain would handle the next few hours, so she made an excuse of taking him coffee and stood quietly at the back of the bridge while he spoke to the members of crew who were qualified to take the helm. 'We'll sneak along the coast amongst the icebergs,' he said, 'and at dusk we'll cut out straight for New Zealand in a direct line.' Then he waved the ship's media liaison, Mark Eaton, into the room. 'There is a thin chance we'll make New Zealand waters before we get caught. We need to raise the stakes on our side.'

Mark was a neat man in his thirties who, Vai guessed, would have worn a tidy suit of a fine cloth if he was on land. He said that the Australian Leader of the Opposition had jumped in like a clever kangaroo and said, 'Enough of Ocean Warrior and her

106

piracy.' This was some backhanded luck: he was supporting the Japanese announcement that they would sink *Taniwha* and take the crew to trial in Tokyo — and that meant thirty years in jail. So now, Mark grinned, the Australian airwaves were running hot with what to do about Australian citizens being taken on the high sea by a foreign navy, and the captain of *Taniwha* was a real Aussie fighter.

'Good,' said Negri. 'I'm buggered.' He pointed to the bench where Vai was sitting. 'I'll sleep there and I want the rest of you to take turns at the helm and wake me for any reason at all.'

Mark stepped in front of him. 'Not yet. We need to get film out to the media of the whale being killed and you need to speak to them now. The world needs to see the exhausted and brave captain.'

Vai thought Negri would object but he beamed with pleasure and smoothed down his beard while Mark wrote some words on his media screen as a teleprompter. Negri pointed his baked and leathery face at a camera held by a crewman and said, 'Japan is a nation without honour. In the face of a global crisis that is engulfing all people and every living thing, Japan chooses to go on with its pointless killing. Japan needs to be isolated and humiliated. We ask the people of all nations to rise up in protest.' And then the film ran of the whale being killed. 'There is no reason for this massacre, this hunting of the innocents.' He held out his hand, palm up and, more softly, concluded, 'This barbaric, slow death.'

Mark said, 'Great. That'll do for now. I'll get it to New York for the team there to drive the public.'

Vai stood for Negri to lie down, and secured a strap over his chest to stop him rolling onto the floor. She let the aching in her limbs have access to her conscious mind and breathed deeply, feeling every strap of the harness that had held her during the battle with the whaler. She knew that if she peeled back her clothes the places where the straps had been would show yellow and purple on her skin.

13

Taniwha slid through the fog with a watch posted on the bow to look out for the icebergs that were like the reverse of ravines in a treacherous forest. The crew moved silently around the ship, the pack hunger that had driven them in the morning now the slinking of a weasel. It was three days' sail from the Antarctic coast to New Zealand waters on a north-west angle, if a fair sea and favourable wind assisted.

At dusk *Taniwha* broke the cover of the icebergs and took silent flight on the open water. All through the short night and the next day she ran straight for New Zealand. In the late afternoon Vai put together a tray of food and took it into the cabin. Still the captain remained asleep in the posture of a corpse. His hands were folded over his scrawny torso and his face looked straight to the ceiling. But his beard rose and fell and gave substance to the rest of him. His toes moved idly in their socks as if a breeze was pushing them around.

Sitting in the big chair with one hand on the wheel was Neelie Ruysch. She was perhaps fifty, and the only woman on board who was even taller than Vai. She thanked Vai for the food and pointed out the window at the rising sea. 'This is getting worse,' she said.

Vai already knew that without looking, her body registering the ocean's changes as if she had a special bone in her chest that moved like a surveyor's plumb bob. Her ability to ride with comfort on the open ocean helped her feel at one with the others, a full member of the pirate crew, but as much as she was competent, she also felt a wide-eyed shock, like a schoolgirl sent on work experience only to find she's careening in a mobile asylum. Frightening, but when she looked inward, frightening-fantastic. The fear of being in a microcosm of the whole mess, seeing it in the dying whale's eye, smelling it, taking the brutal burden of it in the bash, bash, bash of the whaler attack, and then the running, the running away through a building storm of grey and black — and always the anxiety.

The ship ploughed into the evening with a following swell alternately shunting her forward as waves hit from behind and pulling her back as the swell passed under and raised her nose high.

Mark stepped into the room. 'We're having some luck. The public are angry, about fifty-fifty for each side. On our side there's anger at governments hunting an environment ship that blocked pointless slaughter while those same governments fail on every front to stop the world from burning. People are fed up with punishment being meted out to people like us while the leaders don't lead.'

'What I'm hearing,' said Neelie, 'it's like lava boiling. It's like just before a volcano blows. I'll bet the governments are watching their people.'

'Well, that works for us too,' said Mark. 'We can say that Japan is irresponsible. Its pointless hunting is precipitating a crisis between governments. We might isolate it, a pariah state.'

As night fell again the captain stirred. Neelie nudged Vai, who went and arranged a meal. When she returned Negri was in his seat with Neelie beside him, discussing the rising storm. His face was gaunt and he pushed the meal into his mouth without looking up. 'This storm's going to be a terror,' he said. 'I don't know if it will help us. The corvette can run faster than us in a storm. We need something else.'

'We could change course,' Neelie said. 'They'll expect us to do what we have done, run for the Campbell Islands. But we have another option. We could turn for the Antipodes Islands, New Zealand waters to the south-east. They won't expect that.'

Negri lurched to the window, looking across the bow as darkness fell and the storm wind howled in the rigging. He made his way to the rear of the bridge, put his hands on the glass there and peered into the black night like an animal on the edge of a copse. 'All right,' was all he said, and the syncopation of the ship adjusted to the new angle of the swell on her stern.

Shortly before dawn Mark stepped back into the bridge. 'You'll need to shower and change. I've got you onto an important show, run from Hong Kong. It's got a massive audience. You'll be getting to business and political people across the globe.'

Negri was busy fighting the ship, which had become a beast in its own right. The storm-driven waves were crashing on an angle into her stern and shunting her off course every few minutes as she bucked and swerved. Constantly he checked his heading and adjusted for the Antipodes. 'What's changed overnight, Mark?'

'The talk on the mainstream news is that there's a need to decide who runs the Antarctic. Australia's Foreign Minister is talking up the need for stronger governance. Argentina's joined Chile. They both want the big southern nations to straight-out claim the continent, split it up and then deal with any challengers.'

'Any sympathy for us?'

'On social media, of course there is. Win the people, get the politicians. That's our best hope.'

Negri thought about the people. Timid as mice peering at their media screens and registering their support this way and then thinking perhaps their grains of wheat came from that way and changing their vote in accordance. No, Robert Negri, or Black Bob, or whoever the hell he was, didn't much respect the people. He put his attention back on the task of sailing.

Mark was hammering the angle that Japan was a rogue nation, precipitating a crisis. Negri laughed. 'Didn't I tell you about the Indian guy we got hold of in Goa?'

Mark shook his head. 'Don't tally your vices. I'm still coming

110

to terms with your decision to drive your ship into the whaler. India isn't ready to move, but none of the big three will want Japan setting the terms of change.'

'Who've you lined me up with?'

'We have Xu, the host of *Asia Rising*. The show reaches millions of educated people.'

'Good. My guess is India's negotiating flat out for a delay. That might give us a window to jump out of. If the whole thing de-escalates, then the three might be able to announce a single approach later on, which they probably want. I bet they've told the Japanese to back off.'

Neelie buckled into the seat beside the captain. She peered at the radar screen. 'We've got a ship nearby,' she said. 'It might be a fishing boat but it won't be on the route between New Zealand and Antarctica.'

'Go and get changed, Bob,' Mark said.

'Hang on,' said Negri and peered at the point where Neelie held her finger. 'Keep track of it.'

When the captain was gone Mark said, 'If that's the corvette, will it catch us?'

'Yes. It'll be on us soon,' Neelie said. 'But they can't board us in this storm. We have that. We could just charge on. We could still make it.'

Mark set the lights up again for the interview and a crewman entered to hold the camera. Ten minutes later Negri lurched back into his seat. He was looking very smart in a fresh linen shirt with a collar and no creases. The shirt was bright red, his beard gleamed with oil and his dome was freshly shaven. 'How soon?' he said, and settled his beanie on his head.

Mark took the hat and threw it into a corner. 'Very good. You look like a man who has a reliable opinion.' Negri followed the hat with his eyes and then looked at Mark as if he might toss him into a corner of his own.

'We have five minutes,' Mark said. 'I'll get the station on my device and ensure we have a link.'

111

Negri turned to Neelie. 'Show me, where's that other ship?'

She tapped the radar screen and he looked at her with concern. 'It's nearly here. Hey, Mark, we might have the corvette on the interview.'

Mark punched Negri's shoulder. 'That's perfect.' Then he pointed to the screen. 'Here's the studio.' Negri waved at the face peering out at him but Mark said, 'No, that's just a technician.' They sat watching, braced against the storm, until the technician raised five fingers. Mark said, 'Here you go. Look straight at Xu and speak clearly.' He crouched below the captain.

Xu appeared, the master of political media: impeccably dressed, white shirt, red tie, sharp sleeves. Old enough to be credible, young and lean enough to be desirable. He threw a soft scene-setter: 'Captain Bob Negri, thank you for joining us from the Ocean Warrior ship *Taniwha*. Where are you now?'

'Mr Xu, we are near New Zealand waters, in the middle of a Southern Ocean storm, a major storm. It's just on morning down here and we are being unjustly pursued by the Japanese navy. What they are doing is wrong and dangerous.'

'Your ship sank a Japanese merchant ship.' Xu delivered this as an accusation.

Negri leant forward and a flicker of anger crossed his eyes. 'The fault for the sinking needs to be addressed in a neutral court. That is why we are returning to New Zealand.'

'Captain Negri, you can't call into question the facts that have been shown around the world. The fault belongs to the ship that drove deliberately into the Japanese vessel. The collision is *your* fault.'

'They cut in front of us,' Negri barked. Mark gripped the captain's leg and dug his fingers into the thigh bone. Swatting Mark's hand off, Negri said, 'There was no room for manoeuvre. If the Japanese government believes those not to be the facts, let them press charges in New Zealand. What matters is that some governments want to break the Antarctic consensus and begin a land grab because they believe the actions of nations like Japan need regulating.'

112

'Yes, well that is ironic, isn't it? The thing environmental groups have feared for decades might happen because of your actions.'

Vai was following the interview closely, perched out of view of the camera. An idea began to take a vague form in her mind. All these countries scrambling over each other to control the new continent, or just get a little bit. Even little New Zealand, with its cap-doffing, still-colonised personality, had found the courage to have a go. Perhaps there was something for Independence, much further south than she had imagined.

'*Our* actions?' Negri's angry bellow jerked Vai back to the present. 'The countries are lined up on the edge of Antarctica baying for a chance to go in. The issue is the melt, and we're not driving that. Focus on the nations. Who says the Japanese can create endless conflict when the consensus over Antarctica is fragile?'

'So you're not accountable for anything, captain?'

Negri leant forward and stabbed a finger at Xu. 'This is a fucking war. Don't pretend it's anything less.'

'Captain,' Neelie called out, cutting across the interview. 'The Japanese corvette is going to come into view. But we have another ship, from the west.'

'A third ship?' Negri responded with alarm, turning away from the camera to see the radar screen. 'Captain Negri,' Xu called. 'Please ask your crew to turn their cameras. Show us the other ships.'

'Hang on, Xu. I can't see anything yet.' Then the corvette was visible in the light of dawn, riding high on a breaking swell with the sun shafting through wild clouds. The camera captured the greyhound shape through the ship's window and displayed it to the world.

'Thank you, captain. What will you do next?'

'I don't know. We're not stopping. They can't board us in a storm — that would be mad. Neelie, what about the other ship, where's that?'

'You'll see it any moment, captain.' Then, bursting from the north-east with the sunlight behind, came a monster of a ship, massive in its malevolent presence. More than double the size of the corvette, blank sheets of steel and cannon framed against the storming sky.

Negri was silent, pivoting his head between the two other vessels, his jaw working. Mark rose up from his place on the floor so his pale face was visible on the screen and said, 'Mr Xu, can you see that? We need you to stay with us now.'

'Yes, I can see it,' Xu said, sitting very straight in his seat.

Then a new voice joined. 'Captain Negri of *Taniwha*, this is Captain Wang of the PRC destroyer *Shanghai*. We are offering you assistance to reach the port of Dunedin. Will you accept?'

'It's the Chinese!' Negri called to Xu and everyone in the bridge. 'Ha, that'll screw the Japs,' he laughed. 'Neelie, where's that Japanese ship?'

'It's still coming up aft of us, captain.'

Xu was pressing his earpiece and nodding quickly in time with whoever was in his ear, instructing him. 'Captain Negri,' he said. 'Did you know the Chinese navy was going to engage in this situation?'

'What? No. How would I know? What about you, Xu? What do you know? What about your people? What can they tell me?' He was yelling at Xu as if he were a conspirator.

Now the Chinese ship was within two hundred metres of the *Taniwha*, but the Japanese corvette was closer. Hemmed in front and back, Negri told Neelie, 'Hold our course as best you can, but don't slow down. That way they can judge how to miss us and at the same time they'll know we're not quitting.'

He turned back to the screen and caressed his beard. 'You see this, Xu? Now tell me who's a threat to shipping. I've got the Japanese navy sailing hard up behind me and the Chinese navy about to cross my bow. And,' he added with glee, 'I'm in a storm in the middle of the Southern Ocean.'

'Have the Japanese communicated?' Xu asked.

'Not to me, and I haven't heard them communicate to the Chinese.'

'Will you go with the Chinese navy?'

'Just wait. They're crossing our bow, can't you see?'

'Yes, millions are watching. Where is the Japanese ship?'

'It's dropped back.'

'Captain Negri, this is Captain Wang. Will you accept our escort to Otago Harbour?'

Negri smiled and waved his hand to the viewing audience. 'Captain Wang, thank you. You may escort us into Otago Harbour.'

Part IV

14

Taniwha approached Otago Harbour on a big, rolling swell with the sun clear in the sky and the destroyer a mile in front. They were returning to New Zealand in the destroyer's shadow, as a toddler might follow a parent. Media reported that Chinese government ministers were meeting with their American and Indian counterparts in Hainan for discussions on Antarctica's governance. Representatives of smaller nations clustered in Hainan's upmarket hotels.

Two miles out from the entrance to the harbour, *Taniwha* turned landward and the destroyer continued north alone. The narrow, shallow Otago Harbour was no place for a destroyer and Vai imagined its threatening, windowless bulk would be a public relations disaster for the Chinese. Even on the expanse of the ocean, and leading by some distance, the implicit violence of the beast could not be ignored.

Cattle stood forlorn on the brown slopes of the hills, their black bodies scattered like rocks; the hills crowded the edge of the harbour. It was early summer and already the peninsula baked silently in a drought. Only the gorse flourished and refused to be sullen, throwing out yellow flowers in brilliant embrace of the heat. The water beneath the ship sparkled blue and a steady froth of white fell away from the bow. Vai and Paris stood together at the bow, one hand each on the water cannon, their faces shining in the heat. Paris had her chin forward into the breeze and her flock of tattooed birds flew upward to the stitches netted on her cheek. In her mind Vai tried to be a hunter returned from the sea, but the exhilaration of the attacks on the fishing fleet and whale chaser were behind her. Tired little Dunedin city waited at the head of the harbour.

Vai looked up to Negri, perched on his chair, bringing the ship back to land. He looked miserable but waved down to her and managed a smile. She thought back to the attack on the whaler, his willingness to sacrifice everything for the crises in front of him, nothing but now, the immediacy of it.

He had no fear of being refused entry to New Zealand. 'The Japs have backed off,' he said. 'There's nothing to charge us with and we're just here to refuel. We'll just ask for five days. They'll give us permits for that. It's easier than trouble and we'll have a lawyer meet us at the port. He'll be first on. Watch the fat devil — he'll move faster than Customs.'

Negri asked if Vai wanted to continue with the ship, but there was no more to learn from it, she thought. *Taniwha* had been good to her, a respite from the uncertainty and anxiety of advocacy. Now she was going to get five days in Otago, and she had to make those days count. She needed to reacquaint herself with Miriama Hunter.

Mid-harbour the ship rounded the Port Chalmers Head and in front of them lay Dunedin. A disappointment of old buildings and old houses laid over land that was too low and then making their way up a few slopes. It looked like an old towel that had been forgotten at the beach. The cost of protecting the port and managing floodwaters had beggared the city, and the bigger Lyttleton Harbour, a day's sail north, hosted most of the civilian and military shipping to Antarctica. Squatting in cold houses was the growth sector; the low areas were wet and tuberculous.

Crew members bustled around the ship and threw thick ropes to workers on the wharf. The engines shuddered in reverse and the ship kissed up against the gnarled wood of the quay. The Warriors were dog-tired but had had a high-profile success and were jubilant.

120

A gangplank was run out and uniformed Customs staff prepared to come on board. A tall man stood sweating in the sun: he wore a broad straw hat and light cotton suit. The pink of the cloth emphasised the softness of his skin and his lips were unnaturally red, like those of a child in a portrait. He smiled up to Negri and waved a handkerchief. He strode forward quickly, moving ahead of the Customs staff, ignoring their protestations. On the deck he assessed the steps to the bridge and strode on, chins shaking with each upward movement. He stopped at the top of the stairs, breathing heavily and put a hand on Vai's shoulder. 'Oh, water, please, if you don't mind,' he said.

In the shade of the bridge he embraced Negri. 'Captain, well done. No one should harpoon a whale. I *felt* it. When I watched the film, I *felt* the spear go in. My God, the look in the creature's eye.' He released the captain. 'Five days, is that all you need? I could get visas for longer.'

Negri said, 'No, we'll be gone in five days.' He looked at Vai. 'What about you? Will five do you?'

Vai handed the lawyer a cup of water. 'Longer would help. I'm trying to negotiate a settlement in Balclutha.'

'I'm sorry, but if you're not with the ship you don't really have a reason to be here.'

'I know Miriama Hunter. I'm going to see if she can help me.'

'In that case you might be able to stay on.' He threw his hands in the air as if in surrender. 'How rude of me. Captain Negri hasn't said who I am. I'm David Bay, Queen's Counsel.'

Miriama Hunter's voice lifted happily when Vai said she was at the port. 'Good timing. I'm in the city for two weeks. There's a lot happening. I'll send a car to get you.'

Vai took up her small backpack and prepared to say goodbye. Despite the cold and the danger, and the close call with the Japanese navy, the possibility of being locked away for decades, the journey already felt like a memory, a break from the gnawing anxiety of daily life. She was missing the ship already, in the way you might stop as you drive away from a favourite village and look back, trying to hold on to the scent of the place and already rehearsing vignettes of your stay. As was traditional, captain and crew clustered at the gangplank and hugged her and wished her well. She had fought as well as any of them and they respected her obligations. On the pier Captain Negri stepped forward, took a bottle of rum and shot glass from his pocket, and poured a shot. He raised it to Vai's good health and handed it to her to down in one gulp. 'Ha, good luck, girl. I hope you're treated with respect. You've earned it.' Then he poured a second shot and downed it himself. Vai rubbed her head against his beard and he kissed the thick cover of black hair on top of her head.

Paris took her arm and they walked toward the road. They both looked back, just once, and then walked on in silence under the baking sun, the heat magnified by the tarmac. At the road a man in a black suit with impeccable silver hair beckoned to Vai and pointed to a large black car. Paris snorted with derision. 'No way. Who owns that kinda crap?'

Vai was ashamed that her pulse had quickened at first sight of the car. 'Miriama's helping me get a settlement.'

'Well, get a damn good one,' said Paris and they embraced. 'I hope you all get to Balclutha.'

Vai said, 'Yes, we must,' and Paris gave a half-smile, touched the wound on her cheek and turned back to the ship.

Vai watched her walk away, hoping she would turn and wave, call out a last goodbye. But she didn't. Blue hair shimmering in the sun, she trotted back to the ship as if she expected to find it preparing to cast off.

Inside the expanse of the car Vai perched her little pack on the seat beside her. The brown leather was soft and classical music played quietly. The car left the warehouse district and climbed into the coastal hills. Near the top it turned onto a tree-lined drive that wound through a large, private garden, past azaleas and tree rhododendrons, to the house. Warm light shone from inside through the stained glass around the front door and promised rest and welcome.

The driver opened the car door for Vai and said, 'Just go on in. She's informal at home.' As he reversed the vehicle quietly back along the driveway, she looked at her worn boots and the rip in her black jeans and unzipped her vest a little from beneath her chin. She pulled a skein of her lank hair forward and examined it, split by the frozen Antarctic air.

'Hello, love,' Miriama called from the top of the steps. 'Come on in.' She wore baggy pants and a light shirt. She had flowers in her hand. 'I just took these from around the back. I have a shadehouse.'

Vai climbed the steps and Miriama embraced her deeply. 'I've been following your exploits.'

'Oh god, what have you seen?'

'The Japanese took very good film. Great footage of two women on the front of a ship with a sword emblazoned on it, shooting a cannon of water like seasoned pirates. The little blue-haired one would cut your throat, wouldn't she?'

'Could you tell it was me next to her?' Vai asked, colour rising in her face.

'Well, not that I would ever say.'

They stood apart, holding hands. Miriama beamed and said, 'The world is for those who refuse to be frightened.'

As Vai unlaced her boots at the door, Miriama said, 'This house was built by my grandfather. Well, the front of it.' They entered a hall lined with wood. The floor was the same warm timber with a simple blue rug running twenty metres to a room with big windows opening to the ocean below. Miriama paused at the first door on the corridor. A man was tidying the room but when he saw Miriama he left discreetly by a side door. Miriama pointed to photos on the walls. 'There's my family. I'll introduce you to them later.'

The room at the end of the corridor ran lengthways above the cliff. A series of large windows embraced the ocean below and the endless sky. 'I added this wing,' Miriama said. 'The upstairs area has a large portion of the city's collection of treasures. They ran out of money and I'm looking after them. But I could spend my whole life sitting just here, watching the ocean change its mood and the sky carry storms up the coast.' She sighed and leant on the window sill. 'But then I would be old very quickly, and nobody wants that.'

That evening Miriama and Vai cooked together in the kitchen overlooking the ocean. 'Locally grown,' Miriama said as they prepared the vegetables. 'It's very interesting. The weather is becoming impossible, it's so unpredictable and the seasons have gone. We're losing jobs at a disastrous rate. But there's a group I'm supporting that took over an office block near the port. They converted it to a high-rise garden. Vertical farming, they call it. Energy and land-efficient. The productivity is amazing.' She lifted the pallid carcass of a large chicken. 'Organic. I have my own little poultry farm. Naughty,' she said with raised eyebrows, 'but very nice. I'm too old to eat science meat.'

Vai realised how hungry she was as the aroma of roasting chicken took possession of the kitchen. *Taniwha*'s cuisine had been austere. She bent to the oven door and took in the joy of orange pumpkin triangles in bumpy white skin, red potatoes and chunks of white parsnips all bundled in with the bird.

'Follow me,' said Miriama. 'I'll introduce you to my family.' They went through to the room with the family photographs. Miriama stood in front of an old paper map and pointed to the Māori names. 'The oldest names in the region have bound us here for over a thousand years.' She picked up a greenstone cut in the manner of a chisel and smoothed her hands along the curves of the tool. 'Perhaps one of my family carried this when it was first made.'

Then she stood before a small photograph of a large family: the faces were indistinct and the little house behind them dominated

124

the woman who sat on a chair and the man who rested his hand on her shoulder. The sprawling dozen or so children took up the foreground and Miriama named each person.

They moved along the wall and Miriama completed her introductions, careful to name each face and explain how they all fitted together. She pointed out her son, Zeb: 'He's nearly forty now.'

'Do you have grandchildren?' Vai asked.

'No, none yet.' Miriama pointed across the room to a recent photograph. 'Here I am in Guangzhou, near Hong Kong. I'm standing in front of the Opera House. It's an amazing building for acoustics, but it looks like a turtle. I'm not sure if that was the intention.'

'I read somewhere that you have an office in China.'

'Did some homework, did you?'

Vai wasn't sure if that was a reproach. 'Yes, of course. Before I met you in Auckland. Do you mind?'

'I wouldn't expect any less.'

Miriama sat in a large leather chair that had pride of place in front of the fire. The brown leather was worn and scratched; a red wool blanket lay across its back. From the table beside it she picked up a colour photo of a man leaning against a yellow boat in the sun. He had a big moustache that dropped either side of his mouth and his eyes shone with pride and happiness. 'This is my father. A great fisherman. After inheriting from his father, Dad built our company from a contracting business that provided civil construction. Trucks and diggers moving soil, building roads. He took that and made it a national property development company. I'm very proud of him.' Miriama indicated a seat and Vai sat at the edge of the chair, buoyed by the closeness of the older woman's hand, inches from her own, a delta of blue veins beneath wrinkled, brown skin. 'Tell me, Vai, what do want to achieve next?'

'Settlement. I need to get my people here before the door shuts. Balclutha. I want to get us all settled there as soon as I

125

can. You suggested there might be development and jobs. I want us to be part of it. I want us to get a foothold and then see if we can work together — whānau, family, you know. I want to set up one of those family business arrangements. We're not going to be poor. Not for long.'

Miriama smiled. 'It might take time. I'm not sure that I can influence the settlement date. I won't promise and then let you down.'

Vai said, 'I understand. But it's good to know you care, that it matters to you.'

'I might be able to arrange something for you, though. I'm looking for someone to work alongside me. It would be something like an executive assistant. You might have to leave New Zealand again for a few months while the paperwork gets done,' Miriama warned. 'We'd have to see how it developed, but to begin with you could accompany me and help with my arrangements. Once you get the hang of things I could introduce you to property work.'

Vai tried to be professional, the way she imagined an executive assistant might be. She said, 'Oh, thank you so much.' But she'd put one hand to her mouth and squealed just before she managed to say 'Oh'. Her eyes filled with tears and then she gave up and hugged Miriama, who was still sitting so Vai had to kneel, which felt appropriate. Then she gathered herself. 'You have no idea how this helps me, to have somewhere to stand while I tackle all the shit that's facing Independence.'

Miriama laughed. 'Damn good response.'

Vai lifted the roasting dish, laden with its coloured bounty and a scent of comfort, onto the kitchen bench. Miriama took a large glass dish from among a display of glass and ceramic tableware. She indicated to Vai to put the vegetables on that plate. Vai said, 'Really? I thought that was a display of art.'

Miriama said, 'There are some very special pieces, but everything should be used.' Then she took a beautiful glass bowl that swirled red and green and filled it with salad.

The front door opened and a man called out. 'Mum, it's me, with Adam.'

Adam Walker, the Prime Minister's adviser, looked out of place in his suit and tie. He took off his jacket and hugged Vai. 'I saw you on the *Taniwha*. You were fantastic.'

'No, you didn't, Adam,' Miriama said briskly.

They sat at the table and Vai observed the men as she ate. Zeb shared a broad nose with his mother and had the strength of an athlete, but looked slight against the muscular shoulders of Adam.

'Vai's going to work with me,' Miriama announced. 'She's going to be my assistant. I'll have someone get the terrible marathon of paperwork underway in the morning. She's only got a few days on her visa now, but once we get that dealt with she'll come back.'

Zeb studied Vai. She smiled and concentrated on her meal.

Miriama let a moment pass. 'Adam, we're free to speak here. Tell me how your boss is.' She turned to Vai. 'The Prime Minister's a local boy. We were at the same college, but I preferred taller men.' She laughed, then jostled Zeb's shoulder. 'Oh, come on, relax.'

'Prime Minister Chen? Hmm, exhausted I'd say,' Adam said.

'Is that the general collapse of the economy and the migrants on the border?' Zeb asked. He pointed his fork at Vai's plate. 'Or the pirates that have forced the Antarctic issue? Lest we forget, it's open season for mining in Antarctica.'

Adam shrugged. 'So many refugees, a hundred million surging around the world. So many small wars.'

'Come on,' said Zeb. 'What does Chen want?'

'He's a pragmatist. He knows New Zealand will be called upon. He's told me, let me get this right.' Adam put his knife and fork down and looked around the faces at the table, gathering them in. 'He called me into his office yesterday morning and told me to come down here and have a talk with you, Miriama. He's resolved. He seemed like a man who's decided to come out of a trench in battle. He knows the time has come and he's lost the sense that he can protect himself.'

One by one the rest of the group put their cutlery aside and their hands flat on the table.

'Chen looked across the harbour from his office and he was reflective. He pointed one by one at all the major property holdings various overseas companies have, just the ones you can see from his window. It was half of Wellington by value. He asked me if I thought the big three were motivated more by the land-grab opportunities in Antarctica or the fear of war getting out of hand. I said that for China and India it's the fear of what's happening on their borders and the poverty in their nations. That's what's driving them, but all of them are coming for the opportunity, of course.'

'The once-in-a-million-years opportunity. The last continent,' Zeb said, slapping his palms on the table.

'The Prime Minister agreed with me,' Adam said. 'He's been trying to communicate the extent of the crises New Zealand faces, without terrifying everyone. The climate change is easy to communicate. But Kiwis just won't look at migration. We can't avoid taking in huge numbers.'

'No one's going to ask,' Zeb said. 'They've just been getting ready. It's going to be soon. We'll be told how many we have to take and how things are going to be run.'

Miriama's head was up and a smile played on her lips. 'How does Chen want to play this?' she asked.

'He knows it's a long game. Well outside the timeframe of politics. He's focused on the integrity of the nation.'

Miriama smiled. 'Good. He's always been a good leader.'

'What he said was this,' Adam continued. 'He said the strategy, especially for the south of New Zealand, is to accommodate. He wants to get closer to the three, to try to make sure they reach a decent agreement. He knows we're going to lose control of our land and he's not going to focus on that. He's looking at the next

128

hundred years of settlement. He's not focused on who lives here, either. He says we've always been a settler nation.'

'Well, he would,' Zeb said. 'He's from a Chinese mining family. They were outsiders in the 1860s and they've hardly tried to fit in. He pisses me off. What was the word he used, "accommodate"? There's a word with a proud history.'

'What the Prime Minister is focused on,' said Adam, 'is preserving the rule of law and our basic integrity. If we're still one of the better places to live in a hundred years, he thinks people will look back and thank us. We'll be weak in the south by then, essentially colonised, but he hopes we'll be an independent nation still. Whoever "we" are. You can only achieve that by working with the three and keeping them united. We can't afford to have them fall out with each other. Everything else is secondary for the Prime Minister.'

Zeb swore and thumped his fist on the table. 'This will happen quickly,' Adam said, ignoring him. 'The Prime Minister is talking to the Australian Prime Minister. They want to work with Argentina and Chile to influence things as best they can.'

Miriama rubbed her hands together. 'Thank you, Adam. At last we're going to deal with people and stop pretending this is just an energy make-over project.'

'Miriama, you know why I've been dispatched down here. The Prime Minister needs to know the progress of your plans.'

Miriama smiled at Vai. 'And now it begins, Vai. The south is going to be dragged out of the hole it has tried to hide in. And good job, I say. Who are we to think we have a right to avoid the world's suffering? We have a development proposal in place. Antarctica is melting. It won't stop until most of the ice is gone and the world will be unrecognisable after that. But living and working there will be very hard for the next fifty years at least, maybe longer. This is much like Australia. Do you know how much bigger Antarctica is than Australia?'

Vai said, 'About twice as big.'

'That's right. And do you know how Australia functions? At

129

the macro level? It's much like Antarctica. A lot of the good stuff's in the middle but it's hard to live there, so the people are gathered in a few cities on the edge and they reach into the middle and get stuff. Then they turn to the wider world and sell it. One way or another, most Australians are tied into this. Antarctica is the same, just on a bigger scale. But it's too hard for a large population to live there and reach into the middle. The second-best option is to live close and reach in from other locations. Buenos Aires in Argentina is the closest, then Otago in the South Island, then Tasmania in Australia. Otago is the ideal location for us.'

'How big will the population be?' Vai asked.

'Australia has a population of forty-five million, including new migrants, almost all of them in cities,' Miriama said. 'It's not hard to see that one way or another there could be a population of ninety million seeking to make a living from Antarctica in your lifetime. This sort of thing works. China used to be locked up, so the British set up a city on Hong Kong island to reach in from. Commercially it was great.'

'Otago will be huge,' Vai said excitedly.

Zeb laughed. 'Hong Kong,' he said. 'It'll be the size of Hong Kong. The Taieri Plains, next to Dunedin, are about three hundred square kilometres, and the built-up part of Hong Kong is the same size. We're going to build out the plains. As time goes by, Antarctica can host its own cities. West Antarctica and the Ross Sea, they face New Zealand, and they're scheduled to melt first, so we get the advantage there. If another twelve million settle on West Antarctica, we get a quarter of the total in our orbit. Everything falls into place.'

Vai studied Zeb, confused. Apparently he didn't want the migrants but he couldn't wait to build the city. She looked at Miriama, who shrugged. Vai looked at her plate and tried to visualise twenty-two million people. What fraction of that was Independence? Stunned by the enormity of the proposal, she walked to the window as if the expanse of black ocean might help her encompass the change. A sliver of moonlight shone weakly on the ocean and she heard Adam say to Miriama, 'Can you tell me about the timing and staging? When will you get started?'

'I'm not free to discuss that right now, Adam. We're meeting with our development partners tomorrow, as I'm sure you know, hence your visit tonight. I will talk to you after that.'

'Thank you. The Prime Minister will back you if you give him the opportunity.'

Vai returned to the table, but they only picked at their food until the staff cleared the plates away. Vai imagined everything falling into place, more than she had dreamed of, leading her people to a whole new city. She would settle them near enough to be builders and construction workers, and before long lawyers and business owners. Nothing was unrealistic. She imagined the call to her mother, she imagined her mother's calls to her friends, she imagined her mother's calls to her enemies.

Zeb's voice broke into her reverie. 'Adam and I are going for a run in the morning. We'll run along the coast a few kilometres. Would you like to come?'

'I don't have any running gear,' Vai said. She felt the bruising on her shoulders and back from the battle on *Taniwha*. She tensed each leg, felt the muscles hard against the wooden chair. Her lower body was fine and the pain in her upper body was manageable.

'In the wardrobe in your room,' Miriama said. 'There's everything you could need.'

'Really? I don't think ... I mean—'

Zeb laughed. 'Mum never had a girl, and every time one comes around she buys out the shops. It's not just you.'

'Don't run too fast, Vai,' Miriama said. 'My boy doesn't seem able to keep pace.'

15

Lying in her soft, warm bed in the half-light before dawn Vai thought about Miriama's embrace of her. Smiling, she pulled the thick duvet closer and snuggled. She remembered the cold Southern Ocean and the low cloud bank that might have revealed Antarctica and she imagined the slow, steady journey of New Zealand from its mother's arms. The first rent of pain as it broke from Antarctica, not as a country but merely as geography, and the millions of years creeping northward. Wild storms chasing the islands in never-ending chastisement and the storms pounding, pounding constantly on the coast, tearing at the very rock. And, so close to now as to be yesterday, the first small groups of people, the storms clawing at their settlements until a country emerged.

Vai slipped out of bed, resting her feet on the soft carpeted floor. Looking from the bedroom window she could make out some of the hills of the Otago headland in shades of grey and black.

'Mate, Adam, let's go.' Zeb was outside Adam's room, calling for him. Vai stepped into the corridor at the same time as Adam slipped out of his room. The men stared at her as she zipped her sweat shirt and pulled it down to cover the top of her running tights.

Outside the house they gathered quietly under the oaks to stretch. Zeb described the route and led them out to the road where they ran at a smart pace to the last house, then Adam moved to the front and slowed the pace and Vai moved to the middle.

The sky grew light, the palest blue possible, revealing hedgerows and trees laid out across the peninsula. Cattle stood in quiet groups and birds began their morning chorus. A flock of starlings lit from a favoured tree and swarmed in the air before dispersing for their day's foraging.

Downhill along the quiet road they ran, then flat along the valley past straggles of brown grass, and across a bridge where the stream below ran dark in the shadow, on the flat a bit longer and up the far side of the valley. Zeb moved close behind Adam but let him lead. Adam was going to be fine for the first five kilometres, Vai thought, but after that he would look for an excuse to stop. The lighter man knew he could out-distance Adam and by sitting close behind him, pushing Adam's pace, Zeb asserted a little dominance.

Two more times down into valleys and back to ridgelines, then the coast opened in front of them. The steep, broken cliffs taking breaker after breaker from the ocean. The wave-torn ocean was a fearful presence, emphasised by the few fishing boats that bounced, tiny along its swell lines far out at sea. No respecter of men.

Adam pointed to a small knot of surfers floating near a headland, and leant against the wooded railed fence, taking the chance to rest. A wave pitched up in front of the surfers, a white peak forming behind the paddling group and holding up, neither growing nor diminishing. One of the group launched himself forward and with just a few more strokes his board pitched down the face of the wave, which was now forming a fast-breaking wall as it raced along the edge of the rock point. Without waiting to drop the full three metres of the liquid face, the rider grabbed the outside rail of his board and cut straight across the wall of water. Within seconds he was enclosed in a green room, hidden from view.

'Any of your new Chinese bosses out there, Zeb?' Adam asked.

133

Zeb assessed Adam's big frame puffing and huffing and the attempt he was making to look casual, leaning on the fence. 'Don't underestimate this deal, Adam. The Chinese are after Antarctica. We will have a lot of control on the Otago side.'

'From what I hear you're going to be "Made in China".' Adam waggled his fingers to denote the quote marks.

'Yeah, well, I don't know who you're talking to because it's them who are going to be "Made by Te Waipounamu".' Zeb waggled his fingers back at Adam. 'It's this island that's going to give them a secure base to launch from.'

'Let's sit over on those rocks.' Adam indicated an area inside the paddock where they could sit out of the wind but still in sight of the surfers. As they moved to the rocks Adam asked, 'Is your mum really going to pitch for a bunch of refugees?' He glanced at Vai. 'China alone will fill the city and there's Britain, the Europeans.'

Zeb lent back against a rock and looked to the sky. 'This has run on ahead of you and the Prime Minister, Adam. Circumstances, as they say, have taken control. This is going to be the biggest property development in the country's history. Nothing even close. And we're driving it.'

'I wish you all the best,' Adam said, shrugging. 'I mean it. And so does the Prime Minister. He's desperate to see locals capture the gains. But tell me about your mother.'

'Mum,' Zeb said, struggling to contain the anger in his voice. His face contorted as he started to describe the decision to bring the Bangladeshis to Dunedin, five thousand of them. 'We were all on board for that. Of course we were, and Mum went to Bangladesh to meet them before they came over because she was building most of the houses. Do you know about that?'

Adam nodded and Vai said, 'Yes, she told me about the meeting in the tent. It changed her.'

'Changed? That's an understatement. She came back a zealot. She was shaken at how they lived and she'd been to some of the camps that were run like prisons, where people had been born

134

there and there were generations of them locked up.' He looked at Vai. 'Prisoners who'd committed no crimes. Even babies. That's what she went on about.'

Zeb stood up and rolled his shoulders. 'She keeps talking about how there's a need to make a fundamental change. She came back angry that we haven't taken many refugees in Otago, saying we're just hiding down here hoping the rest of the world won't find us. Won't find out we've got a safe, fertile place with almost no one here.' He paced between rocks, his voice rising almost to a shout, his chest heaving against his running vest. 'She wants to bring as many over as she can. She wants to throw the doors open. She sees it as a tide of history thing.' He pointed out to the ocean. 'She talks about a storm out at sea, beyond the horizon. How you don't need to see the storm to know it happened, all you need to see is the big swells rolling in and you know a big storm threw them up.'

He turned to watch a surfer struggling in broken surf near the rocks. 'Mum talks about climate change as a monumental storm. But not as a bad thing. She says we need to push on through. Look to the post-destruction phase, more than a hundred years out. She says it's too late to do anything else.'

'She's right about that,' Adam said. Vai nodded, leaning in and nearly falling off her rock. She couldn't take her eyes from Zeb and his pacing.

'She talks about the pain and childbirth,' Zeb said, 'and how we need shared pain so that we can have a shared global experience. She says, what will it look like after the destructive phase? Who will be a stranger, who will be "other"? She wants to bring as many people here as she can, she wants to build up a community of migrants and refugees. Start them out labouring on the new city and then help them become prosperous and change the whole game. Make sure the widest possible group get a first go at Antarctica. But more than that, she wants to build a new people. She thinks all this pain is making us into the global community that we must be from now on. She wants this future. Everyone else is terrified of it.' Zeb looked from Adam to Vai. 'The only way to deal with this is as a global community, and she loves it.'

Vai's heart was pounding. Miriama wasn't just offering a handout, she was offering kinship. This was the world selecting its own future, driving through the floods and the droughts and the little hatreds and rolling out a new place that made the idea of 'other' a nonsense. New stories raced through her head but she couldn't articulate them, not yet. All she said was, 'We could make that work.'

Zeb spat, 'You can't just look beyond the destructive phase like it's some child's concern.'

Vai thought, *I could twist his neck, snap, like a chicken*; but then she softened toward him. *Boy, little boy, playing the leader role. Too soft and too weak, wishing it all away.* She said, 'When I was on *Taniwha*, the crew couldn't think about this because they couldn't stomach the destruction. They couldn't stomach the storm rolling in and changing history. But the ocean just rolls on. It doesn't ask who drowns or whether they deserved to live, whether a species deserves to continue.'

'You sound like Mum. She talks about the forces of integration working with the forces of destruction. One big process of history.' He crouched forward a little and raised his fists like a boxer in a defensive stance. 'You're as ruthless as she is. Loving the idea of utopia and ignoring the reality of it.'

'We *have* to think about this,' Vai said. 'And even more, we need to plan for it. We're too late to avoid the destruction. But what sort of society is being built through the destructive and constructive forces working together? We can get a good one if we plan. In the end.'

'Are you stupid?' Zeb dropped all pretence of calm. 'Don't you see the broken world we have now? Can you imagine what the world will be like once the melt is fully underway? No. No one can even think about it, let alone describe it.' He pushed Vai, a shove on the shoulder, and she raised her fists, balled-up. She wasn't stepping back.

136

Zeb sniggered. 'Who do you think's going to win this? Not the poor; they get to have last go.'

'Screw you.' Her voice was hard. 'I see you. Protecting what you have. Fending us off. But there are so many of us, living free of the little boundaries of a nation. Across the world, we know we'll be landless and there's a freedom there that you can't know. A freedom to imagine and go after a future that's bigger.' She poked a finger at Zeb's chest. 'You see us in camps and down on our knees, but across the world we're being birthed in a shared fire. We're the ones ready to build the sort of world nature is demanding from us. You're finished, not us.'

Adam put a hand on Zeb's arm and guided him back two steps. 'We understand what you have to do, Vai,' Adam said, 'But I'm with Zeb on this. The poor are stuffed, except maybe a few small groups that can be picked up without changing the general direction of things. This new city Miriama's planning is going to get all the labour it needs from migrants and there won't be much need for refugees.' He said it quietly, without malice. His voice was sad, regretful.

Vai dropped her stance and looked down at her clothes. She wondered if she was just in costume and maybe the men saw a beggar. Her eyes teared up and she had to stop herself from knocking Zeb down. She climbed back up on her rock and said quietly, 'Why are you driving this new city, Zeb, if you have such a negative view of where it's leading?'

'I accept we can't avoid a second colonisation. But do you think I'll welcome it? We'll do what we must. It can't be stopped, but this time we'll position ourselves to be winners.' Zeb wrapped his arms around his chest.

'And us?' Vai's throat constricted as she asked.

Zeb shook his head and turned his back on her, facing out to the surf.

'Fuck you!' Vai shouted, hurried to the fence, jumped it and headed back the way they had come.

137

16

The next day Miriama, Vai and Zeb pulled to a stop in their big, chauffeured car at a gatehouse, entrance to the five-thousand-acre Momona Station. A guard in a light-green jacket and cap admitted them to the South Island base for Chinese state-owned agriculture. The small station sat on the almost perfectly flat, low-lying Taieri Plain, a half-hour south of Dunedin. They were meeting Miriama's development partners.

Flocks of sheep grazed placidly within a geometry of fenced paddocks stretching in every direction from the long driveway that led to the homestead. An irrigation system jetted water low across the ground; green grass glistened in the heat. Where the irrigation stopped the paddocks reverted to burnt dirt. Vai assumed that also marked the end of the property.

Wooden rail fences surrounded the homestead. Hewn from native timber, they encompassed a north-facing garden of azaleas and camellias beneath scattered magnolia trees. Beds of flowering perennials completed the colourful sweep of planting as it reached around a lawn in front of the main building. Behind it and to each side a dense copse of trees ran back perhaps forty metres, blocking the prevailing wind. Dappled light fell on cottages set among the copse, and a squad of brightly coloured birds chased amongst the trees.

Zhou Lai took Miriama's hand as she stepped from the car. He bent to kiss her cheek and said, 'It's good to see you again.' Miriama introduced Vai, and Zhou shook hands with Zeb and asked how the plans were progressing at his end.

'All good,' Zeb said. 'The developed designs from our Shanghai office are appropriate for now.'

They entered the building and Zhou gestured to two young men in matching suits who led the way to a boardroom. One of the young men gave three sharp taps on the large table in the centre and a 3D map emerged in low profile. Zeb turned to Vai. 'There's Dunedin at the top, and we're down here in the middle on this sheep station.' He pointed at another place on the map. 'That's the Momona airport.' Then he tapped his own device and the rural landscape transformed into a grid of roads and coloured blocks denoting different types of property development. He tapped the screen again and the southern area ceased to be a lake and rivers and became a large port; the airport quadrupled in size.

Vai didn't know how to interpret the colour blocks but measured the scale of the project, from Mosgiel to Lake Waihola, against the existing city of Dunedin, and realised that Momona City would leave Dunedin as a pimple on its backside. Eventually Zhou turned away from the screen. 'That looks good. Let's talk further about staging and communicating the proposal.'

'Thank you, Zhou,' Miriama said. 'We can't get over-stretched at the wrong time. Can you assure me we'll get the growth?'

'This is the mother. Easily twenty million people will link Antarctica and New Zealand. That doesn't mean all of them will be based here in Momona City. In time the ice on the continent will be well back from the shore and major settlements will go there.' He ran his hand lovingly over the table and glorious images of apartments and offices sprang to life with people of all hues chatting and waving to each other. 'Momona,' he said languorously, 'the mother settlement.' Then he jabbed a finger at a map on the wall, Antarctica was at the centre in snow-white with colour edging. 'Buenos Aires will be similar. It will be the anchor for another twenty to twenty-five million. Tasmania and Cape Town also. America will lead on Tasmania and will try to lead at Buenos Aires, but the South Americans might resist

139

that. The biggest unknown is South Africa. It has historic ties to India, and India will try to enter from there.' He traced a line from Delhi to Cape Town. 'Depending on how successful they are, we will have to adjust our growth expectations.'

'And you remain confident we don't need Dunedin?' Miriama said.

'We can't make a lot of use of Dunedin. But we need to raise Momona up. It's too low and it floods. We need to dig out the new harbour at Lake Waihola and make a proper cut through the river to the sea. We need all that soil and rock to fill the flat land and raise it.'

Miriama nodded, reassured that his view had not changed. 'The land ownership on Dunedin's port remains too fragmented for us to build a new city there at scale and pace. We would be bogged down in land purchases and protests. And it would be too expensive and small.'

'Scale and pace,' Zhou said. 'That's what it's all about now. The city will need to accommodate about two hundred thousand people in the next five years, perhaps much more if we agree to go fast with migrant housing.'

'Migrants and refugees,' Miriama said, emphasising the latter group.

'Well, then, that confirms the pace of development will be fast. Once the settlement framework for Antarctica is signed we can announce the full scale of plans.' Zhou turned to Vai. 'We intend Momona to be the only first-class offering near Antarctica so it becomes the accepted centre for launching to the continent. Once we have first-mover advantage we will keep building ahead of demand to ensure that other locations cannot compete.'

Zeb stood up and ran his hand across the table, altering the image. 'Here's a view of Hong Kong imposed onto the area where Momona City will be. You can see the urban area of Hong Kong would fit into the area we're looking at. We need to own the major infrastructure, the port, water, wastewater, the toll routes and airport. We need that long-term cashflow.'

140

'We know,' Zhou said. 'We need this to be a joint project with a major local partner. We can't afford for you to fail. We are happy for you to take those assets. We want Antarctica.'

'I don't want to sound like a ghoul,' Miriama said, 'but West Antarctica will continue to melt. We're sure of that, aren't we?'

'Locked in,' Zhou said. The table was silent for a while. Vai stared at the map and tried to locate Balclutha but it was too far south to show on the screen. Zhou said, 'Anyway, West Antarctica would likely have melted at two degrees, just on slow-cook. The time frame gets pushed out, but the result is the same as three degrees.'

'Like roasting a leg of lamb instead of just throwing it in the microwave,' Zeb said.

Miriama laughed. 'I hope to God no one born in the south would ever microwave a leg of lamb.'

'Now we need to talk about bringing these plans to the public and the politicians,' Zhou said. 'This is going to be a tough decade for New Zealand. But after that, people might settle into the realities of rapid change. Hopefully your government will hold up.'

'We can only release the plans slowly,' Miriama said. 'To start with, we'll talk about the need to do our fair share for refugees and the opportunity to capture a larger share of the movement to and from Antarctica. That gives us a jobs angle.'

Eventually the meeting ended and the group moved to a restaurant in the building. Miriama turned to the others and said, 'Get started. I want to walk in the garden with you, Zhou, if you don't mind.'

She and Zhou strolled out onto the open lawns and across to the rail fence at the edge of the garden. Leaning against the fence they had a clear view of the snow-covered mountains. Beyond the green farm and its parched neighbours, the mountains reached into the sky. Miriama looked around at the garden and then back across the paddocks. 'Everything I see here is the re-creation of a part of England. The garden, the fences, the sheep,

141

the pasture. Even most of the weeds are English or Scottish. It used to bother me, but as I've grown older I've allowed myself to enjoy the beauty of it.'

'I'm pleased to know that. I can't stand nostalgia. In my experience, the past doesn't bear much scrutiny.'

'Could you do me a favour?'

'Perhaps. What is it?'

'The young woman, Vai. I've taken a liking to her. I want to help her. She's my assistant, but she doesn't have a visa to live and work here. It will take me a few months to get her one. Could you get her down to Antarctica on one of the Chinese settlements? She needs to be somewhere else and there's no point in her being back on her home island. She can learn things that are useful to me on the continent.'

Zhou shrugged. 'Sure, I'll get her on a site that's just being established. It's going to be our main settlement on the ice.'

With a sudden sigh Miriama leaned against him, her legs inexplicably shaking. Zhou put an arm around her shoulder and she let him take her weight. 'Vai represents everything we didn't do,' Miriama said.

He squeezed her shoulder and nodded. 'We'll get there. China dug itself out of a hole almost as deep.'

17

Pre-dawn light, purple emerging from grey as if a painter's brush had lightly stroked the sky, revealed dry pasture overhung by black clouds on the Taieri Plain. Yesterday's scorcher was replaced by a storm threatening to blow in from the south-west. Zeb, Vai and Adam were speeding silently across the Taieri Plain to Balclutha. 'Do you think the rain will get to the plains and the peninsula?' Adam asked.

'Hard to tell now,' Zeb said. 'The weather seems to come in over the western mountains and rain itself out. The warmer ocean seems to hold it off the east coast.'

The car drew parallel to Momona station and Vai asked Zeb to pull over. She walked to the boundary fence where the dark outlines of sheep could be seen grazing the pasture in the weak light. Miriama had told her that she would be going to Antarctica, to join a Chinese development. She was scared and excited, not knowing anything about property.

Zeb followed her. 'Are you okay?'

'Yes, I'm just trying to imagine how much land is needed to accommodate all of Independence in the new city. I thought about it last night and couldn't picture it.'

Zeb put one hand on the fence. 'Look at the paddock here, next to us. It's a big home paddock, but all your people could fit in the one paddock, in apartment buildings.'

Vai looked at the parameters of the paddock, then west to the high mountains blanketed in rain and east to the hills encompassing the plain. Where the hills were breached must be where Lake Waihola flows to the sea, she thought. 'We don't need much, then,' she said. 'Are we still an hour to Balclutha?'

'About that. It might rain further south, so an hour's about right.'

At Lake Waihola, Zeb slowed the car and pointed to the right. 'That's the wetland and lake. It's shallow. Hard to imagine a commercial port.' He pointed to the fences and some of the higher land. 'See the debris from floods? The outlet for this whole plain is the one river and it's not big or wide enough. Floodwaters back up. The Chinese'll make a big cut to the sea.'

They crossed a river running brown with mountain floodwater, but it had not yet risen high against its banks: no rain was falling here. Sheep and little houses intimated the farm life scattered along the route. The river that cut its way to the sea was modest. The houses were modest. They passed a ruddy-faced farmer driving his tractor along the verge: he nodded a greeting and looked back to check the flat-deck trailer. It had a single sheep tied to the front bar, on its back with its feet bound. As they passed the sheep raised its head and lolled its tongue; it had patches where wool and skin had fallen away.

By the time they reached Balclutha it was raining hard. They entered through the northern hillside suburbs but didn't stop there. From the bridge that took them over the Clutha River they had a good view of the part of town built on the river flat. The streets ran in a grid and were mostly quiet, most buildings looked empty. 'Shall we just drive around?' Zeb asked.

'Yes, let's just look around this area. It's the part we can have,' Vai said.

Adam pursed his lips. 'Remember, there's no guarantee.'

'No one has let me forget.'

They drove down the main street, which was part of the main state highway. It was raised against flooding, but it had been a quick and rough job: some shops and houses were cut off from the road by the flood works. Near the point where the road

144

started to rise to the second set of hillside suburbs there was a shop with a light on and a sign that said 'Coffee and Pie'. Adam said, 'Let's have a talk to whoever runs this place, see what's happening in the town.'

Inside was warm. There were horns of bulls mounted on the walls, some of them wider than a man's arm span. Country music was playing, and a man and woman rose from a table and went and stood to attention behind the serving counter. Zeb looked around the empty tables and said, 'Shall we sit down or do we order at the counter?'

'I'll come over,' said the woman.

They sat by the window and looked at the water pooling under their car with the one streetlight reflecting on the car bonnet. The woman said brightly, 'Hi I'm Sal.' They looked through the menu and agreed to have just coffee. Sal looked crestfallen.

'Hang on, come back,' Zeb said. They studied the menu again and Zeb ordered. 'Fried eggs with fried potatoes and onions. And the bacon.' Vai and Adam said they'd have the same.

Adam waved out to the man and said, 'Good to have some rain.'

He replied, 'That's right. It's been a long time.'

Vai pointed to the road. 'Does it flood? Is that why it's raised in places?'

The man walked over and introduced himself as Brian. 'It only floods occasionally, but every now and then there's a big one washes right through.' He pointed to a dirty mark on the wall of the shop. 'The last one left a stain we haven't dealt with yet. Council's broke, roads are stuffed. Rural people need off-road vehicles just to come in and buy a pie. Lucky petrol's stayed cheap.'

Vai peered out through the rain. 'Are people living in the houses?'

'On the hills they are, but the ones on the flat here are meant to be empty.'

Sal called, 'Food's ready,' and Brian went out back to bring it.

After they had eaten, Vai asked Sal if it would be okay to drive around and have a look in some of the houses. 'Go for your life,' she replied. 'Most of them are rotting.'

'Didn't they get cleaned up after the flood?'

'After the first and second big ones the insurance paid for a clean-up and then they said no more, that's it. We've had two more big floods since then and no one's bothered.'

Zeb drove down Argyle Street, at the end there was a reserve that ran to the river. There was a lot of debris piled up on the reserve: it looked as though a couple of big tractors or diggers had swept along the roads after the last flood and just scooped the mess into a pile.

Zeb drove along another street and pulled into a driveway. They sat in the car and looked at the house. It was painted white and had a brick skirt around its base. The windows and curtains were all in place and the house looked good, except it had a watermark about four feet up.

'Let's take a look inside,' Adam said. They hurried through the rain to the front door but it was locked so they trudged to the back door through the pooling water. Adam gave the door a shove and it opened a little. He put his shoulder to it and slowly it gave ground and as it came open an evil stench of rot escaped the house. The three stepped back, gasping, and gulped at the rain-fresh air in the garden. 'Forget it,' Adam said. 'I'm not looking in there.'

'What'd you expect?' Vai said. 'I haven't come all this way to stay outside.' She took a deep breath and entered the house. Her shoes sank into the damp mess of carpet and, once she'd touched the wall, coloured wallpaper hung in little strips from her fingernails. She stopped to work out the layout of the house, then ploughed on into the middle of the main room. Things were as they had been abandoned: plates in the sink, teacups on the table. The cloth-covered furniture had mould growing in groves of yellow and green.

She walked through the house, bouncing on the floor, testing

146

for weak points. The floor moved and sprang but she thought it was sound. The beds were fetid and when she reached the toilet there was brown water with toilet paper and tampons and stuff she didn't bother to identify. She gagged and ran to the outside door. 'The sewage is backflowing onto the floor,' she yelled. 'There's shit everywhere.'

In the garden she let the rain wash over her face and cleanse her trousers and shoes. She welcomed the soaking wet and flicked the paper from under her nails. The men stood under a tree, hunched with their coats pulled over their heads.

'What the hell is this about?' Vai said. 'I think the house might still be sound, but it won't be for long. How could these houses be left like that? Who's meant to move in there?'

Rain ran off the men's coats and their pants were soaked. Vai had water running in cascades over her face and under her collar. She didn't care. She turned to the car and splashed through the mud, pausing at an apple tree that had fruit rotting on its branches. There was a solitary white flower on a small branch; she snapped off the end to take the flower.

When they were back in the car, water running off them onto the seats, Vai said, 'I need to see the river.' Zeb turned at the end of the street onto a gravel track that led to the top of a portion of the embankment that was meant to protect the town. They could see the river boiling and running fast, swollen but not so much that it might threaten the town. Upstream the embankment was blown out for most of its length and offered no protection to the properties on the low loop of the river.

'Now can we go up the hill on the other side?' Vai asked.

They found their way to a street that looked across the valley. Below them the river flats soaked and the part of the town they had just left looked pretty. Balclutha was a town of big trees and big gardens. The roofs of the buildings popped forward in the poor light of the storm, their reds and blues and whites giving a mosaic of happiness past.

Vai studied the scene. 'I bet most of those houses are basically

147

sound. Who is responsible for them?'

Adam said, 'The Adjustment Office.'

'Well, they're useless,' Vai said. 'We need to get someone else.'

18

On Wednesday morning Miriama, Zeb and Vai drove to Momona airport. They were to meet with Adam, the mayor of Dunedin and the chair of the Regional Council to begin promoting the Momona City project.

The facilities manager intercepted Miriama at the airport entrance. 'Your meeting room over there is ready, but Mr Walker has asked if he can have a few minutes in there with guests. I hope you don't mind. I have coffee available for you in a separate lounge.'

Miriama turned to Vai. 'Go and see what Adam's doing.' She and Zeb left with the manager.

Vai found herself in a short passageway with three additional doors. The door on her right was ajar and she could hear Adam talking urgently to someone. He sounded nervous, Vai thought, even fearful.

'Everything will move fast,' he said. 'China will force the settlement and Momona City will begin very quickly. Will you be ready?' His voice dropped an octave, 'I can't believe Japan made itself a pariah state. Do you actually want in?' A chair shunted on the floor. 'Scrutiny, there'll be more scrutiny.'

Now an Asian man spoke, calmer, more confident than Adam. 'The structure of the settlement doesn't affect our deal, Adam.' Was that a snigger? 'It was never a government deal.'

Vai slide her right foot closer to the door and transferred her weight forward. She could see Adam, back to her, sitting on a

149

plastic chair. Now he spoke with more composure. 'This trouble between China and Japan over the *Taniwha* has made it much harder for me to get your company to be the preferred supplier for New Zealand's mining interests.' He raised both hands, fingers cocked like an American cop. 'I'll need more. The guys in Primary Resources are shitting themselves.'

'You and your friends have drunk from a certain cup, Adam.' The Asian man leaned forward and came into view: short-cropped hair, black and high on his forehead, ears sticking out clear of his skull. He leant into Adam's pistol-hands, fearless.

Adam let one pistol go, lowered it. But the other one held steady. 'I know, and now there may be more friends who need a drink.'

Another, younger man with an Asian accent said, 'The company we will use is registered in London.' The first Asian man stood. He could have seen Vai if he had looked away from Adam, could have seen her eyes fixed still, not blinking. The younger man's arm came into sight, hand pushing forward. 'The company has traded for over a century and has a well-established reputation in the minerals field. We purchased it last week. There is no reason for Japan to be mentioned.'

Adam lifted himself to his feet. 'New Zealand has no time for a tender process,' he said with more assurance, 'and no national companies that can get down there fast enough and at scale. An offshore company will be fine, will be needed.'

'Thank you, Adam,' the older man said. 'And the good thing about all the ice melting is there will be plenty to drink, so if you have someone who really needs a drink, that will be fine.' He said 'fine' in a way that indicated the conversation was closed.

Vai slipped out of the passageway into the airport hall and when she looked back as the Asian men emerged she recognised the older one as the man who had flustered Adam in Auckland.

She went to the meeting room. Adam looked up and said, 'That was quick. I just messaged Zeb to ask you all to come in.'

'Miriama sent me on ahead to check when you would be ready.'

Adam looked searchingly at Vai, so she said, 'I saw the man you spoke to in Auckland leave, so I assumed you were finished. Where's he from?'

'He's Japanese. Where did you see him?'

'In the main hall, as I was walking over.'

Miriama entered with Zeb, the facility manager and two new people. She introduced the mayor of Dunedin, Dr Elsie Inglis, and the chair of the Otago Regional Council, David Henry. 'Vai is my assistant,' she told them, 'but she will be leaving me in a few days because she needs to get a work visa. She will join my Chinese development partner for a few months. They are setting up a new base in Antarctica.'

'That will be interesting for you. Where are you from?' David asked.

'I'm from Independence Island. I'm a lawyer, the Advocate for Independence.' The words rang in Vai's head as if she'd spoken them into a tin drum. She was being thrust into roles she hadn't prepared for and, for the first time, she felt as if she should be older. Or even someone else entirely.

Elsie scrutinised Vai. 'You're very young to be the Advocate. You must be clever.'

'Not just clever. She's determined, a fighter,' Miriama said.

Elsie laughed. 'Well, that explains it. That's why you're making all this effort to get her, Miri.'

Miriama patted her friend's arm and said to Vai, 'This woman knows Dunedin better than anyone ever has. She will fight for Dunedin, first and last.'

'And I lead the region,' David said, looking apologetically at Elsie. 'I think of myself as a navigator, or even the person who checks the map.' He scratched at his grey beard and adjusted his kilt. Vai wondered if he had a wife, someone who could tell him his over-large belly and skinny legs didn't really work with a kilt any more. A daughter would do that; perhaps he had neither a daughter nor a wife. All the others were so elegant: Miriama, as always, but Elsie's dress shimmered between black and red and deep blue as she moved, and she had a pendant of greenstone, two fingers thick and the length of a woman's hand. Vai glanced down at her own simple dress: light lemon with a thin, black belt. She imagined the impact she could make over the next few decades, leading her community's interactions with the mayor and the development company.

Elsie asked the facility manager to bring in lunch and coffee. She sat at the head of the table, facing the door and invited the others to sit either side of her. 'Adam,' she began, 'the Prime Minister appears to believe he has to do as he's told. That's fine so long as he's doing what the voters tell him. I had a very concerning conversation with him this morning. He seems to think we should all accept some sort of international consortium walking into the country and taking over our region. I told him to grow a pair, and if he couldn't manage I assured him we could loan him some.'

'Dr Inglis, the Prime Minister is from Dunedin. I have no doubt he is aware of the public mood.'

'I'm not talking about the mood, Adam. The mood changes like the weather. I'm talking about what the voters want, the sorts of things they come back to when they aren't being frightened by dark talk from their Prime Minister. Things like democracy and self-determination. The environment, for God's sake. Remember that?'

Adam closed his eyes and held the bridge of his nose. 'The aspects of this that the council influences — property development, water quality, community — the council retains control over that.'

'I presume we can work our way through the practical issues fairly easily,' David said. 'I know that we won't, in the end, hold up any approvals, at the regional level. There will be a point of consensus. The region just needs a bit of time to understand the proposal, how big, how fast. That sort of thing.'

There was a knock at the door and an airport staffer entered pushing a trolley with a light brunch.

'David, there is no agreement on anything yet.' Elsie spoke to the chair of the regional council as if he was one of her staff. 'Let's put aside the impacts on the Antarctic environment for now. Although as the city mayor I'm going to work with the environmental groups to ensure those issues remain live. But I accept that my remit only exists within the region. Don't look at me like that, David. I need to consider the region to make good decisions for the city.'

'Let me pour the coffee,' David offered.

'Thanks,' Elsie said. 'And can you pass me a couple of sandwiches? Something for Adam, too. I'm about to chew his ear off.'

'Perhaps I should speak before we get caught up in the roles of various levels of government,' Miriama said. 'We're going to lodge plans for a city of two hundred thousand. To begin with it will grow quickly to fifty thousand and after that we will have to respond to the pace of uptake.' There was a sharp intake of breath from Elsie and David.

'Two hundred thousand?' David said. 'I don't think our people will accept that.'

'The city would struggle to take that many,' Elsie said. 'But we could do it as one very big waterfront development, and I suggest you put some at the airport.'

'We'll put all of it around the Momona airport, out on the Taieri Plain. The land is too hard to assemble in the city. We'd never get the project off the ground and now that the big three countries are forcing the Antarctic settlement resolution we need to move fast. It could happen very soon.'

'None in the city?' Elsie was shocked. 'That'll kill us! The city will fall into ruin.'

Miriama tapped her knuckles on the table. 'We move at the pace the Antarctic settlement dictates. We can't remake Dunedin quickly enough. But there'll be a second wave of development and Dunedin could be part of that.'

'How quickly will the Antarctic settlement be arranged,

Adam?' Elsie asked.

'It's being negotiated now. It could be finished in weeks, but probably months,' he said.

'How is that possible? There are two hundred countries involved.'

'I can tell you what I understand to be the case. But it is confidential.' Adam looked around the table and waited for everyone to nod agreement. 'India, China and America are going to block the entire northern hemisphere. Except themselves, of course. It's going to be a "southern hemisphere plus three" settlement.'

'There will be outrage!' Elsie said. 'Are you telling me that the big three think they can cut half the world out of a deal over the last continent? The last major prize on earth?'

'Yes. The big three are all that stands between many small wars turning into big ones. Maybe one big one. The argument they will use is that the other northern countries have very large areas of low population opening up. They've got big areas becoming available toward the Arctic.'

'And Antarctica is the only place that's new in the south,' David said.

'That's right. What will be proposed is a ten-year period where the big three lead. In that time a federal arrangement of some type is to be worked out with the participating nations.'

'But so many of the northern countries have bases on Antarctica,' David said.

'They will be put into a heritage group and eased out over the ten-year period.'

'Can the three impose that?' asked Elsie.

'The Russians are tied up with the Arctic, making themselves very important there. Britain is under the tutelage of India — it's lucky to have such strong cultural ties and history. The others are too broke and too dependent on the big three to raise any objections. None of them could fund a conflict in the Antarctic, even if they had the ambition to cross the big three.'

154

Elsie placed her hand on Miriama's. 'We've known something was afoot, but not this scale. I'm not sure, Miri. The climate is so unpredictable. Without this, our economy . . . Well, what will it be? But we need to deal with the fact that this Momona proposal is such a big change, and it involves new people. Foreigners. I'm not opposed to that, but we need time to debate this, see how things link together.'

'That's why we are going public now,' Miriama said.

'We're being told. Told, not asked,' David said stridently, 'to become a frontier mining town. What does that mean? Families looking for new schools and playgrounds? Thousands of single men looking for brothels and bars? You tell me.'

'We'll put this to the public. But you're right. There's no stopping it,' Miriama said. 'We need to do our best to bring people along. But there will be a point at which the big players just unload their diggers and get cracking.'

'Well, hang on,' said David. 'There is a rule of law here.' Elsie looked at him as if he was mentally deficient.

Adam said, 'If necessary the government will pass legislation. In fact, it's likely to be necessary. The Prime Minister has made it clear that we either work with the big three or they bypass us. This is being driven by climate breakdown, not democracy. If we wanted things to be different we should have addressed warming thirty years ago.'

Elsie said, 'Miriama, you need to work with others to manage this. Don't think you can do this by charging off with one big power.' She rapped the table. 'And what's more, we need to get a large part of the benefit inside the city.' She grasped the edges of the table. 'The city!'

Miriama put a hand on Elsie's shoulder. 'I'll meet with you as soon as I can. But we also need to talk about refugees.'

'We agreed another ten thousand,' Elsie said. 'You're making me nervous.'

'Yes, that's a very large number for a region our size,' David added, looking around for support.

Vai snorted then quickly looked at the floor, pretending to cough.

Miriama allowed a small smile to cross her face. 'One hundred million refugees. Elsie and David, you're too good to turn your backs. Otago will become a centre of economic activity and we should repay that gift by taking a very large refugee settlement.'

David rounded on Adam. 'Prime Minister Chen won't last five minutes if he lets the big three move in like this! Throwing refugees at us too, ones they can't handle themselves. His own party will throw him off a cliff. I hate to say it, but he is of Chinese extraction. It'll look like he's in on the deal.'

'When the big three decide to move on Antarctica we won't be able to stop it, but we could get trampled by it,' Adam stated calmly.

'You prick!' David bellowed. 'Wellington's not even going to fight, are they? I mean, a city of two hundred thousand is too many. I'm up for fifty thousand. But I won't tolerate Chinese and refugee colonisation.'

'It seems certain there will be mining in Antarctica,' Adam continued calmly. 'But settlement is another question. No one can be certain about that yet. The national interest is to trade and to capture the wealth that will flow from Antarctica. There is nothing inherently wrong with establishing a new town at Momona. It will be subject to New Zealand law.'

'David, I'm sorry you referred to the Prime Minister as you did,' Miriama said. 'Perhaps his experience of Aotearoa is closer to an indigenous, a Māori experience. After the devastation of European settlement we don't have an inherent commitment to the Western way, nor any inherent bias against working with China. We'll do our best with what is in front of us.'

David looked at her in astonishment. 'I can't believe what I'm hearing. Do you think control of the country will be abandoned with no resistance?'

'No effective resistance, David. Nothing effective.'

'When will you make the plans public?' Elsie asked.

'Monday.'

'You've been working on this for a long time, then,' Elsie said slowly.

'I'm sorry. I know you must feel betrayed. But you couldn't have kept this quiet, not in your role as mayor,' Miriama said. 'We were approached a decade ago.'

'A decade!' Elsie exclaimed. Anger and hurt played across her face, and Vai realised the depth of the older women's relationship as it reflected in Elsie's pain.

'Yes,' Miriama continued, looking only at David. 'It was very straightforward. They explained that the ice would melt, at least on the part between the Ross Sea and the Antarctic Peninsula, West Antarctica. There would be opportunity for mining and who knows what else, maybe permanent settlement. They said that Otago would be a perfect staging point. We looked at options to redevelop Dunedin, but the place is in so many little property titles, it was impossible to assemble decent development blocks, and protection against sea-level rise in that context was going to be very expensive. We couldn't give them the scale they were after. So, we agreed on a new town.'

'I have no idea how you kept this quiet for a decade,' Elsie said sadly.

David hissed at Adam, 'There's no way this can stay secret.' He turned to Miriama. 'Don't count your chickens.'

That evening Zeb dropped Miriama and Vai at Elsie's home. Before she stepped out Miriama said, 'You're quiet, Zeb. Often you're quiet.' She touched his shoulder. 'Is it the migrants and the refugees?' He said nothing. 'This isn't just about making us rich.'

'I know, Mum.' He kept his eyes forward, looking down the darkened road. 'But while you're alive I'll keep both eyes on the commercial tasks, and that's where they need to be right now. Once you're gone I will honour your commitments, I promise.'

Vai watched Zeb carefully, wondering how much his mother

believed, what she knew of her son. His jawline glowed gently in the light of the car's dash. Despite her anger at him, Vai wished she could touch him, reach over and run the back of her hand lightly on the stubble of his beard. He was the one who would drive Momona into place. She'd need him as much as Miriama to get Independence settled.

Miriama smiled and each cheek dimpled. 'I know you will,' she said. 'I'm just saying, when the decisions we make now are written into history, it's important to me that we've shown integrity.' She leaned forward and kissed her son on the cheek. 'We don't control the destruction,' she said with a sigh, 'but we need to understand the forces of integration and explain them, help people see what to do next.'

Miriama and Vai hurried along the concrete path that stretched upward to Elsie's home in St Clair. The night sky was blocked by clouds; rain fell. Tree branches arched over the path, and in the dark Vai ducked, unsure of the enclosure. A night owl called to the silence – *ruru, ruru*. Near the front door they paused to look out over the ocean that spread before the house. White caps blew from the tops of waves that were too dark to be seen.

Miriama pushed the front door open and called out, 'Elsie, it's me and Vai.'

Elsie's grey hair hung free and fell to her waist. A light woollen sweater hung to her knees and Vai was taken by its colourful patchwork. 'Haere mai, Miri,' Elsie responded, 'I was just going to sit down and watch the news. Word's leaked about your plans for Momona.'

'The ever-helpful regional chairman,' Miriama said.

'No doubt. I'll have to go to the protest tomorrow and talk with people.'

'We're ready. I knew when I told David that he would be too incontinent to manage himself.'

'I've spoken to Rod Gibson. You must know who he is, the regional eco-protect manager.'

'Yes. He's a good man.'

'He tried to put a brave face on our discussion. To start with, anyway, but he's furious that the nations are going to try and bulldoze into Antarctica.'

'I'm sure. But he knew this was coming.'

'Yes. They're really stuck, the environmentalists. I talked to Rod about the need to settle migrants and refugees. He's a liberal man and he cares. He wants the poor to be looked after. I repeated what you said, we're discovered. A relatively good place to live, with a bright economic future and a low population.'

'It's a seismic shift.'

'He ended up weeping. Not just crying. He was weeping. He knows what's next.'

'The harried, the poor and the desperate. It's difficult for liberals to put the environment ahead of the people. I do feel sorry for him. I hadn't expected tears.'

'Well, there'll be plenty more around the region over the next few months,' Elsie said with a shudder. 'I was just making tea.'

'I'll get it.' Miriama went to the kitchen and came back with a pot of tea and three cups.

'That's a lovely locket, Vai,' Elsie said. 'Beautiful patterning.'

Vai took the locket in one hand and extended it forward to the limit of its chain. 'Mum gave it to me. It has a lock of Dad's hair and one of hers.'

'How beautiful,' Elsie said.

'When Mum was pregnant with me, Dad came to New Zealand for work and they put their hair together.' Vai opened the locket to show them. 'There's a flower from a garden in Balclutha in here too. We're going to Balclutha,' Vai said, looking to Miriama for reassurance. 'It's the new part of our story, our future.'

Miriama poured the tea. Elsie sipped and then set her cup down. 'How big Miri? How big is this Momona place going to be?'

'We plan to make it as big as the market will stand.'

'Half a million?'

'As I said before, Elsie, you're the mayor. Once you know our estimates you'll be obliged to share them. Try and figure it out. Think about the big picture. The global picture.'

'I don't want to fight with you about that again, Miri. I don't believe in predetermination.'

'I'm as sorry for what we lost as Rod Gibson is. But that country is gone. He's just smoothing the pillow for a dying past.'

'Palliative care?' Vai cut in.

Miriama rounded on Vai angrily. 'Did you get that from Zeb?'

'Yes.' Then Vai added, 'I'm sorry.'

'Don't be,' said Miriama after a pause, conciliatory now. 'I used that word once, and he latched onto it. I meant that the New Zealand Elsie and I grew up in, that wonderful country, is gone. What I'm interested in is the future that will come.'

'You look forward to it, don't you?' Vai asked. 'Every time it's mentioned you become excited. I see your eyes. I hear you.'

'Maybe this is how fighters feel when they go into war. Once they know the killing and the blood won't be avoided. But that's not the same as celebrating it. Don't think that of me.'

'What about abundance? Do you think we could achieve that, in the future?' Vai looked from Miriama to Elsie. 'When I was on *Taniwha* there was talk of abundance. Not that any of them would support it.'

'What did they say on the ship?' Elsie asked.

'That left to itself nature tends toward abundance. Most places on earth that aren't abundant were made that way by people. Because people are dominant, we have the obligation to learn and facilitate abundance. Then we survive by harvesting a small portion off a very large total. What we've done under sustainability is seek the minimum point at which a system can survive and then harvest from that. Sustainability has degenerated into the economic idea of consuming on the margin of disaster.'

'We lack the maturity for abundance,' said Miriama. 'It's the right idea but it could only work in a world where people worked with each other in a global, sophisticated way.'

'That's what we need to work on.' Elsie said, triumphant as if she had just got the last clue in a game show. 'Abundance requires maturity. And if we get things right we might not need to move most refugees. As you say, the world can be abundant.'

'We have to act now,' Miriama said. 'To not act now is cruel. Thank God for China's leadership, I say. They're the only community in the world that can act at scale and pace. Your approach is Kiwi bureaucrat writ large. Duck for cover, wait and see.'

'We don't have to open up to China or any other country.' Elsie snapped. 'It's you who's opened the door, Miri. You and the Prime Minister. You get to mix bits of cement together. It's people like me that have to build something that's worthwhile.'

'Mixing cement?' Miriama jumped to her feet and put her hands on her hips. 'Rubbish.' She raised her hands theatrically. 'Here's a funny story. The mayor used to live inside a walled garden. Same house, this one, only it had a big wall around the garden. A brick wall, as old as the occupant, one hundred years.'

'Oh, yes, very important story this one,' Elsie interjected, rolling her eyes.

'Two years ago, a storm knocked a portion of it over. Boom. Crash onto the street. In the morning Elsie looks out the window — and what did you see, Elsie?'

Elsie sipped her tea, saying nothing, looking out the window to the black sky.

'Council workers were climbing over it,' said Miriama. 'Coming in through the hole in the wall. But they weren't white men with Scottish names. Oh, no. They were a Sudanese crew. How about that? Black men climbing in through a hole in the walled garden.'

'Very symbolic,' Elsie said. 'And then they took the whole wall away and I no longer live in ignorance. But I do still live on an island.'

Anger washed over Vai without warning. What did this old woman know about life on an island? Living here in safety.

Obscurity, yes, obscurity. 'When, Elsie, when would you take action?'

'It's on us now, Elsie,' Miriama said.

'Tide of history?'

'Tide of history, that's it. But don't be angry with me. You've been caught out. Vai caught you, seeking to hide Otago from foreigners.'

'Did you?' Elsie turned to Vai, putting on a hurt face. 'Did you catch me? What do you see?'

Vai looked at Miriama, embarrassed. Miriama said, 'Go on, Elsie's just playing.'

'I need to get Independence settled,' Vai said. 'The worry consumes me most days and at night I can hardly move, but sometimes a thought comes into my head and I imagine the landscape is painted onto glass. Sometimes I'm in a garden or a town and sometimes I'm on the edge of an encroaching forest. I wait for the glass to shatter. It's only then, I tell myself, that I will see the real world and get a chance to grab safety for Independence. I imagine a moment, a chancing moment.'

'Hmm,' Miriama said. 'You think it will come down to chance?'

'I don't know. It's just something I've experienced a few times. I have to be ready, always ready. And always pushing on every door.'

Part V

19

It became hot soon after the sun climbed above the ocean. No cool morning breeze stirred in the garden and plants hunkered down, submissive. Vai stood in the kitchen and shielded her eyes from the glare. Miriama fussed over the stove and directed Vai to check through the large pack that held her Antarctic equipment. Sunscreen, ice axe, crampons, clothes, toiletries and on. Clothes that folded into tiny handfuls but nonetheless would handle minus twenty, minus forty, even colder. *Could it get colder?*, Vai wondered.

'Put the pack on, Vai,' Miriama instructed, leaning on a bench, coffee in hand. 'Tell me if it's comfortable.'

Vai swung the pack onto her shoulders. 'Hmm, good,' Miriama said. 'Looks good on you. A good fit.'

Vai looked at herself in a mirror, from boots to hat. If she got lost it wouldn't be down to lack of colour. She hoped this was the right stuff. It looked right, but it also looked like a fashion shoot. Miriama might have made a mistake, might have gone to a high-street outfitter rather than some place you get real Antarctic gear from.

'You'll be spending most of your time with navy people. The navy's leading down there for China.'

'How long do you think I will be down there?' Vai was excited. *Antarctica*. She was going to stand on it, see it. She thought of the days she had spent on *Taniwha*, peering into the fog or looking at distant cloud settled on the continent, wondering if glimpses of mountain were showing through. She didn't think she had seen land, though.

'A month at least. I'm pushing as hard as I can, but a case has to be made that you're a skilled worker.'

Vai nodded. A month in a new settlement. She would be with the navy's property people. There might be a segue into the work China would lead at Momona, Miriama had suggested that, but Vai had thought of it earlier. Both on the same page.

'Once you can say that you've worked on the Chinese project on Marie Byrd Land we'll have a better case to say you have skills I can't get in New Zealand. The new town they're building will be big, eventually.'

'Beijing.'

'Yes, that name tells you something about what they're building. It's going to be their Antarctic capital. I don't think Beijing is the name they'll use officially, but Zhou calls it that.'

Vai sat at the table and Miriama handed her a bowl of food and a cup of coffee. 'If you meet someone handsome and funny, send me a photo.'

Vai laughed. 'Will you get him vetted?'

'Of course. I'm not having you settle for someone with no humour. Humour, always eat your fill of humour.' Then Miriama said, 'Let's get a photo together.' She called one of the staff and Vai put her pack on again and they hugged and posed and then Miriama put the pack on and Vai feigned weeping and then it was time to go.

A helicopter with Chinese writing on its side stood stationary at Momona airport. Vai guessed this was her ride to Antarctica. It was bigger than the helicopter that had taken her off Independence. It was the shape of an insect, although she couldn't think which one. Possibly a dragonfly.

Vai and Miriama were standing at the big viewing window inside the airport. When Zhou called out a greeting Miriama stepped over to him and took his hand. As Vai crossed the room to them she saw how Zhou looked at her, his eyes lingering on her legs. Miriama noticed his look too and said, 'Isn't she beautiful?' A swell of surprise and disappointment arose in Vai.

Zhou led them to a room where three women stood in a group waiting. He introduced them as officers in the Chinese navy, although they were scientists — a geologist, Dr Tu Weiping, and two ecologists, Dr Zhang Yan and Dr Xie Chunhua. Xie looked like family of the older Tu, close enough to be cousins, same jet-black hair tied behind their necks, lean faces and determined mouths. Vai tried not to stare at Zhang, who was altogether different: unusually tall, almond eyes and chocolate skin with frizzy black hair. Only Tu spoke English. After the introductions Zhou left the room, wishing Vai well, saying he would see her soon.

Miriama said to Tu, 'I'm not sure what Zhou has told you. Vai works for me and I am partnering with Zhou in some developments here in Otago. Vai is going to spend a month, possibly longer, at your base in Antarctica. I think you call it Beijing.'

Tu smiled politely. Vai guessed she was in her mid-forties. Her boots were scuffed and her clothes were workman-like: not worn, but somehow more practical than Vai's. Vai wondered again if her own clothes were adequate. She felt like the new girl at school being handed over to a prefect. She'd do better once she was on her own, she thought, strike up some conversation.

'What is your profession?' Tu enquired.

'Lawyer,' Vai said. 'I'm the Advocate for my home island.' Tu looked puzzled and Vai felt stupid, like a parcel that had found its way to the wrong pile.

'She's learning the property trade,' Miriama said. 'I want her to spend some time in the Beijing settlement. It will help her understand what we need to do in Otago, whom we're catering for.'

Tu nodded and smiled with more assurance. 'You won't find much there yet. The navy is still getting started, mostly huts and sheds. Packing cases.'

167

Vai lifted her pack, then couldn't think what to do with it and put it on the ground again. A man came and took it from her. He put it on a trolley with the other bags and wheeled it out the door.

'We're leaving,' Tu said. 'It's time to go in five minutes. Use the toilet. There's nothing private on the helicopter.'

Vai followed Tu and the other women. When she returned Miriama was still there. They hugged and Miriama said, 'Learn all you can. Take every chance.'

Inside the helicopter it was warm with the doors shut and the engine noise was blocked out. Tu directed Vai to sit next to the window, behind the pilot. It was a prime seat, with leg room and visibility the other passengers wouldn't get in the five-hour flight. Besides the scientists, pilot and co-pilot there were three sailors on board, one of them squeezed in among their bags.

Vai relaxed. She loved flying, loved the lift-off, with her stomach butterflying and the improbable physics of it all. Especially in a helicopter, up, up from a standing start. They lifted off the tarmac, paused momentarily and then everything fell away below. Happy in the respite of being borne away, Vai touched her locket and thought of her parents.

For the first time since the storm that threw her away from Independence she had no trouble thinking of her Dad. It occurred to her that she didn't mind that he was probably dead. *Funny,* she thought, *on the ground it feels so sad. Up here, I wonder what he's doing. I wonder if he made it to the boat. If he did he would have lived through the storm, he would have known what to do. But after that he would have drifted.*

Below her she could see the South Island rolling away, like a movie being played too fast. They weren't very high — she could make out most of the features of the land — but there was no time to focus on anything. She caught sight of herself in the window, hands pressed on the glass, nose squished. She sat back, embarrassed. *I must look like I've never flown.* She looked across at the women in her row. 'I love to fly. The ocean, from Independence to New Zealand. I love to watch the ocean.' The women were silent. 'What will you do in Beijing?' she asked Tu.

'I won't go straight there. The three of us have work to do. We'll be dropped off before Beijing. I'm walking inland to an area that will eventually become a lake.'

'How do you know it will become a lake?'

Tu looked at her as if she was a bit simple. 'Because we can scan under the ice. The landform is a bowl.'

Vai's interest was piqued. The practicalities of settlement. She asked all she could think of and told the doctor about Independence. The other women, the ecologists, were following the conversation, asking for brief translations. Vai told them how the storms were damaging the island, how the crops were failing. They were interested, offered ideas for soil management. Vai showed them photos and they looked closely, asking about the coast, offering more advice.

Tu said that the ecologists were going to travel along the coast. They were monitoring the speed with which the ice was pulling back and the way in which the ecology was responding. 'Who will travel with you?' Vai asked.

Tu rolled her head backwards toward the sailors and scowled. 'One of them.'

Vai looked behind her. The nearest sailor had a scattering of stubble on his chin. He looked like a schoolboy, skinny, tight-cropped hair and big ears. The other two looked about the same age. 'What will they do?' she asked.

'Just carry stuff, and if there's bad weather or trouble I need someone. I can't go in there alone.'

'Trouble? What sort?' Vai hadn't imagined the sort of trouble you'd need a sailor for.

'Just broken legs and falling down holes,' Tu smiled. 'No military-style trouble.'

'Just someone to lift the gear?'

'Yes. They're okay, but they're just boys from faraway towns. I'd be as happy with a mule.'

169

Vai wondered if the boys picked up on Tu's resentment. She had thought it would be just a flight to Beijing and then hanging around an office. The tough little woman next to her was doing something more, but she wasn't in control. Vai studied the nearest boy some more. He was just a sprat. She held up her hands. 'I'm bigger than they are. I can carry as much as one of them. And I'm good company.'

Tu looked at Vai with renewed interest. 'You don't want to go to Beijing?'

'If it's just tents and sheds, if it hasn't really begun to be built, then no, there's no rush. I don't need to go straight away. Can I get there after the lake?'

'After the lake, sure, we will walk to Beijing.' Tu ran her eyes over Vai, assessing her build. 'Do you know the ice and snow? Have you been into mountain areas?'

'I'm not a city girl. I know the ocean and I was in the Southern Ocean on a ship until last week. We were in amongst the icebergs, but didn't get to land.'

'Really? Who were you with?'

Vai hesitated. 'An Ocean Warrior ship, *Taniwha*.'

Tu's face split into a broad grin and her eyes lit up. 'And they've let you come down to Beijing?' She put a hand to her mouth and looked around. 'Don't tell too many people that. We all think it's great that the Japanese lost a ship, but most military people are very conservative.'

She sat back, grinning. Vai waited. Perhaps she couldn't go, wasn't suitable. Tu leant forward and spoke to the co-pilot. He looked back at Vai, curious, sized her up. Then he spoke into his headphones.

'We'll have to wait,' Tu said. 'It might take a couple of hours, but we have time. Still a long way to go.'

Zhang stretched her legs out long. Vai took in their slender cut and asked where she was from, Tu translating. Zhang named a place in China that Vai hadn't heard of. Then: 'But you're asking about my skin.'

Vai raised her own hand and turned it. 'Yes, and your beautiful hair.'

'My Mum's from Somalia.' She ran her hands through her tight cropped curls and her eyes sparkled. 'Dad was working in Pakistan and Mum was in a camp near where he was based.'

'The trade route to Africa,' Vai said. 'The road through the mountains with Pakistan and down the river valley to the Arabian Sea.' The infamous route. The Young Nature people had shown a film about it on Independence. It was a warning movie dressed up as a documentary.

'That's right. Dad was an engineer maintaining roads.'

Vai studied Zhang's face, her eyes. Looking for damage, but there was nothing obvious. No signs of suffering, just clear skin, a generous mouth. 'Were you born in a camp?' she asked.

'No, China.'

'That's lucky. We saw a film of the camps on that route when I was at school.'

'Yes. Big camps.' Zhang exhaled carefully. 'I never knew the camps. Only Mum did.' Neither woman spoke for a moment, but they kept leaning forward so they could see each other. 'Mum was at school and Dad was running the team fixing the road at the school gate.'

'How old was she?'

'Fifteen. Dad took a shine to her straight away and Mum thought she'd better take the risk. She'd taken plenty already.'

Vai imagined a skinny, tall girl at a school gate, dropping her head when the older man approached her, wondering what was about to be said. Imagined that Zhang's mother might have had a shawl covering her hair and she would have pulled that tighter and tucked any stray hair away.

'Did you like growing up in China?'

Zhang shrugged. 'We moved a lot.' Her dad was a blue-collar engineer, she said, working on sites, not a desk man. He would

171

get sent all over to build or fix roads, but he wasn't a high earner. So Zhang and her mum never really settled in anywhere and of course that was tough on women, limited chances to form friendships.

'You must have relied on each other a lot,' Vai said. She imagined the mother and daughter being each other's best friends, like her own relationship with her dad. Zhang nodded enthusiastically: Vai could tell that Zhang was thinking of times she'd spent with her mum, some good times.

Zhang spoke quickly to Tu and their voices bubbled and frothed. Vai grinned even though she didn't know what was being said. Tu translated, saying that Zhang and her mum often stayed inside and cooked and made all the family clothes. They were both able to make complicated clothes and whenever they moved to a new town they would go to the best school and wait outside to make contact with the mothers, and soon they were selling fashionable garments.

Vai asked if Zhang went to those schools. Tu translated: she was home-schooled until she entered university. Her dad had taught her mum to read and speak Chinese and then her mum had a thirst for learning. Zhang described it as a thirst that ran the length of the country and all the way back to Somalia.

Up to now the other ecologist, Xie, had kept quiet. Now she joined in and there was more laughter. Vai could see the boys smiling but too embarrassed to lean in. Tu said that because Zhang's dad lived on the road a lot, camping in among the job he was working on, often the mother and daughter were in the apartment alone, wherever that might be, and they would get some words wrong and not realise it. 'One example was that they would meet mothers outside the expensive schools and when they had a commission they would go to the woman's house to see what type of dress she wanted. They had to measure the women up and for years they'd been saying something to the clients and there was always a pause before the client replied. This was to do with measuring the woman's bust and it turned out they

172

were saying something that belonged in the bedroom between a woman and her man.' When Tu gave a rough wording for it Vai burst out laughing. Everyone caught the moment, including the co-pilot and the sailors, all slumped in heaps of laughter, squashed against each other in the helicopter's tight cabin.

When they had recovered Zhang said, 'You should have seen the trouble Dad caught when he got back. Anyway, we learnt that lesson and studied more attentively from then. Mum never wanted to be thought of as ignorant.'

The feeling in the cabin had changed to be like that among a group of buddies going on an adventure together. Vai asked Zhang if she ever camped on the road with her dad. Zhang shook her head. 'No, it was never safe.' There were a lot of people moving through the countryside, Chinese and people from all over the world who were attracted to China because it had the biggest economy. Her dad had to carry a rifle, but he only used it once, and then just to shoot a horse that had fallen into a ditch and broken its leg.

The skinny sailor with big ears asked about the gun. After Zhang explained it he said, 'That would hardly do the job. Your Dad must have put the muzzle right up on its head.'

A second sailor said something, trying to sound authoritative but he had a high, excited voice: he was younger than the first one, with just a scruff of fluff on his chin. Tu shook her head and said something to Zhang and the darker woman put her hand on Tu and the story halted.

Vai sat back and looked down. They were over the ocean now; the land was gone. Above them was high cloud, white, pure white. The sun glittered off the ocean. Vai put her forehead against the glass. There were so many ships. She tried to count them, but the helicopter was moving too fast and they were hard to see in the glare. It amazed her that *Taniwha* had found only two confrontations.

They travelled in silence for a long while before eventually the co-pilot spoke into his headset, then turned around and spoke to

Tu. Vai watched their faces, trying to understand what was being decided. Then Tu turned to Vai, smiling. 'They don't mind. You can travel with me.'

Vai felt a rush of excitement. She thanked the doctor and looked at her again. *Short and wiry, strong*, Vai thought. *Less strength than me, but fitter. I'll struggle to keep up for the first few days.* She asked about the journey, where would they start, how long, the terrain. Tu took out a media device and showed Vai the path they would take from the coast onto a ridge above the lake so they could see the terrain that would feed it, then on to the lake and down to the coast, then Beijing. It looked as though they would have a window of good weather.

After a long time the co-pilot turned and spoke to the travellers. He pointed forward. Everyone craned to see. Antarctica. The ocean sparkled: icebergs stood tall and blue-white, and beyond them mountains rose. Land stretched left and right, as far as Vai could see. The sight of the great continent shook her soul. What lay in front of her was unexpected, endless in the way the ocean is endless, nothing familiar. Nowhere did the land reach out to the travellers: the fecund, fertile lure of land was absent. No luxuriant oasis beckoned, no coastal patchwork of tilled land. The thrill Vai felt at seeing the continent was strangely hollowed by the sight itself, as if she had arrived at a venue expecting a party and found the lights out, no one there, no welcome, no note of explanation.

The helicopter dropped to no more than a few hundred metres and the icebergs and mountains became markers that indicated their speed. Vai thrilled to the sensation. Marie Byrd Land — it was the one large portion of Antarctica not claimed by any of the nations that formed the Heroic Age of Antarctic exploration, the decades after the continent was first sighted, when white men had hurried to criss-cross and circumnavigate the land, raising flags and naming places. The continent had plenty of settlements, but there was no indigenous law, only general conventions and the body of international law. What did exist were detailed maps of topography and, held tightly by each nation, increasingly detailed maps of mineral deposits, rivers and valuable assets such as Beijing's hidden lake.

The helicopter slowed to a halt and hovered. Vai could see a large valley that ended at a cliff above the ocean. Water fell in one long, wind-swept veil from a river, billowing a plume of spray onto rocks fifty metres below.

They landed and climbed out onto gravel. There was a cold wind sweeping down the valley and Vai pulled her hat low and put gloves on. The sailors started unloading the helicopter and gestured to Vai. They had her pack. 'They want to know what to do with your gear,' Tu said. 'You won't be able to bring it all. You need to carry food, the tent and some of my equipment.'

Vai took the pack and opened it. A sailor gave her an empty bag to transfer some things into. Vai looked at Tu, not sure what to leave and what to take. Tu went through Vai's gear, making two piles. She examined Vai's jacket and heavy-weather trousers. They went into the large pile, the leave-behind pile. A sailor brought over replacement equipment and held the clothes against Vai, checking the fit. Then the large pile was put in the spare bag and onto the helicopter.

Vai looked at the remainder of her gear: tent, food, the ecologists' pile of gear. It wasn't much. Vai looked back at the mountains looming high at the end of the valley and then at the snow and ice that ran to near the coastal edge. She and Tu smiled at each other, Vai giving two thumbs up. She felt like jumping up and down with the thrill of standing on a continent that, before the *Taniwha* adventure, had only vaguely registered in her mind, little more than a mythical place visited by strangers. The navy men shook hands with them, climbed into the helicopter and it lifted away into the sky.

Tu and the ecologists studied a map on a reader, switching between views and trying to align what was in front of them with the images on their screen. The mountains formed a significant barrier to the interior of the continent: their towering presence filled the horizon. Looking over Tu's shoulder, Vai saw the name of the range – the Executive Committee Range – and pointed and laughed and asked if that was correct.

'The Little Men Range we call it,' said Tu, forming a small pyramid with her hands. Then turning back to the tasks she directed Vai to help her with the tents. 'Cloud might blow in, or rain. It's best to get them up now.'

The tents were ingenious. Tu simply took one from its bag and twisted a dial and then four base arms extended and screw-shaped pegs burrowed into the gravel. Next the tent filled air-slots along its length and stood itself up. The tent Vai was to share with Tu had two stunted conifer trees behind it, shrubs really, blocking some of the wind.

The three Chinese women began to talk busily again and point along the coast. Vai excused herself and walked a little way up the ridge behind the tents. She lay in the short tussock with her back against a rock, out of the wind. There were several bird colonies near the entrance to the valley, not far from her, while other birds appeared to nest singly on rock ledges. After about twenty minutes she noticed the colony birds rising from time to time and attacking something in anger. Whatever it was it kept among the rocks and was too small for her to see. There were few clouds in the sky and, lying back, she couldn't see the mountains. If she blocked out the cold she could imagine being back in the Pacific.

The three scientists appeared above her, looming large against the sky. Vai sat up and pointed at the birds. 'Over there, where that bird colony is. The birds are attacking something in the rocks. Look, they're at it again. Do you know what it could be?'

Tu translated and the ecologists watched for a few minutes as the birds dive-bombed the rocks, some of them landing and pecking at their target. They talked together and Tu reported, 'They think it will be rats. But they are surprised they have reached here. It shows that the coast is not freezing over for long periods.'

The four women began to pick their way back to the tents.

176

The birds kept up their noise and the ocean sparkled amongst the drifting ice. Vai kept thinking of the rats. She had imagined Antarctica as pristine, although she had no definite idea of what that might entail. Not rats, though. She looked across the valley to where a particularly loud fight was underway. 'The rats must be doing a lot of damage to the birdlife,' she said. 'How do you think they got here?'

'I don't know, from settlements or ships.'

'On *Taniwha* the talk was that the mining companies are introducing animals and plants. They want to destroy the idea that the continent is natural. Sow the seeds for large-scale settlement and mining. I haven't really thought about it until now.'

'Sure, there's rats everywhere. Rats and people always travel together.' Tu spread her arms wide, indicating the valley. 'Only the people who come down here know how it is changing. Up until now, the incentive has been to pretend it's as uninhabitable as it was a hundred years ago.'

'Not now,' Vai said. 'The starter's gun has been fired.' She raised her arms in imitation of Tu's stance, but wider, encompassing the continent. 'I once saw film of a helicopter flying as fast as possible across the continent's ice, and then the shot pulls back to reveal the context and suddenly the helicopter appears to have stopped, only it hasn't stopped, it's still flying as fast as ever. But the scale of the continent is so vast that the helicopter just seems to not be moving. No matter how hard it turns its little blades, the whiteness just consumes any progress.'

Tu gestured up the valley toward the mountains, then toward the coast. 'In its natural state Antarctica is a big ice sheet with birds and seals arranged around the edge. There are no animals native to the inland areas. So answer this: if the ice melts and the rats get inland first, what is their status?'

Vai looked at Tu with incredulity. 'Are you serious? You could contemplate rats taking over?'

'I'm just asking, what would be their status? They would have to travel with humans to live off rubbish. Or, as some of the more

177

adaptive birds moved inland, they could travel with them.'

'What do your ecologist friends say?'

Without asking them Tu said, 'They want to protect the existing ecosystem. But I tell them, it's too late. We're locked into over a hundred years of warming. Even if we then reverse it and the continent freezes again, there will have been one hundred years of change, more. That's plenty of time to wipe out vulnerable species and have others establish. It's an epic reallocation.'

Vai said nothing. Reallocation, reshuffling: she thought about those words. They kept coming up. She listened to the birds fighting for their young and wondered if they were ghosts, like the community on Independence. *Do the ecologists see ghosts?* she wondered.

The women ate an early evening meal together. The Chinese women spoke among themselves and Vai chose not to interrupt. After the meal she tidied up and the others went and stood at the cliff edge, engrossed in a conversation. When they returned they appeared to have resolved whatever was the issue. Zhang asked Vai if there was a date for Independence to move to New Zealand.

Vai scowled, 'They're saying ten years now. We were meant to go when the cost of keeping us up there went beyond a hundred and fifteen per cent of moving us.' She took her media device from her pocket. 'Look what they've done for people who lost their homes.'

The four sat close together and looked at the photos. Vai's mum and siblings were there amid a row of white tents. Sturdy tents, high enough to stand in the centre, and a well-formed path running through the tent rows. Vai sighed. 'We had a good house, a strong house. Then she explained what had happened to her dad and each of the women hugged her and said there was always hope.

178

Tu said, 'I've been in refugee camps. On the border with Pakistan. I was advising their development, helping manage the risk of rock falls in the mountains.' She put a hand on Vai's shoulder. 'The camp that has just been set up on Independence looks very permanent.'

'No,' Vai said, but the tone of her voice said otherwise. Her last conversation with her mother and siblings had left her more scared than ever. Emma had begun to complain about the tent and as she did Vai watched her mother, waiting for Sonya to halt the list of deprivations. But Sonya cast her eyes down and let the girl talk and Emma sketched out what they didn't have. 'And the toilets at night.' Emma's voice turned fearful. 'They're not good. People are there, they wait there.'

'Erfan goes with you,' Sonya interrupted.

Erfan looked more worried than his sister, Vai thought. 'Things happen,' Emma said, 'There's men there. I only go in the day.'

Vai returned her attention to the women around her. 'What do you mean by permanent, Tu?'

'The earthworks, the toilets, the showers, the classrooms. They're quite an investment.'

Vai looked from face to face while Tu translated, hoping one of the other women would dissent. They were quiet. 'The New Zealand government has refused to fix the wharf,' Vai said. 'No one can leave without a helicopter coming to the island. They've made it a camp.'

Vai stood up and scuffed at the stones with her boots and held her hands apart a short distance. 'In New Zealand I had a man show me, in a field, how much land was needed to accommodate all of Independence in apartments. Do you know how much land is needed?' She didn't wait for an answer. 'One sheep paddock. We can all fit in one big sheep paddock.' She picked up a sharp-sided rock and threw it into the night then her hands balled into fists. She nearly lost control of her voice across the dark space. 'The Māori communities in New Zealand have taken two hundred years to recover from the poverty of colonisation. I guess

179

we face the same fight back from the poverty of resettlement.'

Tu said, 'There's a lot to be afraid of, Vai. But there are a lot of good things being achieved. There is a lot of generosity being shown.'

'Is there?' said Vai. 'Really? Or is it just good intentions? What have you seen done?'

'We're generous to those close to us, physically or emotionally, but not often to others. China has built a lot of cities. We can move fast.' She scratched at her nose. 'But I guess one of the things people have started telling each other is to wait for Antarctica to open up. It's taking on the role of a saviour location. All around the world people are fearful that they will either be refugees or will have to host refugees. And then Antarctica starts to melt and people say, Oh thank goodness, that is the solution to the refugee problem, an empty place.'

Vai looked at Tu, unsure. 'Will it be?'

'It will be really hard to live here for a long time, more than a hundred years. Only small populations could live here before that. The cost per person will be high, so it's not a solution for the poor.'

'Is there anything else?'

'Have you heard of century leases?' Tu asked. 'What is being trialled is to lease an area of land for a city of perhaps two million. The lease is for one hundred years and creates a city state. The refugees own the assets in the city and build an economy, which they integrate into the wider global economy. They build wealth. But they have not moved into an existing city, and local resentments and the little prejudices that keep outsiders from success are avoided. Eventually, the support to the cities will be reduced and the population will stand on its own alongside other cities.'

'Have any succeeded?' Vai challenged.

'Only five have been trialled. Three in Eastern Europe and two in southern Africa. Two work quite well. They are surrounded by strong regional economies, and the effects of climate destruction are modest. The sense of confidence from the local population

180

is important. If the locals are confident in their own long-term viability they are open to supporting a new city state. But the three established in places with climate failure, there's little support for them. They are caught up in conflict.'

'What would happen at the end of the lease?'

'The hope is that the populations will have integrated, at least economically. Perhaps they could continue as nations, like Singapore. Sometimes the idea is called a Singapore Solution. There's talk of putting one near Melbourne in Australia. A big one.'

The three Chinese women spoke quietly to each other. The wind had risen and Vai's face was becoming cold. She zipped her jacket to her chin and nestled into it. 'Is China leading all of this?'

'The big three are leading together. There's a lot of coordination. We know how easy it is to fail, to fall into fighting. A lot of work is going into telling people we can succeed together and showing how it can be done.'

'And alongside that a lot of work is going into building camps? Prisons for people who have committed no crime?'

'Yes.'

Vai sat quietly, thinking. At last she smiled and let the tension drop out of her shoulders. She stood up and looked toward the ocean. 'We're real estate agents,' she said loudly, and laughed as if she was drunk. 'Having a look at the new subdivision.'

Tu smiled without any enthusiasm and translated Vai's statement to the other women.

'Thank you,' said Vai, addressing the three women together, slowing her breathing and taking stock of where she was. 'I'm sorry, I don't mean to be no fun. I won't be like this again, I promise.' Again, Tu translated: no one responded. Then Vai said, 'I'm going to sit at the coast.' She walked to the cliff edge and sat out of the wind, isolated in the dark. The Southern Lights whirled crazily overhead, like the world gone crazy, preparing to drop something out of the heavens that couldn't be put back.

20

In the early morning the rocks and tussocks were covered in white frost and the air moved in a light breeze. A few birds began calling across the quiet valley. Vai sat at the entrance to her tent, enjoying the beauty laid out before her. The mountains stood white against the still-dark sky and she began to imagine the land beyond them. Thousands of kilometres; plateaus, rivers, ice, snow, volcanoes, valleys. Little settlements scattered, pioneer outposts of scientists, mineral explorers and military observers. She thought of the hundred million displaced people in camps, on trains, on boats and on foot, all searching for a new place to settle. How was it that a whole continent existed that was almost empty?

Birds were in flight by the time the two parties left the camp. Tu moved quickly, jumping lightly from rock to rock and pushing through the low vegetation. After two hundred metres Vai stopped and looked back. There was nothing she could see that marked where they had camped, and the ecologists were gone from view. Soon the rocky ground turned to snow and ice. The contour remained easy, but Tu explained that they would have to move carefully in case there were any streams below the ice or snow they could fall into.

In the early afternoon sun the pair stopped their trek up the valley and surveyed the indented pass in the ridgeline high above them. The sky was devoid of birds now and the valley silent. They sat down to eat. They would have to climb to the pass but only one section appeared to be risky, as they would have to navigate a narrow ledge with a cliff above and below.

Before they left the valley floor Tu contacted Beijing to advise that they were heading into the mountains proper and to get an update on the weather forecast. She was agitated, gesturing.

'The weather will be okay,' said Tu once she had ended the call. 'It's going to change but we should have the time we need.' She tried to hide her anger. 'There's media interest in our journey,' she said in a tone she might use if she had found a rat in her pack. 'My government is fostering media interest, a human-interest story.'

Vai was nonplussed. 'What type of media?'

'There has been some backlash against China because the government is propelling forward a settlement. People are scared, beginning to view China as too aggressive. I've been told to prepare for a brief interview with a political review show, *Asia Rising.*'

Vai smiled broadly. 'I know that show. The captain of *Taniwha* appeared on it just as we were being run down by the Japanese navy.'

'I forgot it was that show,' Tu said and clapped her hands above her head, remembering the excitement. 'What great viewing! Your captain was insane. The ocean was churning and the sky was black. He was ranting, with mad eyes and huge beard, and then behind, into shot, comes the Japanese corvette, bucking like a wild horse in the storm.'

Vai felt a surge of pride: she was part of the catalyst for the settlement. 'Could I be in the interview?'

Tu became serious. 'I'm an employee of the navy. I will be in the interview representing the government. I must act and speak in a certain way. If you came on, would you just speak as the Advocate for Independence Island and not mention the *Taniwha*?'

Vai felt a prickle of anger against her scalp, being pushed back to refugee status, but she contained herself. 'Of course. I don't speak for Ocean Warrior.'

'Good. Having you alongside me will imply that China is thinking about the small nations. I want to conduct the interview at the top of the pass. The backdrop will be great. If the weather doesn't close in the viewers will be stunned.' They roped together and attached crampons for the ice.

Vai shifted the weight of the pack on her back and crouched low, stretching out her legs, anticipating the climb. The little doctor grinned and held up a thumb and Vai wasn't sure she would keep up. Tu led, zigzagging slowly uphill, sometimes in ankle-deep snow, sometimes on clear ice, and then in snow up to her waist, wading against the cold powder. After two hours they reached the narrow ledge they had seen from the valley floor. There were bluffs above and below the ledge and they had no choice but to take the route it offered. Vai was breathing hard, despite stepping in the tracks Tu had made. Her eyes watered.

Tu pointed along the ledge. 'There's no snow on it. It's exposed to the wind, blown clean. See that clear-glassy look? When it gets warm the ice turns to water, then it freezes at night or when the wind comes up.' She pointed above the ledge. 'Similar thing happening there.' Vai could see big blocks of ice above the ledge with metres of snow teetering on top. She didn't have the breath to put into speaking but nodded her understanding. Tu instructed her how they should cross: 'You bury your ice axe in the snow just here and tie off the rope on it. I'll walk out along the inner edge of the ledge for ten metres and then secure my axe. When I am ready you come forward to me. Then I will go again. You need to brace yourself to hold me if I fall. We should be fine. It's not steep.'

Vai set her axe and Tu stepped carefully onto the ice and crunched her way forward on her crampons. She cast about, prodding the ice looking for a place to set her axe. Once she was done she crouched next to the axe and waved to Vai to cross to her. They repeated the procedure again. The third repetition would require them to skirt around a block of ice that extended from the cliff, pushing them to the outer edge of the ledge. 'When you pass the ice don't touch it. It looks very loose and there's a lot of snow sitting high on it,' Tu instructed before stepping forward to complete the next phase of the traverse. At the block she paused and called back, 'Very difficult here. The ice is loose against the cliff edge. It's warmer.' She passed out of sight, around the barrier, reset her axe and called Vai to follow.

Vai edged forward, legs bowed, thighs protesting from the climb. At the ice block she stopped, leant her face close to the cold blue-white of it, studied the fractures running through it. She ran a gloved hand up the pillar and imagined it had been there forever, believed it could hold no end of the weight of snow. Her heart lifted as her eyes were drawn through the mountain passes and across the enormous expanse of land beyond. She raised her fist and cracked it on the ice pillar and then her heart skipped and she screamed as the ice shattered into shanks beside her, dropping its burden of snow on her. The weight of it driving the breath out of her, smashing her to the ground, holding her head hard against the ledge.

Gripping her axe tight, Vai pushed up onto her elbows to create an air space. She opened her eyes, head encompassed in white. Taking the weight, she hauled her knees under her and worked her fingers up the axe. She held still. The weight wasn't increasing and nothing more was falling. Again, she moved her legs and shoulders and they responded without pain. Her mind moved to the rope around her waist. It had no weight on it. Tu must still be on the ledge, Vai decided. Hatless, she was freezing around her head and boiling through her body. Panic swept in and threatened to turn her arms to water. She flexed her fingers on the top of the axe and drove her legs against the weight of snow and shoved a fist up high. Her arm broke through into the light and she waved it around, creating a tunnel of air. The rope pulled tight and released and then pulled again: Tu was communicating. Vai worked her torso free of the snow and looked along the ledge. Tu

185

was pressed up against the rock wall, feet braced, blood running from above her ear. The women paused and stared at each other, a little pool of red staining the snow where Tu lay.

Tu held up a hand signalling Vai to be still. She pointed up to the remaining snow threatening to tumble. Then she signalled Vai to clear herself free and made slow crawling motions, long stealthy cat motions.

When they were together again they hugged silently, foreheads joined. Then they stood and traversed together, not taking turns, staying close and moving slowly. When they were free of the ledge they sat, arms around each other, nestled into a flat area they had scooped from the snow.

'Thank God you didn't go over the edge,' Vai said.

Tu laughed quietly. 'I hate to tell you, but my instant reaction was to calculate your weight. I thought, hell, can I hold her?'

Vai tightened her grip on Tu. 'I had the same thought. I dived as fast as I could for the inside of the ledge.'

Tu touched Vai's face. 'You are bruising. It's turning deep blue on the cheek.' She opened her pack and took out the medical kit. 'You're not scared?'

'I've had worse from the ocean.'

'War stories,' Tu said. 'All adventurers need war stories and now you have a good one.'

It was getting toward evening by the time they reached the top of the pass. One side of Vai's face had bruised blue, and the half-moon below her eye was yellow. Tu was raising a red welt from in front of her ear up into her hair line. Snow matted into their hair and Vai was hauling breath in and out, sawing like a broken set of bellows.

The top of the pass was narrow, no more than four metres wide before it began dropping into the next valley. They settled into the snow with their legs extended toward the second valley. They set Tu's media device on the snow in front of them. Behind them the view was majestic.

Tu advised Beijing they were ready for the interview, and they were put through to Xu's Hong Kong studio where they could observe his show underway. They had to wait five minutes. Xu was debating the likely structure of the Antarctic settlement, speculating with some experts. None of them had access to anyone who knew what was being planned.

A Chinese man in a purple jacket was arguing that China was taking the only responsible position, insisting on a rules-based future for the continent. His big hands made loose fists beside his jowl, silver rings fat on each finger. A white man was suggesting China was bullying, manufacturing a crisis to force countries to accept whatever it was that China, America and India were finalising on Hainan Island.

Vai watched the middle-aged men argue, angry and not knowing. Then she looked across the ridge to the ocean far away, and back up the valley. Through gaps in the mountains she had glimpses of the continent's vast interior. The men were tense, as if they might be owners of the continent, neighbours fighting over the view. The white man was angry that the nations whose explorers had arrived first were not being honoured. The heroic, explorer nations wanted territory, lots of it. The Chinese man looked confident and impatient, like the biggest kid in the playground.

Someone new appeared on the screen, counting down with her fingers. Tu sat up straight and touched her hair. Xu turned to them and said, 'Welcome to *Asia Rising*, Dr Tu Weiping and Ms Vai Shuster. It is great to have you both on our show.' He paused, lost track, peering at the women's bruised and pale faces. The women leant into the screen, peering back at the men, waiting for Xu, their perspective strange, too large, unexpected, freakish. The snow and long shadows made them look monstrous, a breed apart. Xu recovered, recaptured the moment with his bright smile. 'Dr Tu has a deep knowledge of Antarctica and the actions of one of its biggest actors, China. Ms Shuster brings the perspective of the world's little places. Dr Tu, you've been to Antarctica eighteen times. Today we're discussing the continent's

187

current and future governance. Does it need to change?'

'We're trying to maintain the thin pretence that the continent can't be settled. And at the same time, it's being settled. Now the Madrid Protocol has ended and mining is allowed, we're on the verge of a scramble that'll rip the countries apart.'

'Give me an example.'

'It's a continent and you can travel a long way and not see anyone, but don't let that fool you. Just three hundred kilometres from here there's a private company that's set up a plant nursery and it's just planting its way along the coast, putting in anything it can find to grow. Then it's releasing insects from up around the Arctic Circle.'

'Why? What does that do, except cost them a lot of cash?'

'They're acting upon the land. It's an old European idea. Just sitting on land and doing nothing with it doesn't give you rights, you have to act on it. Basically, farm it.'

'What are they farming?'

'Nothing yet, but they'll have something in mind. Not far from them another company has set up grow-houses and is producing food. They've been selling it to science camps. So they're meeting the basic idea of acting on the land.'

The white man leant forward and introduced himself as Professor Allendale, professor of law at Singapore National University. His jacket and pants shimmered silver then black as he moved. 'Are you saying private companies are claiming land rights?'

'Not in any formal sense,' Tu said, 'but in practice. They're big companies with government backing and they're sowing expectations.'

'What expectations, Doctor? Please elaborate,' Xu said.

'Settlement. They're talking about selling settlement rights. There are expectations taking hold that Antarctica can be used to resolve global pressures of settlement and migration. All of a sudden we have a big empty area that can take a lot of people. Similar to the European settlement of the Americas. Or, more

188

recently, the movement to cities, which was a bit like discovering a new continent itself.'

'And you don't think that will work?' Allendale said. 'People are panicking, but they always panic. Always, as we jump forward, we have to carry the panickers and the weak. But we're doing fine, there's no shortage of us.' He sat back in his chair and regarded the women with a thin smile. 'I'm for the settlement of Mars. Antarctica is just a practice. A step, a catalyst.'

Scorn flickered on Tu's face and then she was back on point. 'It will be a hundred years before people can live here, other than mostly inside.' Her voice rose pleasantly. 'That's a very expensive way to live and unlikely to help the poorest. We have so many millions that need a home now.'

Vai slipped her shoulder behind Tu and, without thinking, raised one fist, palm forward against her bruised face. 'This is new real estate. A place where everyone has opportunity, including the landless and the refugees.'

Allandale smiled again. 'Climate change is the black dog that chases us down the evolutionary path.' Vai's stomach knotted and then a surge of anger washed stinging hot across her face and she remembered the Young Nature people and the ghosts. She grabbed her ice axe and held the wide, sharp blade forward. She lurched to her feet, pressing down on the axe, peering down into the screen. The men peered back, startled at her giant presence, her young face twisting and straining against the bruises and the yellow-purple skin, strange fruit in the frigid air.

Xu touched his earpiece and nodded. 'Thank you Dr Tu and Ms Shuster, that was very interesting. Unfortunately we have to leave you now.'

It was dark by the time they got down from the high pass. They pitched their tent on a knoll that sloped gently. Inside, the tent cocooned them from the vastness of the dark. Tu rested a gentle hand on Vai's swollen face and said, 'You look like you've been trampled on.' Vai pressed her hand softly on the doctor's hand, her cheek stretched tight, throbbing gently. Her legs ached and her hips, her thighs the most, but she had kept up. She searched in her bag for new socks, feather light and snug.

Tu called Beijing and spoke for a few minutes. When the call ended she said that a storm was coming and they needed to prepare, in case they had to stay longer. She emptied their packs of food and cooking gas and surveyed the small pile. 'Let's assume we need four extra days,' she said.

Vai surveyed the small portions. 'If the storm lasts a couple of days, could we be flown out to Beijing?'

Tu looked at her sharply. 'No. I'll never get away from the base again without some of the sailors trailing along behind. It's like being supervised by high-school boys.' Then she slipped out of the tent and Vai followed her into the still night with its blanket of uncountable stars. The silence was absolute, no animal noises, no wind. Nothing intervened, and the women stood silently together and even the cold air helped to empty the space they occupied. They ate their little meal and Vai lay on her back and tried to find a familiar constellation above her. The cold from the snow eased the pain in her body but she thought of the warmth waiting in the tent and her body ached for sleep.

By midnight the storm was howling from the mountains, shaking the tent and driving snow against its walls. Vai and Tu lay next to each other, warm in their sleeping bags. Vai felt her bruised face and stretched against the pains that had settled into the muscle and bone of her. As the wind shifted its pitch, Tu sighed and moved restfully.

'After all the changes take place,' Vai said, 'in one or two hundred years. Do you think it will be reversed? Do you think we will ever return to the way the world was, unpolluted, safe?'

Tu rolled over to face Vai in the dark. 'I don't know. It would take a long time, and things might be similar in some ways.'

'Imagine if we move somewhere that is difficult, no jobs, just poverty.' Vai's voice rose high against the wind. 'We'll have just

190

adapted to our migration and then people might force another set of changes. We might have to adapt twice. I'm thinking about the interview. Thinking about what the professor said. He thinks we're superfluous.' She wasn't angry, just ruminating. 'When I left Independence, I thought the negotiation would be practical and fair, but it's as if, well, I don't know.'

'Superfluous,' said Tu, without hesitating. 'There's a lot of people like him. They're cowards. They like to believe they have a big, brave vision, but really they just can't think about what happens next.' She rubbed Vai's shoulder. 'We'll protect the people we care for and love, that's always been the way. So, what we do next depends on how big we cast our embrace.'

Vai burrowed against her. 'Yes, I guess so.'

Tu stroked Vai's head and listened to the storm. Then she said quietly, 'Do you know the Christian story about Moses in the desert?'

biblical

'Yeah.'

'Moses took slaves from Egypt through the desert to where modern Israel is now. It took forty years, although they could have walked there in a month.'

Vai rolled onto her back and touched Tu's face, running her hands down Tu's brow and nose. 'They went in as slaves and came out as free people.'

'Yes,' Tu replied. 'They had to stay in the desert until they had a free-born generation. Perhaps climate change is the desert we need to wander in. Perhaps there's some transition we need to make. I'm not talking about running away to Mars. I'm talking about something else, something we're missing.'

'Miriama sees it as a spirit of the age thing, that we have to decide if we can choose to work at a global level because that's where the problems lie.'

'She doesn't think it's personal? The spirit inside us?'

'Personal and global. Not personal and national. Arms wide open, bigger than ever, unity or bust.' Vai turned on her side and spooned in to Tu. 'Superfluous,' she said, her voice a mixture of frustration and sorrow. 'It sounds like a void. I imagine being let go in space, just beyond Earth's atmosphere, beyond gravity's reach, beyond anyone's reach.'

The storm blew itself out overnight. They woke before it was light and ate in their tent. Half an hour later they were packed and moving down the valley as the black night gave way to grey watery light. The wind moved slightly and cloud hung in the air. They could barely see twenty metres ahead. The ground was uneven and water snaked under the ice, so they kept to the slope on the edge of the valley.

After four hours of steady walking they came to a barrier of ice that protruded into the valley and stood high above them. After peering into the mist for a minute, Tu said, 'I don't want to go into the valley unless we have to. It's too dangerous. Let's go up. I think we can get to the lake edge that way.' As they climbed there were opportunities to clamber up onto the ice but it was brittle and cut with deep gashes and with Vai's limited experience and the poor visibility Tu was reluctant to commit to any of the possible crossing points.

They carried on for two hours moving slowly uphill. Then Tu stopped and pointed forward. 'We should be able to see the lake. We're at the bowl that forms it.'

Vai couldn't see anything that looked like a lake. The snow rose and fell and the fog dispersed any sense of contour and proportion. Tu took Vai's arm and pointed again. Vai shook her head: no, she couldn't see it. Tu picked up a fist-sized piece of ice and hurled it ten metres. There was a little chink sound and the ice-lump broke through the thin skin on the lake and Vai could see water.

Now that she had located the water the rest fell into place. She could see the shape of the land. The edges of the lake hosted small, sedge-like bushes in sheltered places and a few stunted conifers huddled near where they stood. All covered in white.

192

Tu pointed to the plants. 'It's good to see the vegetation. I'm going to try to estimate the amount of water in the lake.' She took a small drone from her bag. Beneath it was a small black box. She took off her gloves and fiddled with it for a minute then set it on a flat rock. It launched into the sky and they quickly lost sight of it. 'It will be an hour,' she said. 'With this poor visibility, I don't know if we can get around the lake. Let's stop for a while and then go back down. We'll have to look again at climbing around the base of the ice flow, go into the valley floor.'

Vai nodded and they sat overlooking the lake as the cloud intermittently closed and opened their view. She calculated their day's travel and took their small midday ration from her pack and gave Tu her share. Two hours to the lake and almost the same to get back to the valley floor, plus the four they had walked from the overnight camp. The portion of food was dry in her hand, textured like coarse flour. They ate in silence and then Vai heard the sound of the drone returning. It was invisible in the grey sky until it hovered above them. Its motors called out a complaint into the empty space, as if it resented having been sent away, alone.

They stowed the drone and put their packs on before beginning the slow walk back. At the floor of the valley Tu used her ice axe to prod the snow and ice beneath her, locating the cracks. 'If we go into the valley there'll be deeper breaks in the ice. The water will kill us in minutes. Rope up to me. Stay well back and follow my footprints. If I fall you'll have to haul me up quickly.' She took the drone out and set it flying a few metres in front of her. It scanned the ice for cracks, relaying a visual to their media devices: red for areas that were too weak, then orange and green. There was no green path so they edged out along the side of the ice flow, linking orange routes as best they could. With each minute that passed Tu found it harder to locate a path. Eventually she called, 'We're not going to get around the ice flow safely. There's too much water beneath us. We'll go back, keep this distance.' Vai turned and silently retreated along the path of their footprints and, to allay her fear, repeated the prodding and stepping, prodding and stepping that Tu had shown her, even though the drone flew in front.

As they returned to the intersection of the ice flow and the valley edge the wind climbed and by the time Tu was standing beside Vai snow was being lifted around their faces. 'We'll have to go back to where we camped and try the other side of the valley tomorrow,' Tu said. 'I don't want to camp anywhere else. I'm not sure about avalanches.'

The wind continued to rise and cloud blew wet across their faces. The drone couldn't fly so they packed it away before pulling on masks, leaving nothing exposed. Vai determined to lead, defying the wind's strength, pushing forward in the track they had cut that morning. It was hard and she reined in her thoughts until only the sound of her breathing registered in her head. She kept up a slow stepping rhythm for an hour until Tu tapped her shoulder and indicated for her to stop. Tu stepped out of the track and onto the wind-crusted snow, strong enough now to hold her. They continued, easier on the harder surface, but the wind grew stronger and soon both were bent almost double.

Eventually Tu fell. Vai dropped behind her, clawing forward on hands and knees to tug on Tu's jacket. 'Shall we just stop and pitch the tent here?' she called. 'We're hardly making any ground.'

Tu cupped her gloved hands to Vai's ear. 'Just one more hour. I'm not stopping anywhere except the knoll we were on last night.'

They resumed walking with Vai in front. Visibility was hopeless but Tu's device was leading them back along the morning's track and they kept from wandering. The wind threatened to blow them over backward: Vai's fingers were starting to freeze and burn despite the warmth she felt through the rest of her body. And then they were at the place Tu wanted the tent pitched.

Vai dragged it from her pack. Holding tight an edge each they clicked the mechanical mechanism that triggered the tiny anchors to burrow into the snow and ice, locking the tent in place before pushing up the air poles. Wordlessly they scrambled into the tent and dug into their sleeping bags, no more than a few metres from where they had been that morning.

Vai rubbed her hands and blew on them. 'They're so sore,' she complained. 'But don't worry,' she quickly added. 'I'm enjoying it. The lake was magic, or at least the stillness was magic, and the idea of the lake.' She laughed, embarrassed at herself. 'What I mean is, the lake, the quietness, the new plants. The future. We saw some of the future. It's exciting. That's what I mean.' She moved her raggled hair to one side. 'Thank you for letting me see it.'

Tu ran a hand wearily over her face and considered the young woman next to her, the dark bruise and the yellow under the eye shining brighter than the day before. Her hair was lank and beneath that she disappeared, worm-like, into her red sleeping bag. The smell of sweat steaming in a tent and the joy of discovering exhaustion in the wild. 'You be careful of those hands,' Tu said. 'If they get frostbitten they could die from the tips down before you can stop it.'

Vai closed her eyes, the better to feel Tu's warmth, the deadly cold beyond the tent's walls incongruous with the feeling of friendship. With her eyes closed Vai felt free to risk more. 'Tu, some people on my island have TB. The New Zealand government says it has to be cured before they can enter the country, but what if there's drug resistance?'

Tu took a gentle hold of Vai's wrist, careful to avoid her sore fingers. 'It's not you. You wouldn't have been able to make the walk today. Is it family?'

'It's lots of people.' Vai's throat constricted and she shut her eyes tighter but tears squeezed out. 'It's my sister, Emma. We've been hiding it, but now they're living in a tent people will know.'

'There are new drugs.'

'We don't have any money. We can get the old drugs but they're not working on others, so we think Emma's got what the others have.' Vai rolled towards Tu and opened her eyes, hoping, 'Do you

195

think it might be an old type of TB, but the drugs are no good?'

'She needs to see a doctor. It might be a treatable type. The drugs she can get might work.'

'Then she goes on a list.' Vai sat up and rubbed at her red eyes. 'I'm supposed to get everyone to New Zealand. It was meant to just happen when the island was broken, but we're stuck.' Cold crept back into Vai's bones, settling silently as a ghost might move into a host. 'You mustn't tell anyone.'

'I know.'

They ate and then slept for a few hours, huddled together. The wind dropped and the silence disturbed them both. They listened. Nothing.

silence

21

The next day the weather lifted and the two women crossed the valley and by midday were opposite the ice that had blocked their progress the day before. The ice shelf plunged out into the valley like the prow of a cargo ship. Fat and wide and high it commanded the side of the valley and rode up the slope toward the lake. Tu said, 'See how it sits in the slope? The water from the lake must flow slowly and build on that plug of ice. Maybe when the weather warms the lake overflows and the plug melts at the same rate so there's neither increase nor loss.' She pointed toward the coast. 'There's a Chinstrap penguin colony at the coast, about fifty thousand pairs of birds.'

Vai stayed close to Tu as they descended the valley. A river emerged from the ice. In places it clattered alongside them then was gone into some cavern beneath the rocks and then it was beside them again. The river grew larger as they descended and whirlpools threatened where the water was blocked by rocks and dug a subterranean route. Tu sang softly, her voice lilting; Vai imagined creatures, long asleep on the continent, waking to the doctor's song.

They smelt the penguin colony before they could hear it and cut across low hills to stand above it and survey the ocean beyond. The sun came out and the sea glistened. Penguins were clambering over rocks, returning to their nests for the evening. Vai covered her nose. The birds reeked. They looked funny hopping across the rocks and stopping to argue and clack their beaks, but she had not expected the stench. Tu stood very still, her attention taken entirely by the sight below her, then hurried closer to the colony and zipped her jacket across her mouth and nose. She waited for Vai to catch up and said sadly, 'The birds have a disease. It's killing them.' She pointed to feather clusters on the ground below that Vai had thought were birds at rest. 'Those ones are dead. It looks like half the colony is dead.'

The wind was coming in from the ocean and blowing the stench over them like a blanket. Vai felt her stomach tangle up and bile rise. She wanted to say how terrible the sight was but she didn't want to part her lips because she could imagine the smell sticking to the roof of her mouth. Rats ran about among the dead birds and in the scrub. Some scurried from carcass to vegetation and on to another carcass. But others had no fear and they hopped and skipped and feasted.

Tu said, 'Follow me. We'll get downwind, on the edge of the sea.' They trekked in a half-circle around the colony to the edge of a cliff. Vai sucked fresh air and, emptying her lungs, she tried to expel the death from her mouth. 'Have you seen this before?' she asked. Big birds hovered over the mess and dropped to feed on carcasses, jumping around among the rats.

'Yes, it's been moving down the coast from the top of the peninsula. It probably started in Argentina. When it strikes, some birds die immediately and the others don't seem to be affected by the virus but . . .' Tu's voice trailed away.

Looking down, Vai could see rats watching her, just feet away. One broke cover and ambled closer. It was as long as her forearm. Its fur was thick and it was fat, content. Its bright black eyes were fearless, enquiring. Its companions watched her too. Vai imagined being alone, breaking a leg. She could see the rats gather, patiently waiting for her to weaken. The apex predators, for now. Vai imagined putting a dog amongst them.

'Will the survivors breed?' she asked. 'Will the colony survive?'

'The survivors seem to be weakened. There are further deaths, but from secondary causes.'

198

Vai watched the penguins that were returning from the sea. Beautiful swimmers, they had nothing to offer on land, graceless and bickering, stumbling and tripping, ill-equipped for the terrain.

Tu opened her device and called Zhang and Xie. They spoke for a few minutes and she looked eastward along the coast. 'Zhang and Xie are camped nearby. They've seen the birds and taken samples. There's nothing for us to do here.'

Tu led the way along the coast and they found the ecologists settled in a tent amid shoulder-high conifers and tussock. They all hugged and the three scientists talked earnestly. Vai warmed to the conversation despite not understanding a word. She enjoyed knowing that the women were expert and that they had learnt new things and reached new understandings.

They brewed coffee and ate together. Vai set the tent and spread out Tu's and her own sleeping bags. She closed the door, secure against rats. Zhang took off her jacket, her bare arms all sinew and muscle. Xie held her device for Tu and Zhang to examine and they discussed photos and video, gesturing and explaining and debating. Darkness moved in quietly as if it didn't want to frighten the women and settled about them. Xie set music playing gently and the women settled comfortably against each other. Vai thought of the ice ship and the rats and the dead birds and placed her arms so they touched the women either side of her, just a slight touch.

Zhang and Xie told stories about things that were dying and plants that had their origins elsewhere but were flowering along the coast; Tu told stories about things that were emerging from the ice. Vai recounted Adam Walker's story about inside living: Zhang said she had worked in Shanghai as a consultant to a large urban colony with over two hundred thousand people living in the one enclosure. She was employed to assess the ecology and part of the job involved rope work, up high among the structures that held plants. For years these places had been sprayed to get rid of mosquitoes, but spraying stopped once genetic engineering

199

had collapsed the mosquito population. Insects were introduced and butterflies and then geckos and little snakes. Bees helped with pollination.

'Really?' Vai asked, 'Were the hives harvested?'

'Some people kept hives on their balconies,' Tu translated for Zhang, 'but other hives were left to themselves, hanging in the roof structures.'

Vai explained her experience with beehives on Independence. 'Inside living has an ecosystem?'

'Yes. These places are very sophisticated. They make good use of the services a well-managed environment provides. The enclosure was eighty floors high, there were bird colonies and monkeys. School education programmes were based on my work.'

Vai kept Zhang talking, asking for detail on the enclosure and thought about the Warriors and wild nature. The smell from the penguin colony wafted on a rogue wind and Xie took a knife and cut small branches from a conifer, handing out one each and one for herself. They held the scent against their noses. Vai pulled back a stretch of bark and twisted the thick sap in her fingers and held her fingers to her nose for a stronger taste of good air.

They were in the dark with a million stars above them, as good as alone on a continent that had refused people for more years than a person could make sense of. All around and just safely out of reach the rats nestled into the soil and moved quietly in the scrub. Vai leaned back and watched a group of about six rats nestled together, lying over each other, content in each other's warmth.

She came back to the topic that had been troubling her. She wondered whether abundance was a place she could go to, as a person who had been cast out of paradise and had quested for some place new but so far to no avail, or at least not a place that was generous. *Yes*, she thought, *a place that was generous. Balclutha had had its days of generosity, its time of giving.*

Vai asked Tu if she would mind helping with a discussion on the topic. Broken from her own restful quiet, she reluctantly

200

agreed to translate. Shy now, Vai asked whether there might be a time when the earth recovered and flourished. She said she had an idea of what that might be like because since she was small she had worked in her Pa's garden with the rich, red volcanic soil and the bounty it produced.

Tu didn't like to translate this conversation and the faces of all three scientists became sad. They took a long time to reply and they said that it was a difficult thing to know. They talked about it in ways that Vai had heard before, talked about the rewilding of places that humans had abandoned and the places where species hung on in little groups, huddled against the damage wrought on them and the way inside living could cater for some types of animals. Extinction was everywhere and the idea that species could be brought back was just a hope. The scientists talked about the poor dying in large numbers as the century wore on and the space that might make for nature and Tu didn't translate that. And then they talked with Vai about the great reshuffle.

Vai said, 'Don't you think the most important thing is to change the way we think? Because our actions will follow that. What if we had a shared vision of what abundance might be like? What if we all worked toward that shared thought?'

While the other women struggled to think about how this might work Vai said, 'This is what my father showed me. I was his fishing accomplice, his mate on the boat. We would go out over the reef and watch the birds to see if they discovered the big fish chasing the little baitfish into a ball. Then there would be a feeding frenzy, the birds diving on the ball of small fish, the big fish and the dolphins herding them from below. Once when this happened Dad stopped in front of the bait-ball. The sun was out and the sea was calm, smooth as glass. He tied a rope to the boat and we jumped in. He held the rope and we swam away from the boat and hovered in the ocean. Then the bait-ball swam in a wild frenzy straight through us. Dolphins and sharks and sailfish all working together to herd and feast. Birds dropping out of the sky like missiles. I clung to him like a limpet. There were tens of thousands of fish and the bait-ball was twenty feet deep.'

Vai waited while Tu translated and then said, 'Have you ever seen anything like that?' They shook their heads. 'Dad dragged me back into the boat. I was shaking and couldn't stop talking. I'd seen a wonder of the world! And Dad said, "No that's just a sad reminder of what used to be," and he even had tears in his eyes. And I've never got that out of my mind.'

Vai reached out to Tu. 'This is the bit I want you to talk to them about. Dad said to think about this, to think about abundance this way. Imagine if in the year 1900 you collected all the life in the oceans, all of it — fish, whales, shellfish, anything you can think of that was alive. And you weighed it and said the weight is one thousand units. Then let's say that to feed all the humans alive at that time we needed to consume four units per year. Because of the abundance of the ocean it could absorb that consumption and replenish itself back to one thousand units each year. Next, in the year 2000 we still have one thousand units in the oceans, but the larger human population needs twelve units per year. In an abundant way of thinking, we would say, "The ocean can remain abundant, but we have to manage it to that end." But because we approached the twentieth century from the childish perspective that people can only act selfishly and resources are scarce, we said, "The ocean resources will ultimately be scarce and if I don't grab what is there, my neighbour will." Because of this we managed the oceans to destruction, and the best we could do was try to find the marginal point where the ocean life would cling on, damaged and small. If you place abundance and cooperation at the centre, rather than scarcity and self-interest, you go about the practice of living very differently. You identify the very many examples of successful cooperation and you emulate these. It's about adults choosing their future.'

'You're saying we have to choose abundance, and we will only choose that if we have sufficient maturity to do so?' Tu asked.

'Yes. Abundance is the partner of adulthood, while scarcity and self-interest are the partners of childhood.'

202

Tu spoke with Zhang and Xie and then said simply, 'We know abundance works in practice. On its own, nature tends to abundance. Unfortunately, people lack the skill for it. We lack the sophistication. Is that what you think of as maturity?'

'That's a good way of putting it,' Vai said.

Xie placed a torch light so that it shone on her face and spoke earnestly. Tu translated, 'We need to be more purposeful. Look back at the strategy we attempted. We tried to emulate evolution through the market. Every day billions of people prodded at the status quo trying to improve it, and often they did. But evolution has no purpose — it has nothing in mind, no end goal. It can't look up and see a systemic crisis and act to avoid it. And the way the world was run, it took us nowhere in particular. An accumulation of purposeless greed left us stranded.'

'We lacked the sophistication and maturity,' Vai said.

'Yes,' said Tu. 'We need to adopt a much more purposeful stance. We need to decide what we want and how to get there. We need to act in the world as gardeners of wellbeing and wildland managers. Actively tending our communities and the system we live in, evolving and leading.'

'Abundance,' Vai said and rubbed her hand across Xie's shoulder.

Tu placed a hand on Vai's leg. 'Is abundance the land you hope to reach?'

Vai said, 'Abundance isn't a place, it's the stuff of adulthood.'

22

In the morning the Chinese women spoke together without translating. They were angry and gesturing. Sometimes they stopped and glanced at Vai and then kept going. They were reading something and it was making them mad. Some kind of resolution was reached: they were all looking at her now. Xie nudged Tu in the small of the back and the three Chinese women came and stood around Vai, very serious, arms folded.

Tu looked as though she could commit a murder. The other two were a combination of murder and that shoulders down, defeated look of a woman who wants to flee but has nowhere better to go. 'Some friends of ours have been taken on the border between China and Kashmir,' Tu said. 'They were guiding refugees trying to get to India.' Tu gestured to her friends. 'We've done this guiding.'

Vai said, 'I didn't know,' and instantly felt stupid.

Tu nodded her head, hard, as though was banging it on an invisible wall. 'Well, you wouldn't know.' Xie said something that sounded like a gun firing multiple bullets; Zhang pulled Xie's head against her shoulder, running her hand slowly up and down the smaller woman's hair.

Tu said, 'If someone gets taken they have to be traded back quickly or they're broken.' The way her hands were wringing together made it clear what else might happen.

Vai said, 'How did you get involved in that?'

'The refugees don't know how to cross the Himalayas and they are prey to bandits. We three know the routes because we have worked up there and we know how to live in the mountains. There's an organisation of volunteers who guide the refugees. The idea is that the bandits will leave them alone because the Chinese military will protect its own people.'

'You shield them?' Vai rocked back, looking at the scientists as if she hadn't met them before.

'Yes, we carry Chinese flags and pay fees to get through. China doesn't want to take responsibility for the crossings, and India doesn't want the crossing points. But China doesn't want the people stuck in China. India's blocked the sea route and the border with Pakistan. Pakistan lets them in from the Arabian Sea, just to annoy India. Then they go up to China, on the good roads China built.'

Tu picked a stone up and shifted it from hand to hand. 'Some of them are ethnic Indians with a long history in Britain, the poor ones. There are service jobs in India, supporting the inside-living cities. Then there are other ethnic Indians. Seems like the whole diaspora's going home. India has weight in the world.'

Zhang said some more, apparently urging Tu on with their story. They were all scared and angry and it seemed they wanted to talk. Tu said, 'We did ten trips over a couple of years. Having women lead the caravans lowered the tension but if it all turned into a mess, well . . .' She threw the stone hard onto the ground. 'There were thousands in each of the camps and we would take them through, five hundred in a caravan. Walking slowly, pushing carts with pregnant women and babies and the elderly. There'd be meetings in the days before you left. The camp bosses would agree who was going and herd them up together. Ones who couldn't walk properly but were too big to cart, they got held back. Then in the light before dawn we'd all be ready. Chinese citizens would get on the front and rear corners and around the edges and we'd leave the camps. The first river crossing would sort out who were your leaders and who was in the mob that needed help.'

Tu was hitting her pace and she had a new stone in her hand.

205

'It was like an addiction. Once you'd taken one of the caravans you wanted more. There was the fear, and the beauty of being in the mountains, but over all of it was history. Grinding your way uphill, single-file or a few abreast depending on where you were, and all the time the altitude sucking the energy out of the walkers. Looking back from the front all you could see was a straggle of colour, the oddest assortment of rags and good gear gifted by charities. While we walked everyone was silent, heads down struggling, just a clatter of moving rocks and footwear.

'The ones who'd sorted themselves out as leaders when we crossed the first river stayed up front. Others they trusted ranged along the sides and mustered the group. We'd walk for two hours and then stop. Then another two hours, and so on across the day. It didn't pay to stop for another reason, like when you came to the start of a steep climb. That just gave people the idea they might avoid it somehow. We had four different routes that I guided on. Each one had its own villages and bandits operated across the whole area.'

Vai moved to sit at Tu's feet, making herself comfortable in the dirt and put a hand on the older woman's leg. Tu said, 'Every journey we ran into bandits. It wasn't bad luck, there were just so many of them. Really, they're just villagers operating away from the village. Little men, no bigger than me and skinny as anyone you ever saw. Their faces wrinkled like dried fruit from the weather and the hunger, but each one creased differently. There would often be twenty to twenty-five of them with guns and little horses. They would look the group over and calculate a fee. On my first trip I was terrified. We Chinese would stay at the front clasping our flags and confronting them. Behind us would be rows of the refugee men but they had to hold still and not give a reason for violence. Every time, except once, we would haggle over the fee and we would be sweating and you could smell the fear and the caravan was like one person with two big eyes watching the negotiations and calculating whether to stand still or run like a wave to nowhere.'

When Tu paused for a drink of water Vai said, 'What happened the other time?'

'Wait, I'll tell you more about the haggling. From the moment the bandits appeared we called the army for assistance. But often they were days away. They wouldn't send anyone unless something happened, but the bandits never wanted to hang around, so they needed to haggle fast. We tried to slow it down and give the impression the army was coming. We were under instructions not to pay too much, because that would just inflate the whole project. I was one of the negotiators because I was older. I'd get right up close with the leader of the bandits and my translator, and to start with you could smell the evil little man in your face with his rotten teeth. As time went on the whole caravan and all the bandits would be getting worked up. If there was no wind there was a stench of unwashed bodies and urine and wet clothes. I'd push as hard as I could, and they'd threaten to break into the caravan and rob it and take a dozen women away. Depending on what was happening back in their villages there were times when they preferred things other than money.'

Tu swept a strand of hair back from her face. 'I would be up really close in the leader's face and run it like an auction, get a rhythm into my speech and use my hands for theatre. I had to keep all the bandits' attention on me, one hundred per cent. That way they stayed with the haggling and their minds didn't wander down into evil so easily. I learnt I could push it if I kept them entertained, bang my fist, grab a collar and twist it, get them laughing. Then I'd reach a point and quickly nail the deal, pay them and be in command enough to say that's it, show's over.'

She sat back, panting, eyes wide remembering the fear of it all. Xie had her hands clasped in front of her as if she was praying; Zhang was rubbing her cheek hard enough that she might have drawn blood, scratching her gloved fingers up and down and back along her skin.

'The last time it all turned to blood. There must have been an order from India to close the border and frighten everyone off. The bandits rode down on our caravan fast and nearly didn't stop. They were going to ride straight in, shooting all the way through. I was pretty good at reading things by then and I yelled to the Chinese women to hold their flags up and run forward. We cut the angle down so they would have had to shoot through us, and they hauled their ponies off to the side and rounded back in a circle on a plateau of grass.'

Tu was panting again and Zhang was bent in half, holding her stomach and peering closely at Vai, watching her reaction, following the story even though she couldn't understand the words. 'The leader had a big scar that ran up from his chin into his hair and a wall eye that made you look at it more than the one that worked. I motioned to the women with me to come up in a line. We held our flags out in front of us like spears. The leader leaned from his horse and pointed his gun at my head and my legs were all rubber but I kept walking forward. Zhang was next to me and he studied her, then he got off his horse and grabbed her by the hair and twisted her onto the ground. My interpreter said, "He thinks she's not Chinese."' Tu took hold of Zhang's hands and squeezed them. 'I was yelling at him, "She's Chinese! Her Dad's Chinese!" He was looking back and forth between us, figuring it out. I could see him thinking he had someone who mattered but she probably wouldn't get full protection from the army. He started dragging her away and yelled to his men something and they started shooting and rushing the caravan. I was holding onto Zhang's foot and he took out a knife and jabbed into me, just under the eye. See there?'

Vai took hold of Tu's head and looked closely at the scar under her eye. 'It's not big but the point was made,' Tu said. 'I stopped still and Zhang stopped struggling away and changed direction and dived between his legs and he turned to get her and I threw a rock and tipped him over. Zhang was quick and she got on his horse and grabbed me up behind her and we bolted for the track we had walked up. Xie was running in front of us and we got her on and wove in among the shooting and people scattering with their kids. Some of the men were fighting back but most of them were at the head of the pack that was running.' Now Tu slowed down and scuffed her boots and the other two realised where she was up to in the story and hung their heads.

She paused, drifting off for a moment. 'We rode all the rest of the day in the heat. The pony was all bones and wanted to turn back so we left it and walked into the night. We camped up off the track in some trees. We heard stragglers down below, but we stayed quiet and in the morning soldiers came.'

Vai imagined the women talking to the soldiers and not looking at each other and not hurt, except for the nick on Tu's face. She imagined the soldiers listening to the women's story and thinking about whether they'd have to head up into the mountains and risk getting shot just to stamp their authority back on a wild place that was best left alone.

'We travelled with the soldiers for ten days,' Tu said. 'They were seeing out their patrol and wouldn't take us back to a train until their days were up. We walked in the middle of their group and camped in the middle at nights. They were a tribe that didn't need to fear anyone and they barely posted a guard in the dark.' She waved her hand at the other two. 'We talked about it and joined the military after that. Since then we have been in remote places like this, travelling in the troop, if there's a need to.' She looked at the two ecologists, scratched her neck and her story trailed off, without resolution.

The women were reluctant to move. They sat in the weak sunlight and the soft wind blew cold from the ocean and goosebumps stood on their bare arms. They cooked a small meal and ate slowly. Beijing was a five-hour walk from the camp and they were in no hurry to get there.

Beijing was being built in a vast valley that ended at a high cliff. A river dropped off the cliff edge into the ocean. They would hear explosives well before they reached the valley, Tu said. The navy was blasting the cliff to form a causeway and wharf and as the ocean rose the cliff would protect Beijing.

Vai thought about the ocean rising as they set off on their journey along the coast. She thought about the conceit of people and the idea of the Anthropocene age. Everywhere she looked she could see water taking control and people being humbled before it. Nowhere could she see people in control. People could wreak havoc, and mistook this for power, but the age in front of them was an age of water. The creating, the reshaping was the domain of water. The ice sheets melting, the rivers flooding or drying up and the oceans driving the people like ants. There was no Anthropocene, she concluded: Nature was preparing to strike.

With this idea resolved in her mind she concentrated on the journey. Ships passed, some close enough to reveal their form, others low on the horizon. There were more ships than she had imagined. How many ships were required to prepare a continent to be taken? Taken, sullied.

Vai pushed through low vegetation, keeping the other women close. There was no track and they stopped frequently to assess their route options. The vegetation was thickest near the ocean. But in places they could drop to the coast and walk on the pebbly beaches. Fist-sized, brown and grey, the pebbles moved underfoot, each step a crunch of moving stones and a small slide sideways on the slope. Bits of plastic and old nets scattered across the smooth, flat pebbles. Vai took up a few palm-sized stones and skipped them across the waves. The stretch of beach ended at a small cliff and the women scrambled up on their hands and knees. At the top of the cliff they were met by cloud sliding off the surrounding hills, low and white, slipping across them and onto the ocean. They pulled hats on against the damp. The high land they were walking on curved away in front of them and they would have had a big view across a large bay, but the cloud hemmed them in.

A flame burned orange in the mist. Vai couldn't determine

how far out to sea it was. 'I didn't think exploitation was allowed yet,' she said.

'They can go in now,' said Tu. 'The Madrid Protocol only banned mining until this year and nothing's replaced it.'

The mist lifted a little in the breeze and a steel platform emerged, black on its slender legs, the flame giving it life, an imaginary head that might turn and, sighting the women, begin to stride across the ocean. Vai imagined it reaching out a hand to them, curious and friendly.

After midday the fog lifted to reveal a cluster of cargo ships at anchor a mile off the coast. A swarm of helicopters shuttled back and forth between the ships and Beijing, loads strapped beneath those returning to shore. Further out military ships moved slowly along the coast. Xie pointed at the military ships and spoke to Tu and Zhang.

'Two of the Navy ships are Chinese,' Tu translated. 'The other three are American. The Americans are curious, looking at what we are building. Or, rather, they're jealous. The valley we are building in is the best on the coast.'

'Will the lake be piped to the city?' Vai asked.

'Yes, the lake is important. Once we're rested in Beijing I'm going inland, to near the head of the valley. There's a place with very good soil, but it could also be dammed. I have been asked to look at the rock. It is more exposed than last time I was there.'

'Good soil,' Vai said. 'Really? Does Antarctica have good soil?'

'There's a volcano further up the valley,' Tu said. 'It has set down a large area of very good soil. If things warm up enough it can be farmed. Will you come with me?'

'Unless you'd prefer a mule or a sailor.'

23

Beijing was a shock. Vai wasn't prepared for the size of it, sprawling away across the valley in a maze of huts and tents, people and machines in constant motion, bumping into each other and continuing on. Surely, Vai thought, a military settlement would have a pattern, a strict alignment of roads and a hierarchy of buildings. High up a slope would be the officers' accommodation and then everything would descend in order down to tents. But this looked like chaos. Then eventually she saw there was a pattern. The layout of the settlement followed the contours of the valley and the hierarchy ran from the coast inland, not from the hills down. Fronting the coast was the largest building. Three storeys high and spreading over perhaps three hundred square metres, it had a high-spine roof, dropping steeply on either side. It was the only building in what Vai thought of as the front row, its view along the coast unimpeded. Behind it were three rows of solid, significant buildings with large areas between each. After that the spaces between buildings became meaner and roads came to dominate.

Xie spoke to someone in the settlement on her device. Then Tu pointed to an orange hut in the middle of the settlement, near the river. They made their way toward it.

People were busy carrying loads, going places, building. They glanced at Vai and Zhang as they moved through the streets. The noise of talking and building and getting about was disconcerting after the quiet and near solitude of the previous days. *Unbelievable*, Vai thought, *so busy, so many people.* She stared up at the buildings and the stream of helicopters clattering. The aroma of ginger, vinegar, aniseed and other ingredients wafted from larger huts that had lines of mostly men snaking out of them. Hunger twisted her stomach and she realised her feet were sore. The streets were muddy slush, above the toecaps of their boots. Rats, the rats were there, but behaving like normal rats, hiding and scurrying, leaping into rubbish bins and under buildings.

At the orange hut they were greeted by a man who seemed to be running a grocery. Behind him in long rows were supplies of wrapped food, toiletries, general goods and cleaning equipment. The women were signed in and given a bag each of toiletries and food.

Tu led the way to a hut with four bunks and a bathroom and they settled onto the beds in rumpled satisfaction. Lying on her back Vai lifted her legs six inches off the bunk and looked at her feet, bare in the chill air, wrinkled and damp. Tu said, 'Take the shower first, but please don't be too long. There's not much hot water.'

In the bathroom Vai looked into a mirror for the first time since she left Momona. Her face had a racoon-mask of burnt dark skin around the places that her glasses had protected; her hair hung in a single, oily straggle. She sought a word for her hair, tugged it into a few pieces. *Hank, that's the word*, she thought. *I have a hank of hair.* There was grime in the creases of her palms; oil and sweat stuck to her skin. She waited for the shower to run hot before stripping off and hurrying under the weak spray. She rubbed soap into her hands and watched the accumulated grime drain away, then put shampoo in her hair and worked to untangle it. Again the water running to the plughole had the colour of a small stream after rain. She quickly finished and stepped in front of the mirror to dry. It showed a woman who was almost the one that had left Independence but who was also not that woman any more. She carried less weight but there was something that had settled across her like a banner that belonged to an older woman, something colourful and bold.

Back in the bunk room she looked out the window at the press of buildings and people. Things were changing so quickly, but at the same time it was all familiar in a way, all just a mess of people and ideas and things to get done and everyone finding somewhere to live and food to eat and ways to stay warm. She smiled, happy and clean. There was a box on her bunk with the things she hadn't taken on the trek. She searched in it for clean clothes, slipped into them and lay down on her bunk and wriggled her shoulders and back. She wasn't at all weary.

That evening the scientists were summoned to meet with the Commander in charge of establishing the settlement. While she was alone Vai spoke to her family. She told them about her travels and they talked about Moses. They agreed he was lost to the ocean and they all cried together, Vai's mum and the twins hugging each other, far away in the heart of the ocean. There was no boat and no news, but Vai's mum said that her Pa had talked with Moses's parents and they wanted to mourn his passing.

'I'll come home,' Vai said.

'No,' Sonya barked and Vai recoiled at the sharpness of her voice. Sonya leaned forward until her face filled the screen. 'Do you remember Mrs Jones? She has that lump of a daughter. You know, the older girl with the bad hips.' Vai braced herself. 'Well, her boy has gone to Australia. As if anyone would think *he* could be an Advocate.' The two women held each other's eyes. Sonya said, 'Get back to New Zealand and get us a place. That's what your Dad would be proud of.'

Tu and the biologists returned late in the evening. Tu announced they would leave to travel up the valley in the morning. While she was up there she would have to do another interview with *Asia Rising*. She stuck out her tongue and made a rude noise. 'Why is Xu interested again?' Vai asked.

'Xu's not interested, he has been *invited*,' Tu made imaginary quotes with her fingers, 'to interview me. It's marketing. My government wants to be seen to lead the settlement of the continent, and stories about infrastructure portray China as strong and reliable. They want to interview me away from the military settlement.'

Vai punched Tu lightly on the shoulder. 'Okay, partner, I'll be ready at dawn.'

Tu punched Vai back and said, 'You're already on the register. You'll be interested to see what might be developed. You're here for the small countries. Maybe there's something for them here.'

Vai considered being small, an Advocate for small. She thought about Beijing and what it would become. She thought about the noise and the jostling and the development and the spirit that animated people to push on forward, to challenge and take down barriers and to succeed. That spirit was awake too. The people were in motion, frontiers were in retreat. 'Will China really advocate for small nations?'

Tu shrugged. 'I believe in the great reshuffle. You need to be at the table to be considered.'

24

In the darkness before dawn the four women walked through the settlement to a noisy shed where many-wheeled trucks and vehicles on tracks were being prepared for the day's work. The shed was painted grey and its high doors were thrown open, spilling brilliant white light into the cold air. Inside were men busy attending to the needs of each machine, ears attuned to the sounds of rhythm or a broken symmetry, a hand placed gently on a tock-tock-tocking motor.

The women were directed to an eight-wheeled truck with a snowmobile loaded on its tray. Tu spoke to a man in overalls then told Vai, 'We'll go in this one to the edge of the snow and ice. From there we can use the snowmobile to get to the volcano and the area that could be dammed.' The four friends hugged each other and Vai climbed into the truck alongside Tu. Zhang and Xie stood to the side of the shed among engine parts as the truck trundled onto the narrow road that ran up the valley.

The sky was hemmed in by cloud, the night drifted back to a weak grey and the settlement sat heavy on the land. As they left, the road became a cut on the edge of the hills. Water gathered in the angle where the road met the hill and formed into a rivulet; where the water spilled across the road it created a deep mush.

The driver paid no attention to the potholes and slips, pushing the vehicle fast and bouncing his passengers from side to side in the cab. The road drew upward on the side of the hills and the river shrank away below them. Snow replaced the sodden earth and the clouds enveloped the truck. The only feature was the road, snaking its dirty brown way into the white hills until it ended abruptly against a wall of snow. The driver turned his vehicle around laboriously and backed it against a place where the snowmobile could be hauled off onto the snow without it dropping from the tray. Vai and Tu climbed out of the truck, gathered their things and checked the gear on the snowmobile. The driver turned the machine on and stood beside it, listening to the engine. He nodded his confidence that it would carry them successfully and wiped his red-cold hands with a rag.

Tu straddled the machine and Vai slid in behind, putting her arms around her. They travelled rapidly for three hours and when the main valley split into a number of contributing parts Tu turned to the right and they caught their first glimpse of the volcano over the ridge. Within fifteen minutes the valley spread to reveal a wide flat plain. To one side the volcano dominated; on the other the valley was walled by a high cliff. The volcano's white cone had been blown open at the top, forming a 'C'. The river jumbled and rushed near the cliff and Vai could see how this could be shaped into a high and wide dam.

Tu stopped the machine and they climbed off and stretched. 'See what I mean?' she said. 'There's nothing so good as this on the rest of the coast. We've got the best option for a real settlement, a city, one day.'

The flat land was white and deep in snow. The high land was also skimmed with white, like the edges of a cake. Vai tried to find a reference in her mind for the scene that spread before her. She thought of winter scenes in the American west, cattle and cowboy scenes, buffalo and tepee scenes. But there were no animals here, no humans in this vast expanse. An old song began to trundle in her head, one her Dad used to get wrong, 'This land is your land, this land is something, something, for you and me.' He used to sing that to himself on repeat when they were fishing.

'What do you call the mountains that run behind the volcano?'

Vai asked, pointing to the high range that ran parallel to the coast but well inland.

'That range runs from the edge of the Ross Sea almost to the end of the peninsula, the end near Argentina. It's the Executive Committee Range.'

Vai laughed. 'Yes, I remember. Some group of bureaucrats making themselves important.'

'Yes, it's a dreadful name. We call it the Da Hinggan mountains after a major range in China.'

'Which one will be the formal name?'

Tu threw a ball of snow down the hill. 'China will get its way. We're big.'

Vai walked a little further onward, admiring the contrasting slope of the volcano and the sharp cliff edge of the older mountains. 'Does the volcano have a name?'

'No, it has not been climbed. So if we climb it we should be able to suggest a name.'

'Then let's make sure we do climb it.' Vai pointed to the foot of the volcano. 'See the three plateaus? Why does the lower one have no snow?'

'It's being warmed from below.'

Vai looked across at the volcano and the cliff wall. 'Look at the river carrying the ice away.'

Tu swept her hand across the vista. 'All over the continent the rivers are flowing. It's a global collapse. We're in for a century when China is in terrible shape and this land is still harsh.'

Vai looked at her boots and considered Tu's tone. 'Where's your emotion?'

'I'm a geologist at the dawn of the Anthropocene. What emotion should I have? Terror? Excitement?'

Vai grew angry. She rolled a snowball and hurled it far down the slope, then rolled another and bounced it in her hand. 'I don't understand the idea of the Anthropocene. We're about to be taken down by nature, by water. We're about to be thrashed.'

Tu placed a hand on Vai's shoulder. 'I suspect we won't fry the

218

entire planet. China has completed tasks almost as complex as this battle in front of us now.'

'The poor will be thrashed.'

'Yes. The poor don't live in the Anthropocene, they live in nature.'

Vai opened up her lungs and threw a wild howl into the silent valley and hurled the snowball after it. It landed and slid a little way, it sat on the wide slope and was hard to see. Her yell vanished, absorbed in the valley.

'I'll sell you ten thousand hectares over there,' Tu said. 'I assume that's more land than Independence covers?'

Vai looked back to the volcano and considered the plateau areas. 'Ahi kaa,' she said.

'What's that?'

'To keep the fires burning. To have a claim on an area you need to be present and, in a sense, maintain a fire.'

'That's right, yes,' Tu nodded. 'We are establishing a claim.'

'What about me and my people establishing a claim?'

'Independence? Too small. No one's fighting yet, but to hold a stake here you're going to have to back yourself up.'

Vai rested her chin in her gloved hands and walked in a small circle, thinking. Then she took hold of Tu's jacket and shook it. 'The global refugee nation. The one hundred million. The generations of exiles. Why can't *we* stake a claim?' She flared her nostrils. 'This is a tabula rasa, a blank sheet,' she said, waving her hands at the continent in general. 'A place for the ones who have nothing, where they can have their turn.' She lifted her arms high, triumphant. 'Tabula rasa. Refugee homeland, blank canvas for the excluded.' She turned to Tu, hands on hips, feet apart, 'Why not? There are no rules here.'

Tu raised her own hands. 'Why not? Just go on and proclaim the refugees as a nation.'

'Quickly. We need to be recognised in the settlement.' Vai was animated now. She walked the small circle again, this time thumping a rhythm on her thighs. 'Help me think how it could work.' The idea was vast, a refugee nation. How might it work? Perhaps they could federate among camps, some sort of regional groupings, many small camps forming a regional group from which representatives would be elected and together the representatives would form a parliament.

Tu started the machine. 'This is a palimpsest, Vai. There're no blank sheets.' She waved a hand at the landscape. 'All the dead forests turned to oil. All the camps turning into towns, the military.' Tu paused and a tone of resignation slipped into her voice. 'Come on, we need to set up under the volcano.'

Vai laughed harshly. 'Now I can see what I must do. Independence can get refugee settlement in New Zealand and at the same time I will begin to arrange a refugee nation. We'll get standing. They can't cut us out — they'd love it. Somewhere to put us at last.'

Tu looked into Vai's angry eyes and shrugged. 'I hope it works better than abundance. At least this idea doesn't rely on a whole lot of species when we're in the middle of an extinction.'

Vai stepped away quickly and fell. She rolled away from the machine and the angle of the slope took hold and she slid down. She slid for fifty metres before halting against a rock. She rolled onto her side and there, a few feet away, was a rat lying dead. Its body was desiccated, just fur lying on bones, its teeth grinning and a hole for where its eye had been. Vai stared at it. There were no bushes, no vegetation at all. She looked up, as if there might be a clue skyward. She climbed onto the rock with her back to Tu. She sat there for fully fifteen minutes and then scrambled her way back.

'Look,' she said, pointing. 'I can see someone walking.'
'Where?' asked Tu.
'There. He's in white clothes.'
'Yes, I see him now. Stay still. Try not to let him see us.'
'Why not? Won't he be from Beijing?'
'I doubt it, or he wouldn't be walking. There's been American navy ships passing the settlement. I'll bet he's from one of the

ships. He could be moving down to survey our settlement.'

'Can't they see enough remotely? Why would they send someone in on foot?'

'Sneaking around to see if we are putting any special equipment in place, or any military equipment.'

The figure dropped into a stream bed and out of sight. 'Once we're away from here I'll call the base and let them know,' Tu said. 'They might send a helicopter up and try to intercept him. If they do, they might drop a couple of sailors in with us while they do the intercept.'

'Could there be fighting?'

'I don't know. Get on the machine. We're off.'

25

In the morning Vai said, 'Yesterday, I was just thinking with my mouth open. I didn't mean to be angry.'

Tu studied Vai for a while, then said, 'I don't understand you, Vai. You change shape like a mirage. In New Zealand, you'll take a broken town, far away from everything. On the ship, you fight for pirates. On the ice, you want abundance — and then you drop that for a refugee nation.'

Vai pointed a finger at Tu. 'Why do you think that is? You get in do-gooding trouble and run off to join a big military tribe. Well, I don't have a tribe with more guns than just about any other tribe. I've got a tribe with no guns and damn near no land.'

Vai walked off. She had a bitter thought in her head about the way the people who owned things and controlled things didn't see how anything could be made available for people like her, or how nothing could be achieved by people like her. But then she looked up at the volcano and decided she would be first to the top. *First person ever. Conquer that damn mountain. Queen of it.*

She stomped her way back to the tent, where Tu was crouched over a gas burner. Vai watched the little meal simmer — green beans and tofu and brown sauce with other things she couldn't make out. 'What's the plan for climbing the volcano?' she asked.

Tu was embarrassed and hugged Vai. 'I'm sorry I insulted you. I don't know what I would do if I was in your tribe.' She said, 'We'll drive to the side around there,' and pointed in the direction they would take. 'Then we'll ride up the slope and walk when it gets too steep. We can spend as long up there as we want and if the weather is okay we can camp on the slope.'

Vai picked her spirits up, pleased to have received an apology even though she knew she was the one prodding and making things uncomfortable.

'We have an interview scheduled in the morning. Xu will call again,' Tu said.

Further lifted by the thought of telling Xu her new ideas, Vai clapped her gloved hands. 'Good. The little country Advocate has new ideas.'

They rode upward, sun in their eyes, the slope steep enough for Vai to need to push back on the foot pegs to stay in the seat. They halted on a flat area before the slope became too steep and looked out over where the land dropped steeply on the flank that faced the upland valley. The colours everywhere were white and black and blue. They spent an hour just walking from side to side on the slope and being pleased that they were there. Then they took out their ice axes and began the walk to the summit. It was steep and each step crunched on the crust of snow and then pushed through the soft centre to find solid footing. They crunched and stepped in single file. Near the top they paused to share a drink: it ran cold into their throats and the air rose from their mouths in little clouds. The last fifty metres to the top was wide enough for them to walk side by side and Vai stepped up her pace and took the lead. When she reached what looked to be the highest bit she slammed her ice axe down hard, standing it on its point. She leaned one hand on it casually while Tu stepped up beside her.

Then Tu kept walking: each surveyed the view alone. Vai thought how tiny Tu looked in the landscape, tiny in a setting that was almost too big to imagine. Breaking into bits and melting away, a broken giant. Nature, innocent and stranded and uncomprehending of its fate.

They climbed down into the caldera of the volcano and walked to the edge of the blown-out section where the flank fell steeply. Each end of the 'C' formed a peak of approximately the same height and gave the impression of a face looking across at the other peak.

It was just midday but there was nothing further to explore. They sat at the edge of the steep flank and ate, then stretched out and rested. Vai had a wide and long view. She imagined what a dam across the valley would look like, imagined the future running forward very quickly, the cold in retreat and diggers and cranes and the way the valley could be irrigated. She imagined leading a procession of people up the valley. There would be a band playing, a lot of brass because brass always announced happiness: it was the happiest form of music. There would be a lot of small children, bringing an end to the not-bringing children into the world.

They woke early for their appointment with Xu. The night was still and they decided to set up outside, placing the camera on the machine and using the headlights to shine on their faces. They built a bench in the snow and covered it with a bright red emergency survival blanket. Their studio complete, Vai looked around their camp and noticed a small black box. 'Is that yours, Tu?'

'No. I didn't bring that.' She carried it into the light of the machine and examined it. 'This is a little recording and scanning device,' she said with alarm. 'Someone's spying on us.'

Vai picked up a light and shone it around, chasing the darkness. They couldn't see anyone. They examined their footprints. There was a third set, big boots, pressed heavily into the snow.

'It must be that American we saw the day before yesterday. He hasn't gone down to the settlement, he's come up to spy on us,' Tu said.

Vai scanned her light around again. The volcano sloped away and shadow muscled up against the beam, making it easy for a man to lie invisible in the contours of the land.

Vai took up a stone, balled it in her hand. 'Tell Beijing,' she said. 'Call them now.'

They turned to their tent and a man in a white snow suit was there, just standing still with a white mask completely covering his face. He'd cut them off from the tent. He was nearly two metres tall. He spread his arms out wide and his feet apart, a monster. He must have been crouching below the lip of the steep slope, in front of the tent. His voice came muffled through the mask: 'Dr Tu, Miss Shuster. I'm sorry about this, and don't let me scare you.'

The women swore at him in unison and stepped away. 'Who are you?' Tu yelled.

He held his gloved palms upward in a passive gesture that jarred with his blank, staring mask. 'That little box is mine. I need to take it back, nothing more.'

'You're spying on us,' Vai exclaimed. 'What for?'

'We all spy on each other down here. We're interested in the dam, we needed to hear your conversation. I just need to take that box back. I assure you I will head off down the hill and you can go on with your interview. Just remember, the protocol down here on the ice is that we don't talk about spying. No telling Xu.'

Tu stepped back and behind Vai, the man closed the gap. Tu darted for the tent and he grasped at her. Vai leapt forward, driving off her left foot, and swung her right elbow into his neck, just below his chin. Dropping to her right knee, she drove her hand into his groin but he lurched sideways and her gloved hand struck only cold air. Then they were all on the ground, wrestling for the box. Tu wriggled away and got to her feet, circling around the other two still grappling, silent on the ground. Vai hung on and the man kicked her in the stomach and drove forward into Tu, knocking her down again and sending her skidding. Then she disappeared with a scream into the night air.

'Hell,' the man yelled. 'Get off me! She's gone over the edge.' He and Vai jumped to their feet and peered over the edge of the slope into the dark.

'Get a light,' the man ordered Vai. She grabbed it from the ground where it had fallen. Down the steep slope Tu was crumpled on a rock with her head out of view. 'Get your ice axes and some medical kit. We can slide down there on the axes.'

Vai ran to the machine and retrieved the equipment. Just then Xu called out from Hong Kong, 'Dr Tu, we're here waiting for you. Are you okay? We heard a scream.'

Vai stopped, confused, and peered into the camera. 'We've been attacked by an American spy. Tu's gone over a cliff and might be dead. Call Beijing. We need help now — right now!'

Xu sat forward and stared at the dishevelled woman again filling his screen, hair matted with snow. 'Why was she attacked?'

'Just get help!' Vai yelled at the screen and ran back to the man.

'What the hell did you do that for? I'm helping you save her.'

'We need a helicopter. Tu could be dying.'

The man took an ice axe and slung the medical kit over his shoulder. 'Do you know how to make a controlled slide using the axe?'

'Yes.'

'Okay, follow me down.' He lowered himself over the side of the steep slope and used the sharp, narrow blade of the axe to control his fall. Tu looked awful: her head was badly gashed and bleeding profusely and her neck looked as if it might be broken. Her left arm was bent unnaturally around a rock. 'Let's stop the bleeding, but I'm not sure we should move her,' the man said calmly. 'Will that media guy get a helicopter, do you think?'

'He has an audience of millions. I suspect someone has called for help.' They crouched in the dark watching Tu's face. 'She's breathing,' Vai said with relief. She opened the medical kit and took out bandages and they stemmed the bleeding as best they could without moving her head. They moved her arm and laid it in a way that looked less painful, less broken.

'Okay,' said the man. 'That's all I can do. I'm sorry about this. I hope she will be all right. I'm not going to stay — there's no point.'

He picked up an axe and the box and prepared to slide off further down the slope. Eyes barely slits, Vai snarled, 'You're not going anywhere. Murderer!'

226

'Murder? Not me. You caused this.'

He looked over the edge of the rocks and Vai hit him with her axe. Hit him with all her strength on the knee. Over he went, down the slope, screaming, feet flailing at the ice. Vai watched as he dug at the snow with his axe and disappeared beyond the edge of the light.

Two helicopters hovered above Vai. The first lowered a medic and stretcher. The second began sweeping the slope, looking for the man. Then a third helicopter joined and began sweeping the slope also. The medic spent some minutes assessing Tu, unwrapping and replacing the bandage on her head, feeling her neck, checking her legs and the arm that appeared to be okay. Then he bound her broken arm to her chest. Vai looked at her friend, crumpled and white on blood-red snow, such a big amount of blood-red snow. *My friend*. Vai shook. *My friend is broken*. She wondered at the friendship as if it had snuck up on her.

The medic signalled to Vai to help him move Tu and together they lifted her onto the stretcher. There was a lot of blood where her head had lain. Once they were all on the helicopter the other two helicopters stopped below them, hovering close to each other. Then Vai saw the man moving, hobbling among the snow and rocks. The helicopter she was in shone its lights onto the scene below.

One of the other helicopters was American, attempting to rescue their man. As he hobbled under the Chinese helicopter toward the American rescuers, a Chinese sailor swung down on a rope and dropped onto him, sending them both sliding further down the slope. The other two helicopters repositioned themselves. Vai's helicopter dropped lower, keeping the scene illuminated.

The man in white lost his mask, and the Chinese sailor was lying under him with a gun to his head. The helicopters remained in position. No one else descended to the snow. The two men on

227

the ground remained as they were. The radio on Vai's helicopter was rattling off Chinese voices flat out.

The sky began to grow light. The medic had run a drip into Tu's arm and was talking urgently to the pilot, gesturing toward the ocean, but the helicopter remained over the scene. Five minutes passed, and now Vai was gesturing angrily to the medic and the pilot, demanding that they leave. They ignored her. Tu was barely breathing, weaker now, failing.

Then the American helicopter veered away, up over the cliff. Vai yelled at the pilot, not words, just noise, a scream to action. He pushed the helicopter forward and out across the valley. Behind her the second helicopter dropped two more men to the ground, and they hauled the American to his feet.

Pink snow lined the mountains in the dawn light as the helicopter swept down the valley. Vai knelt beside Tu and clasped her hand. Tu's chest jerked without rhythm, each movement accompanied by a rasp and gurgle. Her skin was taking on the waxen look of a corpse. The helicopter settled on the ground at Beijing, the door slid open and Vai was pushed to the side. Quickly medics assessed Tu and lifted her away. The pilot signalled to Vai, come with me.

Her boots slid in the mud. She heard voices, words that she didn't understand; people stared at her as she passed by, foreign. The settlement appeared to be sinking, the ugly little buildings sucking into the mud, borne down by the cold. The pilot pointed to a building, one of the larger ones. They went inside and it was warm, with a bustle of people. Gradually they stopped, first one and then the stopping spread through the room and everyone looked at Vai. Then a man in a uniform with very square shoulders marched over to the pilot and spoke to him but stared at Vai. The pilot saluted sharply.

The man put out his hand. He said, in English, 'I am Commander Li. I'm very sorry you were attacked. That's unacceptable. You are our guest and Dr Tu is badly injured. There will be a price exacted for this.'

228

Vai shook his hand and said, 'Thank you.'

He led her down a corridor to a small room, ordered coffee for them both and asked Vai to tell him what had happened, to remember everything and not leave anything out.

Vai began to cry. Slowly at first and then picking up pace. She looked at Commander Li angrily and said, 'You should have sent someone yesterday! We told you about the American.'

Li didn't reply, just waited, so she told him about the encounter outside the tent, how the fight began and how Tu went over the edge.

'Who caused Dr Tu to fall?'

'What do you mean? Do you think I'm to blame? A threat?' She thumped the table. 'What the hell was I supposed to do?'

'I just need to be very clear. This is pivotal. No one is blaming you. You were brave. You fought for us, for Dr Tu.'

Vai repeated her story, adding that perhaps he might have seen what happened or heard more because Xu called out, was on screen. Li nodded. Yes, he said, they had that information. He put a hand on Vai's shoulder and allowed himself a smile. 'Good work with the ice axe, good hit. A lawyer will meet with you soon. You will have to give a signed statement. I will give you accommodation and I'm arranging a flight back to New Zealand.'

'Is Tu going to be okay?'

'I will make sure you are told as soon as there is news.' He studied her for a moment, her red face and eyes, her defiance. 'Yes, you were brave.' Then he closed the door and left her alone.

After the lawyer had been, a medical doctor arrived. It was Dr Zhu. Vai threw herself against him. He was awkward and surprised and Vai imagined him take a share of her burden. Neither spoke and he led her to another hut, and then only the fewest words. 'Will Tu be all right?' she asked.

'I don't know. She's still being stabilised.'

'I lunged at the man. We could have let him have his box. There would have been no harm in that.'

Zhu nodded. There was a wooden chair and a small table, but

229

he sat beside her. When Zhang and Xie joined them, the women cried together and held hands.

In the evening Zhu returned and took Vai to the officers' mess hall. He had to order her to go and she would have refused but she wasn't sure if she had the right to and she was exhausted. Then he walked back to the hut with her in the gloom and sat beside her and told her that Tu had died. Her head injuries had been too severe.

Vai let loose the sound of an animal in a trap. She banged on the door and yelled and Zhu sat still and provided a calm space for her to implode against. 'Well, you've got the man. Shoot him! That's what you should do!' She was coiled in a corner, spitting each word, as if any one of the words might bring the American down. 'Tu was part of your military. He killed one of yours. So you can shoot him.'

When she came to sit beside Zhu she was panting and sweating, her face was swollen and there were red fingermarks on her neck where she had clawed at herself. 'We were friends, but I was rude to her, I don't really know why. I just wanted to fight a bit with someone who would listen.' Vai looked at Zhu as if he might absolve her.

Zhu said, 'I didn't know her. But I know you shared your travels, adventures. You shared adventures. We are always lucky to have a friend, someone to journey with.'

Vai thought he looked quite ugly, an ugly short man with a kind heart. Grey, thin hair and big eyebrows and hands like bird's feet. 'What will happen to me?' she asked. 'Will I be here long? I don't know if I can go to New Zealand. I'm not a citizen.'

'Plans are being made. The New Zealand government is sending some people to get you.' He crossed to the door. 'I will come by in the morning and we can eat together and I will come back at midday and in the evening. You might like to walk along the coast, but stay within sight of the settlement.'

230

26

The following day the New Zealand party was due to arrive and Vai didn't want to see them. With Tu she had felt something, had felt she was someone, she was part of a project. Now she was just a straggler who belonged on an island and she was supposed to break free of it and take everyone with her. Heroic. Now she was going to be sent home with no achievements. After breakfast she stayed in the hut until it was nearly midday and then she escaped along the coast, walking on the cliff edge.

The sea was grey and cut by a crosswind. Waves broke without pattern on the rocks below the cliff and machines laboured loudly on the sea wall. The steady stream of helicopters continued their task of unloading ships, thwack-thwack-thwacking above her.

A helicopter approached the settlement, alone, outside the pattern of the cargo-hauling squad. It had a black kiwi painted on the side. She wondered what news it brought and why New Zealanders took pride in a bird that couldn't fly, much less attack, a shuffling-in-the-dark worm-eater. Some form of disappointment was implied, some lowering of expectation.

She sat on a rock, exposed on the cliff. If they came looking for her she would be easy to find, and if not, she was happy to avoid them for now. She took her gloves off and allowed her hands to grow ice-cold in the wind. She looked along the coast and out to sea and thought about her first impressions of the continent, how unexpected it had been. She let her thoughts flow back to Otago and then Auckland and home to Independence, to

231

her high-school imaginings. Somehow the resettlement always fell into place, almost of its own accord, promises acted on, and her fantasy focused on the quiet adulation of her elders and the little girls who wanted to be her and then there would be a New Zealand man who was somehow wealthy but didn't care for that and instead he was considering going into politics and they would talk late into the night and be lovers. Vai slipped the frozen fingers of one hand into her mouth and smiled. Perhaps he would help her build her refugee nation.

Two Chinese sailors approached. They stopped ten metres away and beckoned to her to follow them. She sat still, watching them, until one stepped closer and put a hand on her shoulder and pointed to the settlement. She stood up and they positioned themselves one in front and one behind her. In single file they marched back to the settlement where Zhu met her. 'Get changed,' he said. 'We will have lunch with Commander Li and the New Zealand contingent.'

When she was ready he took her to the largest building, the one that was three storeys high. Inside it was warm and there was a frieze running the length of one wall, mountains in winter. Classic Chinese imagery, she thought. It could be Antarctica, it could be a land claim. Thick yellow drapes against the ends of big windows held the room together, stopped it spilling out through the windows and across the ocean. It was a restaurant, almost as well appointed as the one in Auckland where she had lunched with Miriama.

Zhu pointed to a table where Miriama Hunter and Adam Walker sat among the group. Vai called out across the room and hurried over. Miriama clapped her hands and rose to her feet, clasping Vai to her breast. Vai was crying and apologising, saying, 'Thank you for coming down. I had no idea, it never occurred to me you would come.'

Miriama held Vai close and whispered into her ear, 'I'm very proud of you.'

Adam stood up and hugged Vai and then Miriama introduced

232

Vai to the Minister of Foreign Affairs and Trade, Walter Mantell. He bounced to his feet and clasped Vai's hands in his. 'So, you're the young woman.' His eyes swept her briefly and he turned to Adam. 'And here we all are in Beijing. I didn't expect to come to Beijing this week.' He dropped her hand and turned to the ocean. He appeared to be studying the Chinese military ships and then lifted his head. She thought his attention had shifted to an American vessel or further out.

Miriama led Vai to a seat in the corner of the restaurant, near the entrance to the kitchen, a place to talk and cry. Miriama comforted her and said how terribly sorry she was to hear that Vai's friend had been killed. 'I have your visa arranged. Eight months, but that's a start. It was rushed through after the publicity over the attack. I'm sorry that sort of publicity is what it took. But that's some good news.'

Vai kissed Miriama and thanked her and thought, *That'll do, a start, then we go on and save Independence.* And now she was fighting tears with smiles, loss and hope all pitching forward at once. 'Did you come to get me, to take me to New Zealand?'

'Yes, we will leave together. But there are two things that need to be done first. This killing of Tu by an American serviceman, a member of the American military killing a member of the Chinese military, it's difficult. The two countries are trying very hard to work together, to provide global leadership. It's been agreed that New Zealand will take the American. He's likely to spend time in a New Zealand military prison. Not long. The Chinese have extracted a symbolic victory, and there's going to be a ceremonial attempt at resolving the issue.' Miriama gestured out the window to the ships moving on their anchors. 'Also, you might not have heard, but the Antarctic deal, the settlement has been rushed forward. America, China and India have reached an agreement and they want it signed before any groundswell of opposition takes hold. It's going to be signed at the main Argentine base in a few days.'

Vai held Miriama's hand and didn't speak. She wondered about

233

the ceremony and the settlement but she had no strength. Her legs were drained worse than at the end of a long haul up a ridge in deep, wet snow. She wanted to be tucked into bed.

'As recompense for the death of Dr Tu it's been agreed that the Chinese name will be formally adopted for the big mountain range that runs along the peninsula.'

'Da Hinggan,' Vai said. 'Tu told me that's the name they use.'

'Yes, that name. We will all be flown to the volcano where she was killed. There will be a ceremony of remembrance and conciliation, then the mountains will be named.'

'Tu and I climbed a volcano. It hasn't been named,' Vai said. She felt a surge of pride. 'We were the first people to climb it.' As she spoke she remembered marching past Tu, getting to the top first. She felt a prickle of heat on her skin and looked down, ashamed.

'I've been told that,' Miriama said. 'Naming it is so important. Of all the things China could have demanded from this incident, they demanded a name. It says, "We belong."' She paused. 'The volcano will get a name.'

Vai waited. It wouldn't be her role to give a name. At home it would be her grandfather Malakai's role to think of one. She recognised the limits of her youth but she spoke anyway. 'Could the name make links, build unity? There's China and Independence. And, you know, New Zealand is a child of Antarctica.' She looked at Miriama shyly. 'Could a name tie the three together with this ancient place? Is there a way we can remember Tu and make those links?'

'Tell me about the volcano. What does it look like?'

'It sort of stands alone. A strong cone shape, except it has a ridge that slopes off at a lesser angle than most of it. We rode the snow machine up the slope. Halfway to the top.' Vai groaned and ran her hand over her face. 'It's where we camped. The fight was there. Beyond that the top is blown half out. The caldera looks like two people facing each other.'

'Commander Li mentioned that, the faces on the caldera. It must be a real feature.'

'Yes, the two faces have a great view,' Vai said, remembering the sense of grandeur.

Miriama patted her shoulder. 'I spoke to my uncle just before lunch, after the Commander told me about naming of the mountain range and the un-named volcano. We had the same thought you did, about binding people together. He suggested a name that binds us in the way you've suggested.' She paused for effect. 'Ngā Wahine Toa. The warrior women, facing each other.'

Vai turned beetroot-red. She kept her eyes on the ground and furrowed her brow. The memory of her was going to be placed on a mountain. She couldn't look at Miriama — her eyes would have given her pride away. Would her mother be proud? Yes, and disapointed. Her mother and her sick sister, and her family and everyone else. Shit, she was being sent home with nothing but a name that no one else could use. *A claimed volcano in the ice.*

Vai took a place at the table beside Miriama. They had been joined by an American navy captain, Alex Ryan; the head of the American delegation, Maria Martinez; and the Argentinian director for Antarctica, Luis Favaloro and his senior military officer. Adam was engrossed in conversation with Maria and Luis. Crab soup was served and Vai attacked it, hungry and happy not to be invited into the conversation.

The talk was about the settlement and Vai observed it as if it was a movie she didn't much care for. Luis Favaloro was assuring his listeners that the Argentine base would be ready for the historic settlement event. Cariló, the oldest real settlement on the continent, he said. Modern hotels and conference facilities were in place and the luxury cruise ships had arrived to accommodate guests and of course the corporate yachts were flooding in. He laughed: 'The event is likely to make a profit.' He gestured around the restaurant and said that although it was excellent and the host was to be commended, such an event couldn't be held in Beijing. It was too recent. No infrastructure. 'No roots on the continent, when you think about it.'

Maria Martinez smiled. 'It's also convenient that Argentina

has no role in global leadership. China and India have been fantastic partners to work with. We share a sense of responsibility, an understanding of the historic moment. And it's been very important that the partner nations have supported the settlement.' She held Favaloro's gaze. 'Argentina must be happy with the south-plus-three deal. It gives you a role you're unlikely to have achieved otherwise.'

Loud voices clattered into the room from the foyer. They broke over the polite murmur of the diners like a jet of cold water. The tables went quiet and Commander Li looked over to the source of the noise, his face set harder than granite. A junior officer was at the door desperately making a 'quiet down' signal with his hands, glancing with fright toward the Commander. The source of his panic were four men in their twenties, civilians by the look of their bright, tight-fitting shirts and gentlemen's adventure trousers and boots.

Commander Li took in the ruckus and glanced at the Argentinians at his own table. Making a quick decision he signalled the frightened officer to bring the noisy group over. The four men approached, swaggering and grinning. 'Hola, Commander,' the first one said, waving his hand airily.

Li set his jaw and nodded to the four newcomers. 'Señor Juan Hernandez, I assume.'

'You know my name? That is good news. Let me introduce my compatriots,' said Juan. 'Eduardo Moreno, César Creevy and Ariel Correa.'

Li shook hands with the four and attempted to contain them with his rigid presence, but they had no stake in conforming. He turned to Favaloro, who was steaming beyond red, heading toward apoplectic purple. 'Perhaps it would be good if we can seat the entire Argentine group together,' Li said. 'May I suggest they sit next to you, Director Favaloro?'

Immediately the table stood and began to shuffle seats, making room for the young men. 'No, no,' Juan said. 'No need. We can fit down here on the end.' He sat next to Adam and his friends took the adjacent seats. 'Juan Hernandez,' he grinned, leaning in close to Adam.

'Adam Walker, from New Zealand.' Adam took the hand offered and squeezed until Juan flinched.

'We are honoured to welcome you to this little island that we were born on. My father used to be the elected representative of the Argentinians born here.'

'I see,' Adam responded with a thin smile, standing to shake each Argentine man's hand in turn. 'You are, what is the term? Natives?'

'Natives!' Juan exclaimed with a sharp laugh. 'I suppose you could use that term, but it implies you are colonials. I was born here, as were my parents and their parents. They still live here. But things change, visitors are welcome. You know, change is not always a bad thing. For instance,' he said, raising his voice and looking around the table to see who was listening to him, 'last summer for the first time these boys and I surfed here. Can you imagine how cold it was? But let me tell you, there are some good spots down here. Not far from Cariló there is a point break to rival your surf at Raglan. How many more places like that do you think are undiscovered?' He tapped his index finger loudly on the table.

Adam smiled politely. 'Are you with the Argentine delegation for the ceremony at Cariló?'

'No, I'm not part of any delegation,' Juan responded, this time with an attempt at a solemn voice. His friends grinned. 'This is a funny place, you know, Adam. While I am Argentinian, and Argentina has settlements here, as do China, America, New Zealand and so on and so on, there is no law as such, no sovereignty, no nations. Which leaves me, could we say perhaps, roving, unmanaged by the law. So, I'm not really a delegate. But I do feel a deep sense of responsibility, a guardian of the continent, as one of the few born here.'

'That sounds like an eighteenth-century condition.' Adam smiled, apparently enjoying his barb. 'Natives, unbound by the law. In, perhaps, a savage condition.'

Juan pulled back, feigning hurt, 'That's not very polite, coming from a diplomat.'

'I'm not a diplomat, I'm a negotiator. Not the same thing.' Adam glanced at the half-eaten meal on his plate. Vai could see his disappointment at the intrusion, could imagine how much he would have looked forward to the high company and good food. He looked out across the bay and she thought he might as well say what was written on his face: *Goddamn babysitter for a scared kid and his mates.*

Juan's loud voice interrupted her thoughts: he had begun insulting the Americans across the table: 'I hear the woman who nobbled your man is here somewhere. Missed his balls and got his knee, I'm told.'

When she heard this she let out a delighted, high laugh and quickly sat back out of sight.

'Let me introduce you to Mrs Hunter, here,' Adam interjected quickly. 'Her son's a surfer too.'

'Yes, and much more than that,' said Miriama. 'He's our CEO. He runs the largest property development company in New Zealand.'

'Works for the Chinese, does he?' Juan picked up a glass of wine and swirled it, watching the liquid rotate. 'I mean, from one about-to-be colonised person to another. Oh, except, twice colonised for you.'

Miriama leant across Adam and pointed a finger at Juan. 'Listen boy, I don't care where you were born. Your parents are still alive, so my respect is for them. Until they pass on you're just in short pants to me, and you can either behave or go and sit outside.' Juan held her stare for a few seconds then sat back quietly and turned to his friends.

The mood at the table lifted and Adam dug into the food with gusto. Juan and his little crew focused on their meals. While Miriama and Maria discussed the proposed settlement, Adam grinned to himself, clearly thrilled. Vai had to admit she was thrilled too, sitting at the top table discussing the settlement of a whole continent. A continent, she thought. *It's like being in the eighteenth century, except the moral taint of stealing other people's stuff, not to mention killing them, isn't in play.*

'I guess it will be tough working down here,' Adam said. 'The snow and ice and bad weather are going to remain for decades. In fact our thinking is that this place will always be inhospitable. Liveable, but basic. The real base of activity is going to be New Zealand.'

'Yes.' Maria studied his face. 'You're moving to a central place in the world now. New Zealand is well located for West Antarctica, and West Antarctica is where we can get development underway first.' She jiggled the ice in her whisky glass. 'Are you ready to be in the middle? China has played a long game with New Zealand. America's looked to you for support in other parts of the world, but China's looked to work with you on your own land. The way I think about it, you've taken on two husbands at once. One husband has been busy overseas, but he'll be spending a lot more time with you from now on. Do you think you can manage two?'

Adam laughed nervously. 'Well, no one's put it to me like that before. I think it will be a test of your willingness to cooperate. We'll house you in separate cities.'

'Don't underestimate the challenge, Adam. New Zealand used to be too small, too distant, as the saying goes. You could hide from the world and all its ills. You thought you could hide from climate destruction. But you're moving to the centre of the map now. America needs resources, and we won't tolerate missing out down here. China and India have population pressures very few Kiwis could imagine. I know you understand this, but I'm not sure the rest of New Zealand understands what they're going to be asked to accept. China and India will look to build cities down here, but that's going to be tough. Building cities in New Zealand is not hard at all. I think your Prime Minister understands.'

'Lebanon, my friend. Lebanon is what you are facing.' Juan laughed loudly. 'Your little country has tried so hard. You've been so accommodating. But the world is not nice and it's getting nastier.'

Adam ignored this, so Juan jabbed him in the ribs with his elbow. 'There's no hiding from now on. The world's coming for you, mate.'

Maria said, 'Don't be ashamed to accommodate. Don't resist the role geography has assigned you.'

'We're not resisting,' Miriama said. 'The Prime Minister understands what's required. He has no fear of the global order that's emerging.'

Maria smiled. 'Good. That's your only option. Be part of what's emerging.'

'The Prime Minister has a big job in front of him, though. He hasn't done enough to prepare the country for its role. The people don't understand. He should have described in detail how the global order might emerge and how that can be positive. He ducked that for too long.'

'New Zealand's fate was sealed decades ago,' Adam said impatiently. 'Tell me, Maria, will the northern countries just walk out of Antarctica? They essentially took possession one hundred years ago. I can't believe they'll just go.' His voice rose. 'Do you think the interim governance deal will hold? Will the north go quietly?'

'Yes, it will hold,' Maria said, dropping her fist on the table for emphasis. 'The next fifty years will see the worst of climate breakdown begin, and we've committed to India and China that there will be no political crises here. We won't tolerate it. But more importantly, if we handle Antarctica right, we could use it as a basis for a better governance system elsewhere. I hope we can build some type of federal arrangement, get it working and maybe it could become the new best model. We have a chance here because there is no real history of war or race or conquest. The resentments and fears that pass on from generation to generation in other parts of the world have not taken hold here.'

'Except for the north. They're excluded,' Adam said.

'We had too much push-back from the south,' Maria replied. 'They rightly pointed out that there are vast areas in the northern

240

hemisphere to take migrants. I believe we have an experiment for Antarctica that is right-sized.' She looked around the room and returned her attention to Adam. 'I wish there was a map here of the continent. Are you familiar with the pattern of settlements, Adam?'

'Broadly,' he said. 'Most of the settlements are on the coast, with a few inland where some geographic opportunity or scientific opportunity exists.'

'That's not the important point. What is really interesting is that the settlements of the nations are scattered and intermingled, so New Zealand has eight settlements, but you couldn't put a ring around them without encompassing at least America, Indonesia and two others. Australia has twelve settlements, and again you can't put a ring around them without encompassing four or five other nations. And so it goes for the rest of the nations with bases down here. Now, you could think of this as a problem. How do you federate when the individual units can't arrange discrete territorial units? Do we exchange and move around? Maybe, but that would foster resentment. And what about the southern countries with no existing bases? Do you see another opportunity?'

Adam held his hands open, indicating he had no answer. 'We don't federate on a territorial basis,' said Maria. 'We just federate on a rule-of-law basis. We agree the most important rules for working together, and these need to be built around general outcomes. The land and ocean are held as common pool resources. From there we operate like a club. You must be a member of the club, abide by the rules, pay your fees. Violating the rules or not paying fees draws a minor penalty, with the penalties able to be escalated if needed. Where there are disputes they are referred to the club's governing body, which has membership from all parties. If there is a dispute that cannot be resolved, then the big three decide.'

Adam nodded. 'A club, yes. I'm thinking a country club writ large.'

'That's it,' Maria said. 'A membership group and a governance system. The alternative is to draw little boundaries around the existing settlements, add in the new nations and from day one you have moved from an ungoverned continent to a Balkanised mess. Antarctica is not a blank sheet of paper, but it *does* allow new thinking.'

Captain Ryan entered the conversation. 'Think about the mixing of nationalities that has occurred over the last two hundred years,' he said. 'It's unprecedented and it's going to happen more. What will matter in the long term is migration and demographics. You wait, I'm too old, I'll miss it, but the ties of family and ethnicity will be like a ball of string that the cat's got hold of. This intermingling, this unity in diversity will drive us toward federalism.'

'Demography,' Maria smiled. 'It gets you in the end.'

'And a good thing all of this is,' Miriama said. 'This chaotic climate process and migration are as much about integration as they are about disintegration.'

'That's a good way to view things,' Commander Li said. 'It takes courage to view the future positively. The wars we have scattered around the planet have been contained so far by the big three, but the whole thing is an inch from exploding. What we need to do is try something new — and Antarctica provides that opportunity.'

27

Before dawn the next morning the group gathered at the helicopter pad, preparing to leave for the volcano. Juan and his mates stood away from the group and then, before the others were ready, took flight in their own helicopter, ensuring they arrived first. As Miriama and Vai flew up the dark valley rain fell softly against the windows.

They alighted at the campsite where Tu had died and gathered in the helicopters' lights. Sailors turned on more lights that cast a yellow glow out into the dark. A large rock had been placed at the point where the tent had stood, a plaque on it covered by a cloth. Vai took Miriama's gloved hand and held it tightly. The helicopters lifted off and the group were left to the silence and the soft rain.

Thin light was appearing on the horizon and the mountains were beginning to glow. Vai led Miriama to the place where Tu had fallen. The rock she had landed on was barely discernible, sunk in the dark.

'So much spirit. The depth of this place,' Miriama said. She placed her hand at the back of Vai's head and drew them together, cheek to cheek. 'This is the continuation of our journey,' she whispered. 'The Polynesian journey from Taiwan to the Pacific. To the islands, your people. Then on to the south of New Zealand, Aotearoa. We've waited so long in Aotearoa.'

Vai spoke in her own language and Miriama nodded, cousin languages, family. Miriama switched to te reo Māori acknowledging that New Zealand was a child of Antarctica, split away from Gondwanaland. She whispered to the mountains, ancestors, the volcano also and the animals and birds that belonged to the land laid out before them. She imagined the ancient history of the land and its many inhabitants, animals and plants, and acknowledged that they had lain beneath the sheet of ice and snow, sleeping for many millions of years, but now the time was coming for them to wake up and for their spirits to flourish and the abundance that had once been theirs to shine again in the world.

Miriama held Vai tight and they turned to the large rock that had been placed to memorialise Tu. 'We earn our bonds to the land,' she said. 'Everyone will remember you both, your courage. That you earned the name. History will remember you.' She held her hands toward the rock and spoke to it, acknowledging the pain that accompanies birth and the massive extent of the pain the world was being subjected to, but also that in recompense there was an opportunity for a flourishing of unity across the globe in a manner never seen before. And finally she spoke to the volcano and asked it to accept the name that was offered — Ngā Wahine Toa — and stand as an emblem of unity and courage, a beginning to people and nature waking up and moving together. She ended her greeting to the dead and to the mountain, and the rain fell down harder and the wind ran cold across their faces. Vai wasn't sure how loudly Miriama had spoken: their heads were together and Vai had been holding Miriama tight. They turned to the rest of the party and realised they were all waiting.

Commander Li gathered the party together and announced that the Antarctic range would be named after the Da Hinggan mountains in China. He spoke briefly about the history of the mountains then, as if he had listened to Miriama, he told the story of the first human migration to Taiwan and the epic migration into the Pacific that followed, the emergence of Māori from those migrants and the weaving together of all the strands, here on the ice. He faced the mountains and spread his arms wide and proclaimed their new name. As the group shook hands Vai could see the Americans simmer.

Now it was Walter's turn. He spoke proudly about the role New Zealand would play, hosting those in need and remembering the lengthy history of New Zealand adventuring on the continent. He acknowledged Vai's courage and expressed his sorrow at the effects a misunderstanding has and the need to work together, now more than ever. Then he took an exaggerated breath, filling his lungs and, bouncing on his toes, said, 'Land!' loudly. He repeated the word again, drawing out the vowel and clipping the last letter. 'I feel something awakening in me, a ghost from the past.' He raised both hands to the sky, spread them far apart. 'The sun only ever rises on potential, on opportunity. We're here for the adventurers, trailblazers, the builders and the makers. The people whose names will be remembered.' He looked at the solemn group assembled around the stone and his face dimmed a little, perhaps a shadow of doubt, or even a future regret. He swept one hand upward toward the peak of the volcano and proclaimed its name. Then he grasped the cloth and flipped it off the rock.

Vai looked around at the leaders and military men, all of them seeking a way forward together, and then up to the top of the volcano. *I can see Tu,* she thought. *All of us together. All this world in danger and we're facing up to it at last.*

After the early start at the volcano they had a quick, light meal together at the restaurant. They were going to Cariló as soon as they were packed. There was no discussion of global affairs. There was the excitement of heading to a party, a week away. A gathering.

They flew east, along the coast, and saw the gathering of ships before they saw Cariló. The flotilla sported colour and power and wealth. The ships that carried corporate logos were the largest; those that flashed the most ingenious names were the sleekest. China, America and India had their biggest naval vessels gathered like prize stallions, moving slow and taut on the herd.

Cariló made an attempt to be fun. The buildings facing the coast had a seaside holiday look, painted in blue and yellow pastels. The streets near the coast were lined with posts, each one with a bright flag of primary colour that stood to attention in the steady breeze. But after a couple of streets the town gave up and got on with managing the cold and the wind.

When they landed there was no one there to meet them. Walter told Adam to get them a vehicle to take them to the hotel. The group stood under the canopy outside the airport and watched the buzz. It was like a ski-resort town: women wore bright colours and sported fur collars and puffed-out boots; the men swaggered around in colours that weren't so bold but the outfits were expensive, high-tech and business-casual. Military people didn't let anyone down, striding with clear purpose, giving the impression they were the preliminary owners. There was new paint on the utilitarian sheds around the airport, and the huts and workplaces that lined the wide road to the business centre were doing their best to look as if they always knew they would host the last great land deal.

Adam found a guy with a six-wheel vehicle that had plenty of room and ripped seats and they clambered up into it. Up high in the old vehicle they looked like a hard-pressed business delegation riding toward money.

After they were settled into their rooms Vai met Adam in the foyer. He had offered to buy her a dress for the signing ceremony and reception that would follow. When he made his offer Vai had glanced at Miriama but she shrugged and smiled so Vai accepted. They set off on foot in the direction the concierge had pointed, huddled in their warm coats. They splashed across the street and then shuffle-walked along the icy path.

Adam pointed out the architecture and streetscape as if he had been to Cariló before. The street they were on was fronted by warehouses that had been hurriedly converted to bars, restaurants and shops. The dress shop they'd been looking for was full of women making last-minute arrangements for the week ahead. The harassed shop assistants sat them in a queue to wait, and Vai cast her eyes over dresses of all imaginable colours and cuts, imported, she assumed, from boutiques in Buenos Aires.

Before they could settle there was a tap on the street window. It was Juan, beaming his smile into the room. Vai waved and gestured to the door, inviting him in. Adam looked as though he'd just stepped in dog poo. Juan hurried across to Vai, attempting to kiss her, but she ducked away.

No sooner was Juan seated next to Vai with Adam on her other side than she was called away to try on dresses. The two men studied separate areas of the shop, until it became too uncomfortable not to speak. Juan asked casually, 'Are you an outdoors man, Adam? Perhaps we could do some surfing together before you leave. I think Vai would like that. She must love the ocean.'

Adam looked over at the young man beside him. Maybe Juan's family had imagined that being born on the continent, part of a government breeding-programme-cum-status-claim, would result in actual status for themselves. 'No, I don't surf,' he said. 'I'll return immediately after the conference. There's a lot to do. New Zealand will get as much business as Argentina, staging access to the continent.'

'That's a shame. You know, this is the most beautiful place on a good day. The coastline is wild. I have fished in places where the schools of fish take an hour to pass by,' Juan enthused. 'I circumnavigated the coast with the Argentine expedition two years ago. We discovered beaches that swept away in front of us for miles. But then there were the places where we spent days climbing along ridges, up and down, ice flows that still reach to the sea edge. It was dangerous, but the biggest challenge was to keep going day after day. We did not rest. We were determined to make the journey in the fastest time. I was fine but some of the older guys, maybe in their early forties, they struggled to keep up. Antarctica is for young men, I think. How old are you, Adam?'

Adam thought about Juan's future and without rancour said, 'I'm forty-four.'

'Oh, okay, a lot older than Vai. But I guess you're just friends?'

'I'm buying her a dress because she needs one and has no money,' Adam replied quietly.

Juan sat back, smiling contentedly. 'We're indigenous here, you know, the ones who were born here.' He looked around the room, the women swarming among the dresses, the line of bored men on the seats. Then he returned his gaze to Adam and said sadly, 'But no one seems to notice.'

The men returned to silence, staring hopefully in the direction Vai had taken. And in a mercifully short time she appeared smiling with a parcel under her arm. 'I'm not going to show you,' she told them. 'You can see it on the day. Adam, thank you so much. I hope you don't mind the cost.'

'Of course not,' Adam said. He took her by the arm and walked with her to the checkout.

'I'm sure it will go on the government credit card,' Juan said, appearing on Vai's other side. While Adam paid Juan suggested they go for a drink at a bar across the street.

Vai clapped her hands and rolled her eyes happily. 'I haven't seen the inside of a bar since I left New Zealand! Will there be music?'

'Of course, it's an Argentine town. There is always music. And who knows, for the event there might be some good bands flown down.'

'Music and beer,' Adam said without rancour. 'Who could object to that?'

The three of them stepped out of the dress shop arm in arm and hurried across the slushy road to the warmth of a bar. Inside, tables were set out in a grid around the bar itself. Chatter and laughter rose from across the space which was busy with people

248

of every hue. Juan waved out to the men who had been with him in Beijing, took Vai's arm and guided her toward where they were sitting. Adam followed closely behind. The men rose to greet the three newcomers with hugs and laughter. A waiter in a black T-shirt emblazoned with the bar's logo approached and took their drinks order.

'Look at us drinking here with a proper hero,' César said. Vai protested that no one knew who she was, but he said, 'Your fight was on global media. Xu is a big star. Don't underestimate your warrior status.'

'Absolutely,' Ariel said, 'and the Japanese hate you. They know you were on the *Taniwha* and began this whole thing. Probably every northern government hates you too. So watch out.' He laughed loudly and looked around as if scouting for assailants. He pointed across the room. 'See those two Japanese men? They might be assassins sent down to even the score with you.'

Vai's pulse quickened. Adam had his head down and she wasn't sure if he had seen the men. They were the two that he had been conspiring with at Momona Airport.

'Really, though, you wrecked things for Japan,' Juan said. 'Who knows, they might have had a seat at the table. But the publicity against them has been unrelenting.'

The banter continued and eventually a band appeared at the end of the room, setting up their equipment and checking their sound. Adam seemed relaxed, enjoying the company. When the conversation turned to the settlement that was to be signed off everyone's voices rose together, animated and excited. Vai thought, *It feels like we're winners in a giant lottery.*

Juan stood and raised his glass. 'Who would have imagined we would be part of this moment?' he yelled into the hubbub. 'This moment when a continent is settled. The last continent, the greatest. Here we are on the frontier of a new world, when everything changes. The whole weight of the world shifts to the south, where everything is new.'

All six came to their feet and raised their glasses shouting 'Sí, sí, sí!' in unison. Laughing and united they fell back to their seats. Juan called for more beer and this time shots of bourbon too. He slipped his arm around Vai's waist and she leaned against him and swayed in time with the music. 'Something good will come of this,' she said, cupping her hand over his ear. He grinned and stroked her hair. Vai proclaimed to the group, 'Damn the climate, here's to a future for all of us. A big abundant future.'

'Damn guilt and fear,' Juan said. 'We call it the grey wolf, present at every meal, watching to make sure we are feeling guilty and scared enough. I don't live like that. That's a British idea because they are morose, but I bet they've been like that forever. It's not the weather that made them that way.'

'That's right, we're about making the future,' Eduardo said. 'Not being frightened into a half-life, where every change is bad and we're supposed to feel guilty about it.' He slapped the table. 'We're going to be abundant, like Vai says.'

'Yes, abundant!' Juan yelled. 'That is courage, that is about saying we don't quit, we don't accept the half-life that's been handed to us. We demand a full life.'

'Yes, that's right. To Vai, the wahine toa!' Eduardo roared.

'To abundance!' Juan shouted. And then turning it to a chant he called, 'Abundance, abundance, abund-bunda-bundance.' Everyone at the table stood and began chanting along with him and then tables nearby joined in and soon everyone in the room was either standing and chanting or banging their own tables in rhythm.

Once the chanting stopped Vai, Adam and the four Argentinians staggered out the door and stood sucking in the cold air. Darkness had fallen on the town and the thinly spaced street lights struggled to hold their own against the mist and damp that settled on their jackets, light as feather down.

'It's still early,' Juan said. 'Let's carry on. There are other bars, better ones.'

'Not me,' said Vai. 'I'm too drunk already and I need to get this dress back to the hotel before I lose it.'

'Come on,' pleaded Juan. 'Don't leave me here with these ugly guys.'

'I'll walk back with you,' Adam offered, his voice slurring a little. 'Just one minute,' he continued, his voice turning dark. 'There's someone I know. I should just speak to him briefly.'

He crossed the road and approached a group of men. Among them stood the Japanese men from Momona Airport. They were clearly waiting for him. He squared up to the group. Legs apart, shoulders back. The Japanese took the same stance: a confrontation.

Juan looked at his mates and gestured to Vai as if asking, 'Should I go over there?'

Things were being said, Adam was poking a finger as he spoke and the men he was with were pointing back at him, telling him, emphasising what they wanted and he was letting them know the same. Abruptly Adam broke it off and marched back to Vai and the Argentinians. He was angry, no longer slurring his words. 'Sore losers,' he said as if that summed it all up.

Juan grinned and thumped him on the back. 'Send them back north, ignorant whale-killers. They never belonged, never understood this place.'

Adam's shoulder stiffened under the young man's backslap. He wasn't laughing now; he was finished with the evening. He said to Vai, 'I'm going back to the hotel. Are you coming?'

She took him in, abrupt and demanding. 'Not if you're going to end the evening like this.'

'Let's end with a light meal and some good wine,' Adam said more kindly. 'I didn't mean to dampen the fun.' He looked back over the road to the Japanese group. 'Don't think the north is finished just because their governments are out of the deal. This was always about commerce and there's no boundaries to that.' He motioned toward the hotel. 'Shall we go?'

Vai gave the other men a quick peck on the cheek and the air went out of them as she moved off with Adam. When she glanced back they seemed momentarily stranded. The yellow

251

street lights merged with the little puffs of cold air coming from their mouths, forming little boxes for speech, but empty. Then Juan punched Eduardo's arm and Eduardo punched César and Ariel and the four of them spluttered back to life and words found them and they turned away down the street.

Vai turned her attention to Adam. 'I saw you with those men at Momona.'

'Which men?' Adam replied, taking Vai's arm as if he might stumble.

'The Japanese. Two of them were with you at Momona.'

'Were you listening?'

'Not listening, but I nearly walked in without realising you were meeting. I stopped at the door and then left.'

Adam was silent for a while as they walked, keeping hold of her arm but not for stability. He held her, directing her steps as if she might veer away from the hotel. Eventually he said, 'Look at all these people. Business people, money people, finance. Military people and ex-military. Commercial security services. Where are the scientists and Antarctic explorers?' They stepped onto an icy patch of footpath and Adam stumbled, nearly losing his footing. He swore and rubbed the back of his thigh. 'Bloody nature. If it's not killing us it's going extinct. I'm fed up with it.'

People like him are going to win the battle against the climate, Vai thought, *just by staying indoors. That's what it's come to.*

They stopped across the road from their hotel and looked up at the restaurant on the second floor. The bright light and clear glass brought the diners into sharp relief. They took the lift to the restaurant and followed a waiter toward a table away from the window. The room was busy and warm. Fresh vegetables on hot plates, *green* vegetables. Vai hadn't seen fresh green vegetables since she left Otago. The vegetables at Beijing were frozen, they had that wateriness, but here the green was authentic green, flown in fresh. Cuts of meat and savoury sauces and aromas passed by. Adam patted his stomach as a steaming plate of fish and vegetables passed him.

252

Vai had lamb and roast vegetables and Adam settled in front of half a roast duck with a mix of happiness and contentment. He turned it on the plate and carefully drizzled it in brown sauce and moved the vegetables away so that the sauce would not be interfered with. He smiled, sliced a portion of the breast, dabbed it in the sauce, lifted it to his mouth and chewed slowly.

Vai left him to his thoughts and focused on the task she had set herself for the settlement period. She had spoken with her mother again, and this time her Pa was there too. Not her siblings — Emma and Erfan had gone to the coast. New Zealand was settling refugees on Independence from elsewhere, holding them there for a while. Pa thought they were sick. It was likely New Zealand wanted a quarantine island. Then there was the self-culling: he suspected there was some of that happening. They had buried four elderly couples in a month. In each case the deaths made it easier for the remaining family to qualify for resettlement, if New Zealand could be convinced to move the settlement date forward.

Sonya had talked freely with Vai about Emma, who had chest pains and fatigue and was losing weight. Vai asked if doctors were available now that refugees were being housed on the island. There were, Sonya confirmed. Vai asked about the risk of having Emma diagnosed with an incurable strain of TB, against the risk of not trying.

As if she might engineer an escape, Sonya said, 'People can get to parts of South America. Even if they're sick, they can get in with a bribe.'

'Who told you that?' Vai wondered what links Juan had. She thought of her cousin Leon in Auckland. Of all the people she knew he was the one who was most likely to engineer an escape.

'Some of the new people,' Sonya said. 'We could find somewhere, inland.'

Vai prodded the remaining half of her lamb. She had Miriama and Adam together for a few days, plus the Minister. She needed a special reason to bring Independence forward in the queue. She stabbed a broccoli floret and pushed it through the gravy.

'Do you want to talk?' Adam asked.

She set her fork down. 'I need your help, Adam, you know that. I need it now. Do you know that Miriama's arranged an eight-month visa for me?' She placed her hands flat on the table. 'That's very good of her, but it's not enough. We can't wait on Independence for ten years. People are getting sick, people are killing themselves if they think they're blocking their family's chances of resettlement. You know what happens.'

Adam smiled, thin lips pulled sideways. 'That's your opening? You've betrayed your position. You have no special case. We can't just gift you a place at the front of the queue. There has to be a reason. What's the answer to the question, "Why is Independence special?"'

At the next table half a dozen women were laughing and eating dessert. Vai looked around the room. Every variation of human was present. Big ones, fat ones, skinny, all the colours and heights. All sitting on the back of power and wealth.

'There were promises!' Vai could barely control her anger. 'We were told and told and told. We would come to New Zealand when the island was finished, and it's finished.' Her thoughts went back to Herieth, Andrew in Auckland, the other public servants. Where did they all go when they were needed?

'You didn't lock anything down,' said Adam. 'Those are old promises and none of them were binding. Now here you are at the end of the world, cast out.' He waved his hand to the large window. 'Casting blame. That's all this amounts to.' He leaned forward and said quietly, 'None of the people you've met promised you anything, and each time you asked we said there was nothing we could do. Not me. Not Miriama. Don't you go asking the Minister. I won't let you embarrass him. He's not a favour-dispenser, not something you drop a coin into.'

Vai clenched her fists. 'For God's sake, Adam. We're dying.'

He remained unmoved. 'This is a test of your character, Vai. Ten years isn't a long time. Get close to Miriama, she will help

254

get your mother and siblings over. That might take two years. Then you need to look at people's family trees. Find some in their thirties with skills. Get them here on work visas, then help them get their kids, nieces and nephews over. Then the ball's moving.'

'Don't patronise me! We've been doing that for generations and it's not enough.' Tears brewed and she struggled not to let them show. 'Ten years is bullshit. In ten years the world will be in chaos. The powerful countries will take New Zealand and use her as they wish. She'll be a teenager stuck in an alley at night. You don't have ten years to offer me.'

Adam said, 'We're already in the alley.' He sounded bitter and hurt. He shut his eyes and lifted his wine glass to his nose, inhaled. 'I'm moving to Prague soon. I'm setting up a consultancy business. Business deals between the EU and other places.'

Hell, he's going to leave. Run away. Momentarily Vai was shocked, but then thought, *Why wouldn't he?* 'Japan,' Vai said. 'Japan, am I right?' She looked at the nearest waiter. She imagined punching Adam, feeling his nose crush. What would happen? Nothing — and that was her problem.

Adam remained as he was, eyes shut, wine glass close to his nose. 'Miriama is your only path, Vai. And it's a damn good path. Of all the poor young women in the world, you've found a billionaire sponsor, one who actually values you fully clothed. Work hard and you can save your family.'

Vai pushed her fork firmly against his hand on the table, pinning it. 'I heard you at the airport,' she hissed. 'I listened in. You're doing some sort of illegal deal that lets the Japanese get big mining contracts down here.'

Adam jerked his hand free, looked at her as if she was a dog that might bite but small enough that he might just kick her. He was undecided, and she was holding her fork in a stabbing position.

'Forget treating us as beggar refugees,' she said. 'You need to help us become migrants. Migrants get status, get jobs, get to choose where they live. We need to get to Momona.'

255

Adam looked around him. The room was busy, tables were placed close to each other. 'Not here,' he said. 'Come to my room.'

Adam's room was double the size of Vai's and looked down along the main street. Vai opened the thick white drapes and stood at the window, watching people hurry through the cold. Small, dark figures in the weak, yellow street lights.

'You're not here for sightseeing,' he said. 'Sit down.' He pointed to the smaller of two chairs in the room. He stood over Vai and said, 'Don't think you will survive if the people you noticed are exposed by you.' He crouched at her eye-level. 'Just outlining your parameters.'

'How much does a person need to pay to get a visa?'

'If the lead applicant has skills, such as construction skills, which Momona will need tens of thousands of, then it's one hundred thousand for a permanent migrant visa. Thirty thousand for a five-year visa. Once they're in, they can expect to bring family members who will contribute to the economy, young people who aren't sick.'

'There's twenty thousand people on Independence.'

'Just focus on some working-age people. Once they're in they can bring family.'

'Three thousand.'

'Don't be ridiculous. Ninety million dollars. Twenty migrants, that's realistic.'

'Twenty? I'd be ashamed to go home. I'll expose you.'

'You might be able to force me to postpone. But the only one at risk here is you.'

Vai stood up and pushed past Adam, sending him jolting onto his backside on the floor. 'How do I know you'll transfer the money? When could you do it?'

Adam pointed to his briefcase. 'I have the account details in there. I can do it whenever I want.' He spread his arms wide and laughed. 'Fuck, I've got forty million to spread around. That's money to die for. There's a lot of people needing to see a share of that.'

Vai sat down on the big chair and curled her legs under her. 'Fuck you, Adam.' Her voice was thick and angry. 'How much of that's just buying you a good life?'

'We're all rats, Vai. Scramble onto New Zealand for what? You'll be a peasant worker on a construction site. Well, not you. You've got Miriama. But your people.'

Sprawled out on the carpet, Adam's belly showed between his belt and his untucked shirt. He had the look of a fat fish, belly-up on the sand. Vai imagined slitting that belly, belt to chest plate, then getting a purchase on his ribs and ripping the knife up to his throat. Blood running like red wine. Fish flapping around, shocked, not anticipating that, life bleeding out.

Her blood ran cold. Then it flushed through her hot, as if a machine had pumped hot water into her pipes. From out on the street the sound of a rubbish truck broke into the room, a mechanical strain of a bin being lifted and then the clatter of junk.

'I'm going to use your bathroom,' she said. But she walked over to the kitchenette. She opened the top drawer. It just had cutlery. The next drawer down had a bigger knife, a breadknife with a heavy handle. She went into the bathroom and closed the door, sitting on the toilet seat, looking at the shower with its scrubbed-clean white plastic and spotless door. Then she needed to pee. She sat there and then she stood in front of the basin and wet her face, forcing her breathing to slow down.

She walked back into the room. 'Tomorrow night. I need to transfer the money tomorrow night.'

Adam's face twisted in a mixture of condescension and anger. 'All you get is twenty people.'

Vai studied him coolly. Took in his big shoulders and his size advantage and now he didn't remind her of a fish. He had her thinking about the big pigs that roamed free on Independence, the boars, snuffling along doing whatever the hell they wanted,

257

taking no notice of the dogs or the kids and then one day there they were looking very surprised with their throats cut and their legs tied on an iron rod over the coals of a fire. 'I'll be here at eleven, once Miriama and the others are in bed,' she said.

28

Vai woke early and lay in bed alternating between resolve and feeling as though she would wet herself. She conjured up Adam's arrogance, remembered him sniffing his wine and shutting her out. She got to the restaurant early and drank coffee while she waited for the others.

Miriama arrived with Walter and Adam, engrossed in discussion. Walter waved to a man across the room who walked over and introduced himself to Miriama and Adam. They halted in the middle of the room, talking earnestly. Another man approached them and Vai wondered if she should go over to Miriama, but she wasn't armed with facts or papers so she stayed at the table.

When the others arrived they talked fast and ordered coffee. Adam sat next to Vai and put his hand on hers. 'A big day today, Vai.' Miriama took her other hand and said, 'You come with me. You'll find out just how big Momona's going to be.'

Adam set a map on the table. It had a fat red line drawn around China and down through Thailand, Vietnam and on to Indonesia. The red line formed a funnel and from the narrow end a line was run across to Momona and then to West Antarctica. 'This diagram's got all the appeal,' Adam said.

Walter tapped his finger on the map. 'Yes, keep it simple. That's communicating better than anything else.' He turned to Miriama. 'I'm promising we'll deliver the Momona infrastructure without a hitch. How's your finance standing up?'

'China's been waiting for this for decades,' Miriama said. 'We

259

can move forward as soon as your government passes enabling legislation.'

Coffee arrived in a silver pot with a small plate of pastries. Vai stood to pour the coffee and took a deep breath. 'I guess this might be the last time we have a few moments together before the signing ceremony and then we'll all split up around New Zealand.' Her hands were shaking and she spilt coffee onto the tablecloth. A brown stain spread toward Walter, who pushed back his chair and stood, snatching up the map.

Vai stammered, 'I'm sorry, swap places,' and scuttled around to Walter's seat. 'Could we talk about Independence?' Now she was rushing. 'It's just that it might be our only chance.' Adam leaned toward Walter, putting his forearm out as if he might fend off a blow aimed at the Minister.

'Leave it with me,' Miriama said. 'We'll talk tonight.'

Walter put the map back on the table and took a call. Miriama beckoned to Vai and said quietly, 'There's no shortage of work. You and I have a full day of meetings.'

They reconvened at the restaurant for dinner. Walter and Adam were beaming. 'The Koreans are going to take over the site of that old aluminium smelter at Tīwai. They'll build a state-of-the-art iron plant,' Walter said. 'More jobs.'

Miriama rapped the table. 'Good work. Momona and Antarctica will need all the steel they can get. I've been worrying that the Koreans would go to South Africa.'

'Quality migrants,' Adam said. 'Otago can wave goodbye to a stalled economy.'

'India's going to be South Africa's partner,' Walter said. 'We'll have America in Canterbury and China at Momona. That secures our safety. We'll bring in their migrants plus their main allies' migrants.' He rubbed his cheek. 'The governance and access agreement we need to sign with America and China's going to be tough.'

'The Treaty?' Adam asked.

'If that's what it turns out to be. The public are going to hate it.'

'It's a boom economy from here on,' Adam said, happily pouring wine for everyone. 'The public are desperate for all the things a settlement with the big three will bring. I'm not so sure they'll hate it.'

Miriama squeezed Vai's shoulder. 'We had a good day too. I've received commitments for enough housing and commercial floor space to get stage one of the city financed.'

'It's going to rise on the flood,' Vai said. She knew she shouldn't provoke them, the rich and the powerful at their carve-up. Earlier in the day she'd been walking with Miriama between meetings when a pod of AI racers swooped past. Ochre in the mist, ski racers built in human form so they could compete fairly with the best human racers the nations could muster. Miriama had stopped mid-sentence, hand at her throat, as the pod sped down the road on their skis. Were they showing off? Vai wasn't sure the idea was relevant. But she smelt the anxiety rising like steam from the human watchers on the street, the cold hands of resentment reaching out, uniting them. The humans never won, hadn't won in years, but they couldn't *not* race later in the week, couldn't not face the inevitability of losing. It gave her some satisfaction.

Walter waved the waiter over. 'We're ordering now,' he said. He instructed Adam on what he was to do the next day and when he returned to New Zealand. Walter discussed the port with Miriama. 'We're in a race,' he said. 'You need to get that port open, Miriama. There's no point in having an inland city. We can't rely on air transport alone. Show the world that we're serious.'

They finished their meal quickly. Adam had most of the wine and Vai listened to him talk more about inside living. He described the shopping mall near where he grew up in Wellington, the place where he'd met his first girlfriend, a shop assistant. Miriama called for dessert menus and Adam got another bottle. Vai drank her glass quickly and felt her head go fuzzy. Adam poured her a second. Miriama glanced at her coldly so she sipped only when Miriama sipped her water. Sip for sip.

Walter waved to a slender woman in her fifties, long black hair and shimmering pink silk dress: he excused himself and joined her table. Adam recognised a woman at the bar with a group of men: he went over to join them.

Miriama used her spoon to break the last half of her dessert into little pieces. Miriama ate each little piece, one by one. Vai felt the locket at her neck, remembered how she had felt when her mother put it around her neck, standing by the ocean. Her four grandparents and two siblings there to see it. Even now, in the snow and on the steepest slopes, it was the locket that weighed the most.

Miriama was watching her fiddle with the locket. 'There's no magic, Vai. We have to be methodical about this. We get you settled and then your family and then we take it from there.'

Tears ran down Vai's cheeks. 'It's not getting closer, it's slipping away. This settlement's not a door for me. It's just drawing you away.'

'That's not true. It was always going to be a long walk. It's neither easier nor harder than it was ever going to be.' Miriama stared hard into Vai's eyes. 'You need to be hard, hard as rock. Calculate every move, build success block by block.'

'There's so much to do and I don't have traction. We're getting more stuck.'

Miriama's face brightened. 'Here's Zhou.' She smiled and held a finger up to Vai. 'See? Opportunity, always opportunity.'

Zhou embraced Vai, held her a little too long and kissed her cheek a little too hard. The two property developers grinned at each other and Miriama recounted the successes of her day, gesturing to Vai when she wanted endorsement but moving on before Vai could do more than nod. Zhou had his own stories and pointed to a group of older Chinese seated in the middle of the room. 'Come and join us.'

Vai said, 'Give me a minute. I need to visit the bathroom.' Miriama walked off arm in arm with Zhou.

Vai locked herself in a cubicle and listened to the sounds of other women moving in front of the mirrors. She thought about Miriama and Zhou and anger fizzed like nitrogen in her blood. The memory of Zhou's touch caused her to double over. She pulled out her device and called Juan.

Juan met Vai in the foyer of a hotel a block away from her own hotel. He hugged her and kissed her cheeks, saying, 'This place has a great bar and there's an Argentinian band playing.' She kissed his mouth and put her arm around him. His face lit up.

'It's cold and I've been spending too much time with old people making themselves rich,' she said.

They found a table at the back of the bar where they could glimpse the band through the movement of bodies and Vai was happy to find that the music wasn't loud, it rushed and withdrew with the sound of surf on a pebble beach. Juan's tanned skin reminded her of people she knew from home. People who spent their days outdoors and were at home in the ocean or working under the sun. He was tall, broad-shouldered and lean, and his brown eyes were the same colour as his hair. His eyes were watching her in a hungry way and she remembered him chanting in the bar the day before.

'I don't always live here,' he said. 'I have an Argentine passport. I was born here and I think of myself as Antarctican, or something. There's no proper word yet. But all the time I meet people from around the world, they come here as scientists and adventurers. Now there's lots of miners and military people.' He stopped and asked Vai if she wanted beer. She said no, she'd had enough alcohol tonight. She lifted her knees and rested them against the table, and leaned on Juan's shoulder.

'I helped a group from Georgia, in Europe. They were over here kayaking and exploring the coast. I arranged transport for them and gave them some advice. They were away for about a month and when they came back we spent a few days together.

Yetim was one of the men in the group. He loved poetry and had a good singing voice. A good voice but not a great voice. He sang too much.'

Juan paused while a group of people pushed past their table. He squeezed closer to Vai and she kissed him again, this time on the forehead. He grinned and ran his fingers down the scar on her neck. 'Yetim invited me to visit him in Georgia. He lived in the mountains, the Caucasus. It's a very mountainous country that runs down to the sea, I can't remember which sea, just a small one. I went there three years ago and stayed for two months. It was late summer and then autumn. I've never seen anything like it. The leaves on the trees turned into the most spectacular colours of red and orange and brown. Sometimes they turned purple. They have a lot of rivers, not big ones, or not where I was staying, and we canoed. In deep ravines and across open valleys and all around us were these beautiful colours.'

Vai snuggled against him, enjoying his voice. 'I've only been to New Zealand and here. I had a friend on the protest ship I was on, Paris. She told me about all of the wild places she has been to.'

'You should travel. It's great. You should keep going.'

The band stopped playing and Vai took a sip of beer from his glass. Juan touched her nose with a finger. 'We drove up high into the mountains with the intention of spending a week camping and canoeing down a river. On the first day we set up camp and prepared our boats. There was a camp nearby, people moving from Iran and Iraq, maybe some Syrians. They were walking up to Russia, to the better climate. We set up near the camp and people were coming to the river for water and we tried to talk to them. Just being friendly.'

'They must have thought it was strange to have people playing on boats in the middle of their crises.'

Juan looked embarrassed. 'Life goes on, it persists. I think it's important to remember how to live.'

Vai put her hand on his leg and shook it, encouraging him to continue. 'I agree, no grey wolf.'

Juan had lost the mood of his story and he hurried now. 'Well, the thing I was going to get to was that Yetim followed one of the women back to the main camp and in the evening he approached her. Just to talk to her. Some men chased him him back to our camp. We were sitting there in the dark, looking at the stars and Yetim comes running and yelling out for help. We had a bit of a standoff and then we couldn't decide whether to stay for the night. We thought if we went to sleep they might attack us. So we packed up and under the starlight we paddled to the bottom of the valley, before the river flowed into a gorge.' He was quiet for a minute. 'I guess it doesn't sound funny, but it was at the time.'

Vai stroked Juan's face. 'Come back to my hotel. Just for a couple of hours. Then I'll kick you out.'

In the lift on the way up to her room Juan held her tight and tried to kiss her, but she was distant. She saw his disappointment and twisted her hand in his shirt, holding him but not close. 'If I came to Argentina, as a migrant, could I work?'

He dropped his hands from her waist, his disappointment settling further. 'Yes, of course. We will have more development from Antarctica than New Zealand. A lot more. But why would you? You have Miriama, it's perfect.'

'Miriama can only help me. Not everyone.'

The lift door opened and Vai took Juan to her room. She held a hand to his forehead, halting his embrace. 'One minute,' she said and smiled softly. 'I want to go to Argentina. I want to see it. An adventure.'

'Sure,' Juan said, sounding unsure. 'When would you like to go?'

'Soon, after the signing ceremony. Miriama won't mind if I take a week. How do I book a flight from here?' She gave Juan her device and he opened the booking page for her and marked it. The wind was out of his sails and she was checking the time.

She grabbed him by the hair, pulling him against her. 'Don't sulk. I just needed to ask for that.' They both laughed and he kissed her and lifted her into his arms and dropped her onto the bed. He stripped her naked and threw his own clothes onto the floor, ran his fingers gently across her cheek, along the length of her neck. She closed her eyes and let the lightness of his touch melt her world of worry.

Afterwards, in the dark, she stared at the ceiling, counting the minutes as if she was alone. Juan raised his head from where he had snuggled into the small of her back and rolled away. Vai got up and checked the time. She looked across at Juan, spread-eagled across her bed, one leg tucked under the twisted sheet. He had a scar running from shoulder to elbow on his left arm. She fixed her gaze on it, imagining the way it might have cut, the blood. She wondered if he had seen the bone inside his arm and what he might have thought when he looked down and saw it sliced open.

She braced herself and took a deep breath. He gave a rueful smile. 'So strict?' She nodded and he climbed off the bed and dressed. They kissed again and he said, 'Tomorrow?'

She avoided his eyes.

29

At 11 p.m. Vai stood outside the door to Adam's room. The hall was empty, barren of furniture and people. She wore a grey sweat top with the hood pulled over her head and matching grey track pants. There was a mirror on the wall with a crack in the glass. She imagined the crack racing across the mirror, the glass shattering. She knocked.

Adam was drunk. He grinned and said, 'You look like the little match girl.'

Vai said, 'I don't know what that means. Let's get this done.'

Adam took a folder from his bag and placed a sheet of paper on the table. 'Where should this go?'

Vai handed him a slip of paper with an account number and name. The account was in the name her father's parents had given her. She'd never used it: it was too long, too hard for people who didn't speak her language to pronounce.

'Six hundred thousand dollars, twenty people. You're on your own from there.'

Vai watched Adam open the account. Not bothering to hide any details. Disdainful of her.

'I'm the only one that's actually helped you!' He glared at her. 'Think about it when you're spending.' He finished the transaction and put the papers back into his bag, zipped it shut.

Vai's knees went weak and she sat on his bed, her heart racing. She thought she might faint. She imagined him as he was the previous night, lying on the floor with his belly exposed. Then she thought of the glass shattering.

'I didn't want it to end like this. Not this way,' he said, his voice roaming off. He'd imagined her pale and scared, but there she was calm, distant. He'd always respected her. Even her extortion. He'd given her more than he needed to, not from his share. But he'd shown her pity and respect. Now, looking at her, he wondered if he'd done too much, provided some false comfort.

'God, Adam, how did we get into this mess?' Vai said.

Adam snorted. 'Really, you're going to stay over and chat?' He bent a little at the waist, hands out to the side, fingers splayed, pushing his face toward hers. 'If you want to blame someone I always find the Paris Greens convenient. The climate-change deniers were transparent liars. They realised climate breakdown would lead to the situation we have now. They're the ones sitting off the coast tonight in their corporate yachts, reaping what they sowed. Good for them.'

Vai smiled, encouraging him to go on.

'I draw a distinction between the scientists, the climate scientists who did real analysis and screamed panic, and the fraudsters who made a living selling sustainability snake oil.' Adam walked to the window, pulled the curtain to the side and peered down to the street. 'The killers were the ones who told the public that science and technology were just over the horizon, riding to save us. No question. A combination of free-market economics, green technology and riding electric bicycles with full facial beard, that was the magic formula. Consumerist crap. Consequently, the public slacked off, they never panicked, they never drove their politicians hard, because they were lulled into thinking the fire was nearly out.' He was pacing the room now. 'The real scientists did the maths. Coming out of the Paris climate meeting in 2015 they knew we were an inch from being screwed. But then a new lot arose, armed with a little information. They were eager to find good news. Solar costs plummeting, electric vehicle use leaping in percentage terms. Rubbish like that. They gave capitalism the escape hatch it craved, so there was plenty of money to fund the anaesthetists.'

He took a bottle of red wine from the bench and filled a glass. 'They didn't know how to assess the scale of change required. They couldn't assess scale against the time remaining, because they were amateurs.' He spat out 'amateurs' as if it was rotten food.

'Then what happened?' Vai asked.

'*This* happened.' He jabbed a finger at her. 'People like you happened, refugees. A hundred million of you, at least.' He paused to consider her. 'At least you got out. And I mean that. I like you, Vai. Even though you robbed me just now. But I respect that. Unfortunately, the rest of you refugees are going over the cliff. No one wants you.'

He poured another glass, swayed over to the window and pulled back the curtain again, just a crack. 'Look at those rich bastards out on their yachts, retailers of anaesthetic.' He steered for the bench and plonked the glass on it. 'I need a piss.'

Vai gasped and he looked at her questioningly. 'Don't you vomit in here,' he said.

Her heart raced, but now she was cold. She looked at her hands and they looked distant, hands she might have seen on someone else.

Adam went into the bathroom and closed the door, not quite shut. Vai leapt to her feet, kicked her shoes off, dropped her pants and threw her top onto the shoes. Bra and knickers remaining on. *No fucking refugees in my family*, she said to herself, and repeated it, chanting it in her head. *No one I know's going over the cliff.* She walked to the kitchenette and took out the breadknife, ran her finger along the blade. She stood at the door to the bathroom. She could hear the stream of his urine into the toilet bowl. She pushed the door open. He was head down watching his piss flow.

Vai had never killed a pig but she'd killed plenty of fish, so she thought of a big fish and the slide of the knife across the gills and she gripped his hair tight and yanked him backward. He yelped out and dropped to one knee and she hacked the knife forward and in under his jaw, across his throat, where his gills would be. Made a big cut, *a fucking long cut*, but not very deep. She sawed back again. Then he was wrestling away, grabbing at the gash on his throat. Vai brought the knife up high and smashed the handle end down on the top of his head. He stopped still and she slipped the blade back into the cut, held his ear on the other side and sawed back and forth, back and forth, getting deep now. He went weak and she knew she had him done. She stepped away and let him bleed out on the floor, thrashing to start with and then just weak movements. Blood all over, his pecker flopping sideways out of his pants like an old sausage.

Vai breathed in deep, kept breathing, big breaths. She looked at her hands and now they looked like hers again. She was elated, she'd done it. Done. Adam wasn't moving: she couldn't see any breathing. The blood was just trickling, no heart pump.

She listened. Had either of them cried out? If they had, it might pass for sex. She couldn't hear anyone.

Right, she thought. *Next thing*. She stepped into the shower and ran warm water over her head and lifted her face to embrace it. She washed off the knife and set it on the shower floor. Stripping off, she applied shampoo and soap everywhere. Everywhere twice, thrice. *Get rid of the pig*. He looked like a pig on the floor, not a fish. *A pig carcass*.

She towelled herself dry and went into the main room. Put her clothes and shoes on. Hands shaking, bile in her mouth. Opened Adam's bag and took out the sheet of paper. She opened the account and couldn't believe what she saw. She sat on the floor and studied the account. Almost forty million dollars, just sitting there. She moved the whole lot. *Why not?* She had a flight to Argentina at seven in the morning and from there she could move fast. She took a deep breath: she was going on the run, permanently. But if she could keep moving for long enough she could move a lot of people off Independence. She thought back to her lunch in Auckland with Miriama, standing there like a schoolgirl reciting the poem. She put her hand on her chest and measured the race of her heart. *Carcass in the shower, woman on the run.*

Back in her own room she collected her back pack then returned to Adam's room. She went into the bathroom, careful to avoid the blood that was spreading, and retrieved her bra and knickers. She checked the time. Midnight. She wouldn't go to the airport until five. Now she paced the room, thinking only of settlement. There would be a settlement for Independence.

The door to the bathroom was open. Adam was on his back, legs bent either side of the toilet. The knife wound was exposed and she could make out bits of yellow and white fat against the meat. They had five hours together. It was like a vigil for the dead. *On vigil duty.* She put on some music.

30

Vai reached the airport at five in the morning and scurried through the wind and sleet into the calm of the building. The airport was warm, no high-roofed architectural gestures, no big windows. The smell of coffee and baking was being forced through the air vents. Her stomach churned at the thought of food: she saw the thick blood on the bathroom floor, the fatty, chunky bits on Adam's neck, and bile rose to the back of her mouth.

She ran her tongue around the inside of her mouth and spat into a bin in a corner before approaching the check-in counter. There was no queue. She guessed that the flights in would be full, but who would leave until after the signing ceremony? The woman at the counter smiled politely and said, 'Unfortunately there will be no flights out this morning. It's too windy and the visibility is too poor. Come back after midday.'

Vai's blood rose quickly, flooding her face red and tears pushed in the edges of her eyes. All through the night she had kept her emotions in hand, not always *in* control, but *under* control. She turned quickly away and hurried to a quiet area of the airport. No one would look for Adam until seven at the earliest, and they wouldn't check his room until eight. She looked up at the ceiling. There were cameras scanning every angle. She identified the sign for the toilets and walked casually over to the door.

She sat down on a toilet seat, rested her pack against the door and shut her eyes against the little creature that threatened to appear. What was likely to happen after eight? They would find her missing and Miriama would call with the terrible news. Vai pinched the skin on her forearm to focus. She could imply that she was still with Juan and tell Miriama that she wanted to stay with him, that she was upset. That might get her to midday.

She exited the airport and looked out into the snow. It was blowing harder and she wouldn't be able to stand against it in the open. She needed to stay close to the airport but not in it, but there was nothing open, no café or shops. She walked past a restaurant and a shaft of light fell onto the alley to the side of the building. A door was open to the back of the restaurant: food was being unloaded and rubbish removed. Two women moved past her along the alley and through the door, bundled tight against the weather. Vai figured they would be workers coming to prepare for the day. How many of them would be temporary? Surely most of the service staff were only here for the surge of demand brought about by the signing ceremony. She walked quickly to the door and looked into the open storage room with the kitchen beyond.

'Hello,' she called. 'I've been told to come here and get started. I'm a contract worker.'

A man came out, smiled, spoke to her in Spanish. She shook her head: 'English.' He beckoned her in and pointed to a huge stack of dirty pots and then to the sink. She took her heavy jacket off and turned to the pots, scraping them out. Then she ran boiling-hot water into the sink. Steam rose into her face and music began to play and she looked at the stack of dirty pots and her thoughts turned to Independence. She relaxed and smiled and imagined she was in the school's kitchen that doubled as the community's events kitchen. Swaying in time to the music, she put on gloves and plunged her hands into the hot water to scrub.

Soon after eight-thirty Miriama called with the news. 'Thank God I've got hold of you.' She was rushing her speech, panicky.

Vai took the call outside and leaned against a bin in the alley, snow piling on her hair and shoulders. The cold stung and her voice quavered. 'How was he found? Do they know who did it?'

She convinced Miriama that it was best she stayed with Juan until after midday. Then she would return to the hotel.

Back in the kitchen she switched off her device. The man pointed to a pile of carrots and demonstrated peeling and cutting. The pile was daunting. There were buckets of extra carrots and potatoes under the bench: he pointed to them as well. Vai worked for half an hour then went to the door and put her face against the window and looked up to see if the wind was strong. In the alley the snow blew softly but higher up the snow was being driven almost parallel to the ground. She checked the flight information and saw that her flight was postponed until the evening. Turning the device off again she went back to her pile of carrots.

At eleven-thirty Vai turned the device back on and, as if on command, Miriama called again. 'Where are you?' she asked. 'I need to talk to you. I'll come and meet you.'

'I'm out walking.'

'Juan says you weren't with him after midnight. The police told me.'

'I was with him until dawn. He was asleep when I left. Then I went walking in the town. When you told me about Adam I was upset and wanted to stay by myself.'

'They've found a bank account, Vai. A sum of money has been transferred. It looks like a robbery as well as a murder. They want to talk to you.' Miriama sounded as though she was going to cry. 'Vai, did Juan do something? Is there something I should know?'

'Juan? I don't know. The truth is I fell asleep before midnight.'

Miriama was silent while she processed this information. 'Well, Adam and Juan couldn't stand each other. The police are going to pick Juan up. Where are you?'

Vai heaved a silent 'thank you'. Miriama was still with her. 'I don't want to come into the middle of this. If Juan's done something bad, then I'm staying right away from it. Let me call you tonight.' She ended the call and turned her device off.

Everything rested on the weather. She returned to her tasks.

The restaurant was open and busy: she was cleaning plates and pots now; the chefs were yelling and the eating room was bustling. She kept toiling through the rush of lunch and into the early afternoon. The storm was constant and she gave up hope of flying out. The man who ran the kitchen came to her and asked her questions but she wasn't sure what he was asking. He called over a woman who spoke English and she said he wanted to know if Vai would work through the evening until the restaurant closed. Vai smiled and grasped his hand, pumping it way too long. No one would think to look for her in a restaurant kitchen.

At midnight Vai picked up her backpack and stepped out into the storm. She hurried to a late-night café and went through to sit in a toilet cubicle. She turned on her device and looked at the messages. Local police requesting she contact them, then demanding she contact them. Her mother. Miriama.

Miriama's messages gave the story of her discovery. 'They think you're involved. Call me.' 'They say the money went to an account held by you. What have you done? Call me now.' 'Don't be a fool, contact me, I will help you. You need to trust me.'

Vai turned her device off and hugged herself tight. She didn't take her mother's messages, but her heart hurried, fearing that her memories, moments, might melt. Might fade to filigree, thinned through distance and all that might remain would be her mother's bitter voice. Vai's long labour had delivered no issue. No, never, never her mother's messages. The immensity of her failure brought Vai to her knees. She looked at the white walls of the cubicle and up to the white light hanging by its cord from the ceiling. After a while she stood up and held her hands out, touching the sides of the cell. Making a fist, she pumped it into her other hand, then again, feeling the hardness of bone, muscle and bone.

She took hold of the top of one wall of her cubicle and lifted herself off the floor. Hanging in the air, feeling the strength of her shoulders. *What next?* she thought. She wouldn't be able to use the airport and there were no ships she could get on. No plan took shape. It was best to be away from the airport, she decided.

She walked out of the café's warmth and back into the storm toward the door of the airport where a few vehicles were gathered, looking for customers. Before she stepped into the light of the airport's entrance she paused, looking at who was nearby. There was a snowmobile across the road with a thin man on it, other vehicles touting for business and a few workers. One of the workers turned to study her. Vai pulled the hat of her coat tighter and looked away. The man hurried inside the airport and Vai walked as fast as she could on the icy path, back the way she had come and then onto the empty road, into the driving snow.

The snowmobile pulled out from the curb and turned to intercept her. Vai started to run, her heart jumping. The road was impossible, a slick of ice with a swath of snow skating on it. The snowmobile revved loudly and cut in front of her. Vai slid, her pack tipping her over, flat on her back. The driver was small for a policeman: maybe she could throw him from his machine. He took off his snow goggles — it was Zhang. Vai looked back at the airport: it was shrouded by blown snow. She couldn't see anyone watching. Zhang typed onto her device, tapped the text for a translation, showed the words to Vai: 'Get on, safe with me.'

She drove to a large shed near the airport that had been rented by the Chinese government. There was no one else there. They dismounted and Vai bear-hugged Zhang with all her strength. Zhang tapped a message into the device and held it up: 'I waited since early afternoon. Freezing.'

Vai tapped, 'Thank you, all my heart.' Zhang responded, 'Where now?'

Vai sat down on a small chair and looked around the shed. It was full of boxes and machines. The roof iron was exposed and no ceiling kept the cold out. Her breath blossomed in front of her in little clouds. She thought about crying, she thought about turning herself in.

Zhang tapped on her device, 'Outside of each settlement, no law. No one can arrest you.'

Vai hadn't thought of that. If she left the settlement she was in no man's land, literally. She tapped, 'Where? I die in snow ice.'

Zhang turned her hands up and shrugged. Then she tapped, 'Go along coast, ask your government for trial at home?'

Vai considered the option. Independence didn't really have a government and she couldn't ask them to risk their relationship with New Zealand for her. But the coast was her best option. Then she remembered the volcano. The warm soil that was free of ice and snow. If she got there she could stay for as long as her food lasted. After that she would have to make another decision. She wondered if she should tell Zhang her plan. She tapped, 'I will go along the coast. Can I have food?'

Zhang smiled and took Vai's hands and gripped them tight. She tapped, 'Take the snowmobile and hide it.' She pulled up a map on her device and pointed out a road that led out of Cariló westward toward Beijing. It ran for thirty kilometres. After that, Vai assumed, Argentine influence ended.

They loaded the machine with food and cooking equipment from boxes. Zhang filled the fuel tank and located a tent. When it was done they stood close and Vai ran her fingers over Zhang's face, feeling each detail as a blind woman might do, inhaling her scent, studying the curve of her eyes and the rise of her nose. Zhang took Vai's head in her hands and rested their foreheads together, sharing their breath. Zhang cried warm tears onto Vai's cheeks. She shuddered along the length of her body and turned away. When she had regained control she tapped, 'I go now. You go before three in morning. Make this look like robbery.' Together they busted the door lock. Zhang threw her arms around Vai's waist and they held tight, then she hurried into the dark.

Alone, Vai paced the length of the shed, listening to the storm raging and hissing on the roof. She tried to plan her next move. She thought of all the people who might help her. Miriama would direct her to the police. Who else? Leon came to mind — perhaps he had contacts, but he was a petty thug. Captain Negri? A petty pirate.

She sat down in the chair. Her head was pounding and she let the pain behind her eyes surface, just for a little while. Her hands sat leaden in her lap and wouldn't rise, not even to comfort her head. The thought of handling the heavy machine on the snow-covered road brought an ache to her arms and back. There was no option of sleep: if she fell asleep she wouldn't wake before three and if she turned her device on for an alarm she might be traced to the shed.

She turned to her dad and said to him, 'I know you made it to the boat.'

He put his hand on her head and stroked her hair. 'Yes, I got there. I hung on until the end of the storm.' She waited for him to tell her more but he looked into her eyes and said nothing. She held his face and studied it. His skin was vibrant and his cheeks were full of life and she could see, in his soul, how settled we might all be if we had the courage.

She released his face and stepped back and looked at the machine, loaded heavy with all that she had taken. She switched on her device to check the time. Two-thirty. She switched it off.

The noise of the storm was loud and uneven. Metal banged on something just beyond the shed and Vai imagined Nature gathering itself for vengeance on the animals that had turned on all other species. She considered calling her mum and struggled not to let go, not here. Her chest heaved and she fell to her knees vomiting across the slick concrete floor.

Her hair fell forward into the vomit and she pushed at it, scooping the yellow mess away with her hand. The door opened and she looked up, terrified, to see a woman in red snow boots, high to the knee, red trousers and a red hooded jacket, white goggles and mask standing out like a shock against the red.

Miriama closed the door and pushed a wooden crate against it. She stood over Vai, feet wide, hands on her hips, breathing heavily through the mask. Her breath drew and exhaled in a thick robotic wheeze. She had a stick in her hand and jabbed Vai on the shoulder. Dug it in hard. Vai slapped at it weakly and Miriama brought it down smack on her head.

Vai squatted, wiping vomit on her trousers and pushing her hair clear of her face. Miriama took off her mask and surveyed the frigid room. All the paraphernalia that made settlement practical, spilling out of crates and stacked on shelves, vehicles and replacement parts and supplies of food, carefully packaged.

'Just another greedy girl.' Miriama stood closer over Vai, who braced herself, splaying her arms and knees wide, as if she expected the earth to quake. 'That's all you turned out to be.'

'Not true,' Vai said, her neck craned at a sharp angle. 'It was never for me.' Vai thought of her sister, Emma, she thought about revealing her illness to Miriama. But here? Now, as it all broke apart? No, that could only be a betrayal.

'Don't lie!' Miriama's voice rose high above the shrieking of the storm and her stick slashed against Vai's arm. 'I was building a safe harbour for you all, putting all the pieces into place. What did you think? Did you think it came in a box and I just had to open it?'

Vai crawled out of reach of the stick and leaned on a crate, low against the floor.

'You have no idea. No idea how many things are broken. No idea what it's like to look at a system in collapse and begin to think about how to pull it back together.' Miriama crossed to a large tractor, its wheels reaching to her head. 'I choose people first. I chose you ahead of everyone. It was working. It will still work. But you?'

'Which part of it is working?' Vai spat each word slowly at the older woman. She thrashed her fist down on the crate, splintering its top, and blood trickled from her wound.

'You have a visa. Gone now, though.'

279

Vai's eyes were smoking with anger. 'You got me an eight-month respite.'

'Eight months turns into a year. A year's skilled work turns into a skill set that is indispensable.' Miriama waved her stick forward. 'You were home safe. Idiot.'

'And everybody else? The void has its big mouth open and the poor are tipping in there like so much trash, so don't give me an answer that includes *later*.' Vai stood up and wiped her blood slowly across her face. 'The wealthy and their helpers will make it. You gave me a minor spot as a helper. But the clock ran out for the rest. There was never room on the lifeboat for everyone.'

'Not for everyone, no. But eventually I would have got most of Independence safe. I could have done that.'

Vai raised her fists over her head. 'We've been given another role, another place in the world. A camp, for God's sake. They can't move us now and you know as well as I do that the next decade will see a racing cascade of calamity. We can't wait ten years. The richer nations will need to ship their people to safe havens and after that the middle nations will get a turn. There'll be no turn for us.'

'So, you lost your nerve? I thought you were made of more.' Miriama approached closer to Vai. 'I won't panic. I'm getting real things achieved, making deals that help. Building.'

'Oh, all the gifts to the poor. Hasn't stopped the drowning.' Vai moved within striking range of the stick, not caring now, fists balled at her waist. 'You and all the bureaucrats like Adam have no end of things you're planning or working on but none of it amounts to anything. Only Adam had the guts to admit that the poor are over the cliff. The rest of you can't bear it, so you live behind your lies and your promises, and they don't matter now. It's all irrelevant.'

Miriama stepped back, resting one hand on the tractor wheel. 'Don't you ever think of me as irrelevant! That's a label I'll never wear! That's the only sin I'll never commit.'

'Well it's the sin that's been committed. All this could have been dealt with but it wasn't. It's too late now, too late for plans and promises.'

Miriama unzipped her jacket and took out a tiny silver pill box. 'You'll kill me, love. You'll kill me.' She tipped a pill into her hand and swallowed it. 'I'm not as strong as I used to be.' She took three deep breaths and her anger evaporated. 'It's the destructive phase, it won't last forever. We'll be better people. Afterwards.'

Vai crossed her arms. 'I'm going to miss the *afterwards* bit. Lots of us will.'

'I know. We've been so ineffective. We knew what to do, we just couldn't find the spirit. The best we managed was to be well-meaning and mostly kind.' Miriama lifted her hands to the storm. 'Listen, now the world is shunning us. It despises us.'

Vai wiped at the blood on her face. 'It's so cruel. We could give so much, but there's nowhere for us.'

Miriama took a scented cloth from her pocket and carefully cleaned Vai's face. 'Yes, so much,' she said.

But that's all, Vai thought. *A chasm is forming — the journey taking shape isn't for everyone.* The metallic banging outside distracted her again. Now it was urgent. She walked over to the snowmobile and in her mind she settled on her next step. 'Quickly, Miriama, what time is it?'

Miriama held her device for Vai to see.

'Oh, it's that time.' Vai stepped back. 'I can't stay. I need to get to no man's land. I could call you later.'

'Yes, let a few weeks go by.'

281

31

Snow piled high on the road and the machine sounded too loud in the sleeping settlement. Vai navigated with the machine's map, riding fast to the end of the buildings. The street lights created a dome of yellow light in the dark. The wind had suddenly slackened; the snow fell softly now. Vai thought about Miriama and a wave of regret rose in her stomach. Adam entered her thoughts and she waited for the emotion that would come, but there wasn't one. She thought about him dead on the bathroom floor and listened to the things he had said to her. She wondered what she might be like if she had been born in a different time or nation. She shook her head: how hard the world was, how hard she was.

She halted at the coast. Ten days to Beijing, she calculated, and then two more to the volcano. *Are you ready*, she said to her dad. A dozen days alone together: she was looking forward to it. Opening the throttle on the snowmobile she let out a whoop and it rode high on the snow.

When the map indicated she had reached the end of the road she stopped the snowmobile and climbed off to stretch. The sun was making a weak effort to shine through the cloud and the coast stretched away beside her. She was out of sight of the settlement. In front of her the wild coast was snow-covered, lonely white. It would stay that way until a full day of hot sun arrived. She looked back at her tracks and realised she should keep riding. She needed to be well away from the area Argentina claimed influence over. Her arms were sore already but her dad urged her on. *There's no prize for stopping*, he said.

Off the road she had to move more slowly, study the map more carefully, looking for contours that were rideable. In the late afternoon she came to a bluff and nearly gave up. But Moses urged her to climb the bluff on foot and look for a route from up high. Together they traced a way through, relying on a half-hour diversion inland. Then they had a good run through to the evening.

Moses called a halt when Vai's arms started to shake with exhaustion. *Get the tent up*, he said. *No one's going to chase you this far. Truth is, they're probably happy to see you gone. They'll tell themselves you'll die out here.*

She put the tent up and ate a small meal. Then she collapsed into the shelter, exhausted.

The next day the snowmobile ran out of fuel before midday and Vai spent half an hour repacking her bag with supplies and throwing snow over the machine so it wouldn't be visible from the air.

While Vai readied for the trek Moses told her about the boat. He'd swum hard for twenty minutes, always with the boat just out of reach, blowing along in front of him in the wind and then a wave would stall its progress and he would catch up but not quite get there. Vai laughed with him as he described his efforts to climb onto the boat once he had caught it. *Think of an elephant seal*, he said. *That was me. And my arms were done for. I hadn't swum so hard in years.* She didn't say that she thought he'd given up when he jumped off the platform and went into the water, a suicide.

They walked on together for days. It was the longest time they had spent together by themselves. They stuck to the coast as best they could, moving inland only if their way was blocked. There were some good hot days and the exposed snow on the coast melted away, leaving rocks and plants. They came upon colonies of rats wherever birds were gathered.

283

Then, when Vai was thinking they must be no more than two days from Beijing, the weather closed in. At first it was low cloud and wet. Then the wind picked up and it was raining hard. She wanted to keep going, had her mind set on getting to Beijing without a break. Moses urged caution, *The rivers are up*, but she was determined.

They came to a small gully and agreed there would be a stream at the bottom, running under the snow and ice. They climbed down carefully, sliding on their backsides. Vai told her dad to wait and prodded her way forward with the ice axe, the way Tu had shown her. Prod and step, prod and step. It was slow going and she couldn't see much. She was about in the middle, probably right over the stream. Bang, the ice snapped and gave way beneath her. She screamed and lunged backward but the snow folded her into itself and she slid down. Terrified, she was waist-deep in ice-cold water, so cold it felt as if it was biting her legs and feet. She lifted her feet one at a time. She wasn't hurt and Moses was up above calling to her. 'Stay where you are!' she yelled. 'Don't come out here!'

The top of the hole was ten feet above her. She bashed some snow and ice away from the edge of the stream, creating a shelf to kneel on. Her feet and legs were burning with cold. She looked up at the sky, it wasn't too far, but the cold was killing her. She bashed away at the hole, cutting a new shelf, snow falling onto her. She climbed onto the new shelf and cut another one, stomping the snow that fell on her. Up again and then she scrambled out of the hole and lay flat, wiggling on her stomach to the far side of the gully. Moses hugged her, tears running down his face.

She climbed up the gully side, her feet aching. She got the tent up and inside she took off her boots and socks and trousers. Water ran from her boots and started to freeze on the ground in a shallow, brown puddle. Drying off quickly she put on new socks and trousers and climbed into her sleeping bag. Rubbing her feet hard. Warming up.

After a while her legs were warm but her feet continued to

ache. She couldn't decide if her feet were burning or freezing. They felt bruised, as if a car had run over them. She cooked a hot meal of beans and rice and was grateful not to be alone. Moses kept up the talking, telling her just to rest and eat. *Stay warm, girl.*

Vai stayed put for the rest of the day and that night. Her feet and legs seemed to be okay, except for her toes. The toes refused to warm up. *Better keep moving*, Moses said. *We'll leave at dawn. You need to get to Beijing and see a doctor.*

They went on as fast as they could. Vai started out hobbling and thought her feet would warm up but the pain got worse and they stopped often. In the evenings her feet throbbed and she cried like a child in her dad's arms. When they reached Beijing it was just after dark and the last part of their trek was guided by the lights of the settlement. They climbed a hill above Beijing and looked down on it spread across the valley. Moses was impressed: *I can see how a city could be built in a place like this.*

Vai's toes were turning black at the ends and her lower legs ached as if the blood wasn't moving. Moses tried to convince her to go to the doctor. *Sneak in and see the one you already know.* But she wouldn't risk it.

They skirted around the edge of the settlement and dropped down to the valley, beyond the edge of the light cast by the street lamps. Twenty minutes along the road they came upon the settlement's rubbish dump. The entrance was lit by two street lights and they stopped to see if anyone was there. No one appeared to be on night watch and they walked cautiously into the pool of light.

They wandered around looking into bins and piles of wood and plastic and the debris of construction. Vai was leaning into a bin that was full of food scraps. There were rats everywhere and they didn't bother moving away. Moses said, *The food's no good.* But Vai said, 'There's potatoes,' and held up a handful. They were a little soft but otherwise perfectly good. She collected all the good ones and put them in a canvas bag she found near the bin. Moses said, *You know what, you could plant those potatoes in the warm soil you say is up on the side of the volcano.*

Vai nodded. 'We could take some of that strong, clear plastic and make a tunnel house.' She collected a big length of plastic and some long sticks of wood, bundled them up and tied them to her pack. Then she weighed the potato bag in one hand and decided she could carry it all. They headed off up the valley, side by side, Vai limping but chatting happily, relieved to be near the end.

32

It took them another two days to get to the warm soil Vai had told Moses about. Her feet were getting worse and on the second day she was in tears. The first thing she did was to dig her hands into the rich soil and hold it up for Moses to admire. It crumbled beautifully. Then she pointed out the extent of the good land. *Massive*, Moses said, and she noted with pride the awe in his voice. He hugged her tight and said, *Land, new land, the soil… it's sacred. I'm proud, love. You've made us all proud.*

Over the next week Vai set up the tunnel house and planted the potatoes. She walked and crawled the extent of the territory that was to belong to Independence and set up marker rocks. She was in constant, throbbing pain, but she was proud and had no trouble seeing how it would all work out.

To start with, there was a problem watering the potatoes. She checked them by carefully scraping the soil aside and saw they hadn't started to sprout. The water she had was bitingly cold and she thought it would kill the sprouts. Then she hit on a solution: she could crawl along inside the tunnel house and pee on them. That way they got warm water, plus some more nutrients. It just meant she had to drink a lot.

They were all set up. They had her tent looking out over their territory, the tunnel house was working and they still had supplies. She wanted to take her dad up to the top of Ngā Wahine Toa, but she couldn't walk well enough for that now. He said, *Don't worry. We'll go one day soon.*

On a warm day when Vai and Moses were sitting outside the tent talking they heard a snowmobile coming up the valley. They stood near some rocks where they wouldn't immediately be seen. There were two machines with one person on each. The machines stopped a distance from the tent. There was a sailor with a gun strapped to his back and a second man.

The second man called out and, lifting a bulging bag, walked across to the tent. Vai stepped out and confronted him. He removed his hat and she recognised him as Zhu. He smiled and extended his hand to her. 'There's food in the bag,' he said.

Vai took her tatty gloves off and extended her own soiled and cracked hand. He shook it warmly and put an arm around her. 'It's good to see you again,' he said. 'How are you?' Her hair was matted and her face was grimy with soil. She smelt of urine and faeces.

'Not bad, doctor,' she said. 'We've staked our claim up here and we're getting things under way.'

He looked around her sparse camp. 'I saw you hobbling. Are your feet all right?'

'They're not the best. But I'm still getting a day's work done.'

'Can I look at them? I might be able to reduce the pain.'

Vai was happy for his help and sat down on a rock that she had made her own. 'My dad's nearby,' she said. 'He isn't used to having anyone around so when we saw you coming he decided to take a walk.'

The doctor nodded and helped her off with her boots. Vai shook like a dog that wasn't sure of being touched, but couldn't resist the company. Her feet stank and her socks were stuck to her skin. Zhu asked, 'Are your feet painful?'

Vai laughed. 'Hell yes, just look at them.'

Zhu helped her peel down the socks and ran water over the soggy skin to reduce the smell before he touched them. Tears trickled down Vai's face as he put his hands on first one then the other swollen ankle. He touched her toes tenderly and watched her face as he wiggled each one. Vai moaned with each touch and swatted at his hand. 'My ankles are the worst.'

'Come down to the hospital with me,' Zhu said. 'You need these feet looked after. It's urgent for you.'

'You know I can't do that,' Vai said. 'I can't abandon this settlement.' She waved her hand to the tunnel house and then the yellow tent that was her home. She smiled through her tears. 'The soil is amazing and it's warm. The tent is warm, even in a storm.'

Zhu looked at the torn plastic pinned tight by rocks and the stained little tent. He reached his hand to her cheek and brushed it gently. 'You can't settle here Vai,' he said. 'Come with me.'

Vai jerked away from his touch, shocked. Eyes wild, she spat at him, a glob of yellow. 'This is our land! This is Independence!' She laughed loudly into the wild mountains. 'You think you can claim what's already been claimed? I've got marker pegs here, all around the valley, all the good soil.' She smiled at him triumphantly.

He nodded. 'I'll leave some ointment for your feet and return in a few days to see if they're improving.'

Together they gently put new socks on and replaced her boots and then Zhu returned to his machine.

Vai struggled to her feet and swayed, defiant with the volcano rising behind her and she surveyed the valley stretching out a long way behind Zhu and the sailor. The sun was beating down hot. The whole continent was sweating its layer of white, and all across the landmass rivers tumbled and the plants and birds and rats pushed at the edges of the ice. She noted the landmarks where she had placed her boundary pegs, then looked up to the broken caldera and lifted her hand to her friend. Hunching forward, she limped slowly to the tunnel house where the potatoes were nearly ready to push their shoots through the warm, red soil. She paused at the entrance to the tunnel house to wave a dismissal to the doctor, sank to her knees and crawled in under her plastic.

Printed in Great Britain
by Amazon

16934645R00166